Praise for Elena Hartwell

TWO HEADS ARE DEADER THAN ONE

"Chava, the mother, is a hoot and Franklin is about as loyal and intelligent as a big dog can be. Chance, the now maybe lover, is attractive and the mystery is indeed mysterious pretty much up until the end. There are enough quirks in the characters and twists in the development of the story to keep things satisfyingly interesting all the way through. Elena Hartwell has conjured up a plausible protagonist and done a good job of plunking her into a setting and plot that nicely suit her."
—Diana Borse for *Reviewing the Evidence*

5 Stars: "The characters are likeable and believable and Chava, Eddie's card-dealing mom, is especially charming. It's impossible not to root for them all through the story. Author Elena Hartwell showcases a delightful heroine in a story that promises pleasant romance and a hint of danger with a twist of an ending. This will keep one from ever putting this book down!"
—L. Kane for *InD'Tale Magazine*

"An engaging mystery that will keep you stumped to the very end. This novel had many twists and turns so that I was kept guessing all the way to the surprise ending. The characters are quite impressive and I enjoyed getting to know them. I could relate to Eddie and loved her quirky mother, Chava. However, Dakota's character brought back unpleasant memories of high school and she made a great antagonist [....] Although this novel is part of a series, it is a good standalone. For those who are fans of whodunits, this is a great read."
—Susan Sewell for *Readers' Favorite Reviews*.

"*Two Heads are Deader Than One* is the second title in author Elena Hartwell's Eddie Shoes Mystery series and continues to demonstrate her genuine flair for writing carefully crafted, impressively entertaining, and original mysteries."
—Helen Dumont for *Midwest Book Review*

"A great mystery from the get-go, packed full of interesting characters. Eddie and her mom make a great team and for once the first person narrative, usually a turn off for me, kept the story moving on a steady burn. What was most remarkable for me though was the interesting presentation of mental health issues. The author's writing style gave me a modern Mikey Spillane vibe and was quite enjoyable from beginning to end."
—*I Read What You Write blog*

4 Stars: "The stories move quickly, there's always danger, moments that make you laugh, and you worry about Eddie. She's a good PI but she's not real careful about her own safety. The author has her sticking her nose out a little further than necessary but it sure makes for a fun read."
—Aloe for *Long and Short Reviews*

"Eddie Shoes is back in another page turner. Haven't read book one yet? No problem. New readers to the series should be able to jump right into the story. Hartwell provides enough detail to get them up to speed without slowing down those who have read book one [….] Eddie's witty no-nonsense personality and Hartwell's well-paced writing style make the chapters fly by."
—*Readeropolis*

"Private investigator Eddie Shoes needs to buy some sneakers. Danger is coming at her that fast in *Two Heads Are Deader Than One*, the excellent new installment in Elena Hartwell's mystery series. A friend from her high school days shows up out of the blue, needing bail and trailing trouble. Nothing's what it seems

in this tense crime novel, though at least Eddie has the aid of her card shark mom and the company of her giant dog Franklin. Fascinating characters and a story that dares you to put the book down make this book a winner. One murder follows another, guns multiply and Eddie gets put in a frame. Mystery fans will be carried right to the end by this crackling tale."
—Rich Zahradnik, author of the Coleridge Taylor Mystery series

ONE DEAD, TWO TO GO

4 Stars: "Hartwell has created quite a winner in the unique and clever Eddie Shoes, and this first case features not only a twisting, turning, fast-paced plot, but also a number of nuanced, quirky relationships, making for a story that is fun and increasingly absorbing, especially as readers learn more about this headstrong heroine's past…. This is a clever and well-paced mystery that will have plenty of readers eager for the next installment."
—Bridget Keown for *RT Book Reviews*

"I thought that this was a thoroughly enjoyable story, well written with fresh and interesting characters, hopefully this is the first of a nice long series…. Moira Driscoll was an excellent choice for this book, she gave each character a distinctive and easily identifiable voice. I thought she captured Eddie's character perfectly, lively and feisty when appropriate, I especially appreciated how she conveyed all the hidden undercurrents of emotion in the relationship between Eddie and Chava. An all round high quality production." (Review of the audiobook.)
—*Audiothing*

"Mystery, murder and mayhem collide in this intriguing new series! An original, well written gum-shoe, readers will find an easy ebb and flow of sequences with just enough mystery to keep them guessing. From their strained past to their bumbling investigation skills, this quirky combination of a mother-daughter

reunion turned crime-fighting duo will captivate readers.… Avid Alphabet series connoisseurs should flock to this kick-off series."
—Roberta Gordon for *InD'Tale* Magazine

"*One Dead, Two To Go* is smart, page-turning fun, with the most feisty and likable P.I. since Kinsey Millhone. Looking for your next favorite detective series? Look no further."
—Deb Caletti, National Book Award finalist and author of *He's Gone*

"The writing is cinematic and vivid, the characters well-drawn, but the dynamic between Eddie and Chava, which reminded me fondly of Cagney and Lacey, is what makes the story. Fans of the Stephanie Plum series by Janet Evanovich should definitely check out *One Dead, Two to Go*. Recommended."
—Max Everhart, author of the Eli Sharpe Mystery series

"Oh, Eddie/Elena—please don't stop. You've got me hooked, snooked, and ready for another long and lovely rain-drenched mystery-reading night from the pitch-perfect pavement-pounding Eddie Shoes."
—Carew Papritz, author of the award-winning bestseller, *The Legacy Letters*

"Private eye Eddie Shoes and her cardsharp mother plunge the reader into a tale of fractured relationships, mayhem, and thrills. I look forward to the next Eddie Shoes adventure!"
—Deborah Turrell Atkinson, author of the Storm Kayama Mysteries

"In Eddie Shoes, we have a character who is smart and sassy and doesn't make a big deal about herself, but who lights up the pages."
—Bharti Kirchner, author of ten books, including her latest, *Goddess of Fire: A Novel*

"Playwright Elena Hartwell mines her glorious dramatic talent in her debut novel, where Eddie (Edwina) Shoes, a Bellingham P.I., solves the double crimes of money-laundering and murder with dedicated detective work, done with subtle sleuth's irony—and the expert help of Chava, her humorous, clever, light-fingered, poker-playing mom."
—Robert J Ray, author of the Matt Murdock Murder Mysteries

"Unlike the standard-issue PI, Eddie seems allergic to guns and violence and worries about a bad haircut as much as stalking danger. Funny, clever, and full of grabbing plot twists, Elena Hartwell's *One Dead, Two To Go* takes the mystery lover into unexpected territory.... A fast, memorable, and entertaining read. Warning: you'll want more."
—Scott Driscoll, author of *Better You Go Home*

"Elena Hartwell doesn't just burst onto the scene with this clever mystery novel—she kicks the door in and holds the reader at gunpoint."
—Peter Clines, Award-winning author of *The Fold* and the Ex-Heroes series.

"Ms. Hartwell is a terrific writer with fine control of the genre, an ear for sharp dialogue, and a smart mouth that makes her work a pleasure to read."
—Jack Remick, author of the California Quartet series and co-author, *The Weekend Novelist Writes a Mystery*

Three Strikes, You're Dead

Three Strikes, You're Dead

An Eddie Shoes Mystery

Elena Hartwell

CAMEL
PRESS

Seattle, WA

Camel Press
PO Box 70515
Seattle, WA 98127

For more information go to: www.camelpress.com
www.elenahartwell.com

Cover design by Sabrina Sun

Three Strikes, You're Dead

ISBN: 978-1-60381-727-1 (Trade Paper)
ISBN: 978-1-60381-728-8 (eBook)

Library of Congress Control Number: 2017959365

Printed in the United States of America

To my father, John "Steven" Hartwell.

Who led me to the mountains.

———•———

Also by the Author

One Dead, Two to Go

Two Heads Are Deader Than One

Acknowledgments

———◆———

W**RITING MAY BE** a solo pursuit, but finishing a novel takes a community. I'm grateful to everyone who gave of their time and experience to help me continue to explore the world of Eddie Shoes. Any errors are mine.

As always, the Issaquah Police Department, especially Detective Diego Zanella, whose insights and assistance in understanding the real world of homicide investigation and crime continue to be invaluable. You make the world a better place.

Eastside Fire and Rescue: Battalion Chief, Ron Walsh, Community Liaison officer, Captain Steve Westlake, Lieutenants Thomas Tull and Michael Tjosvold. Ricardo "Rocky" Martinez and all the firefighters at Station 71, Issaquah, WA. When I grow up, I want to be a firefighter.

For assistance in various areas of expertise: Dr. Beth Carothers, Samantha Engberg, John "Chris" Grall, MSD, USA Retired, John "JD" Hammerly, so glad you are my hubby … and that you know so many interesting things. John "Steven" Hartwell, Michael Marinos and Bigg Dogg Firearms, Dr. Jose Rios, Luisa Rios, Jacqui Seyers, Amy Ungerleider, Cat Warren, and last, but not least, Malissa Winicki, can't wait to discover what I have to ask you for book four.

Every manuscript needs outside eyes. I was lucky to have three sets on this one. My long-time writing partner, Andrea Karin Nelson, I couldn't do it without you. Sherry Hartwell, best travel companion and proofreader a daughter could have. And my fellow novelist and friend, Mary Honerman, (aka Mary Angela), author of the Professor Prather Mysteries.

My thanks to Aftershocks Media, especially: Phil Garrett, Aubrey Anderson, and Becca Eskildsen. I'm immensely grateful to Harlequin Worldwide Mysteries for their inclusion of *Two Heads Are Deader Than One* in their mystery subscription program and to Audible for their recordings of the first two novels in the series. To Brian Rink at On The Brink Designs for my beautiful new website. And to everyone at Camel Press, especially Sabrina Sun for her stunning cover, Catherine Treadgold for her leadership and exceptional editorial skills, and Jennifer McCord for her hard work and developmental editing.

To Paul and Kim Goldenberger, Krystle Decker, Connor Deutsch, Andrew Oakley, and everyone at BasePoint Fitness in North Bend, Washington, for helping me to balance mind and body.

To the Buse family. I couldn't have found a better real-life person to model my own Debbie Buse after. Thank you for your generous donation to Serenity Equine Rescue and Rehabilitation. Debbie Buse continues to be one of my favorite characters; I know we're going to see more of her in the future.

And to author Drusilla Campbell, who always had faith and left our world far too soon.

Chapter One

As a private investigator, I often deal with the misery of others. And while that's way better than dealing with my own misery, I was still looking forward to a few relaxing days surrounded by the beauty of the Cascade Mountains. My plan was to worry about nothing more serious than whether to have a latte or a cocktail in the late afternoon.

Besides my clients and the attention they required, the circle of people in my life were demanding more and more of my time. I wasn't sure how I felt about not being as footloose and fancy-free as I had been for so many years. Relationships require care, and I wasn't totally convinced I was up to the challenge.

Being a grownup wasn't all it was cracked up to be.

Back in March, my mother Chava had started working security for a casino not far from my Bellingham home. She excelled in her new job, able as she was to sniff out shuffle trackers and con men with the instincts of a bloodhound. Recently rewarded for her vigilance with a hike in pay— after her three-month probationary period ended at the beginning of June—she had generously offered up a mother-daughter getaway weekend to celebrate at the newly renovated Wenatchee Valley Hot Springs Resort and Spa.

Her success was further proof that she had no intention of returning to her beloved Las Vegas anytime soon or that my guest room would return to being my home office in the near future. Apparently I now had a full-time roommate.

Currently that roommate was crouched over the wheel of her bright red Mazda 6, zooming up the road toward our destination.

"You've been down in the mouth ever since that thing with Dakota Fontaine," she'd said last week when she brought up the idea. "I thought you could use a long weekend away."

Just before Chava started her new job, an old friend from my Spokane childhood had shown up in Bellingham, bringing *Sturm und Drang* with her. The whole adventure had made me a little cranky.

Besides, I'd thought at the time, why turn down a mini-vacation with the added bonus I could make my mother happy? And, as the resort was dog friendly, we got to take Franklin, my one-hundred-seventy-five pound, Tibetan mastiff-Irish wolfhound cross. So I said yes.

An hour into our drive, we passed through Monroe, a town of slightly under twenty thousand souls. It had sprung up around the railroad a hundred years ago. Once we got through town, we stopped for lattes at the Coffee Corral, a small, roadside stand in the parking lot of the Reptile Zoo. One of these days I'd stop and visit Reptile Man and his animals, but today we were winging our way up Highway 2, heading into the mountains.

Road trips always felt like an opportunity for a do-over. A "restart button" to erase life's inevitable, messy complications. Especially if my destination was a place I'd never been, a place where no one knew me. I could begin afresh. A new romance, a new job, I could be an orphan—

Chava began singing loudly to the radio and I slammed back

into the here and now, her presence tethering me to my current existence, regardless of our distance from home.

Life could be worse though. I could be paying for this little getaway.

I was more excited than I wanted to admit. Chava and I had rarely been on destination vacations together. We'd visited each other in our respective cities over the years, but seldom gone to another location entirely. I'd found excuses to tell everyone I knew that we were going: my best friend Iz, because I had to cancel our Saturday morning workout session at the dojo; Debbie Buse, in case she'd been thinking about meeting at the dog park on Sunday; and Chance Parker, my ex-boyfriend from Seattle who'd taken a job as a police detective in Bellingham last December.

After several tries over the course of the week, I'd "run" into him at Rustic Coffee in Fairhaven and asked him what his weekend plans were. I figured social etiquette would make him ask me about mine.

"I'm taking a few days off and going up to Orcas Island," he said. "Do a little carpentry. A friend's cabin needs a new roof."

Chance was pretty good with home repair projects, so I wasn't surprised, though I wondered about the friend.

"Should be lovely up there," I said. "What's the cabin like?"

And more importantly, who's the owner?

"Primitive," Chance said, with a laugh. "We won't have electricity or cell service. It's not everyone's cup of tea, but James is used to surviving in the wilderness, and a few days of roughing it won't hurt me."

I remembered James. He lived in Alaska and took people out to look at bears and walruses and live on sticks and berries.

"Very manly," I said.

"What about you?" Chance asked, proving my expectation about social niceties. I explained about the trip Chava had planned for us.

"Sounds like fun," he said. "You'll have to tell me all about it when you get back." That was a good sign, right? Almost like asking me out on a date.

"Why don't we get together?" I said, emboldened by his easy manner. "When we're both back. Compare notes on our respective long weekends."

"Sure," he said. "We'll figure something out."

That was a yes, right?

"You're smiling," Chava said as we reached the outskirts of Sultan, the first small town after Monroe, and had to slow down.

"I'm content," I said, a little surprised to discover it was true.

The distinctly Western Washington small towns whizzed by outside the windows. Startup, Gold Bar, Baring—places with grocery stores and ski rentals mixed in with taverns and restaurants, all of which had seen better days. Not to mention the string of funky espresso drive-thrus, including: a windmill, a barn, and a tiny brick building, all with clever names. After Google and Amazon, coffee was the most popular business in our area. Or maybe all that coffee was why we had the tech business to begin with.

Stands of evergreens mixed with deciduous trees covered in moss stretched out along the banks of the Skykomish. The rushing, westbound river competed for space with a railroad track and the road we were on in the corridor up to Stevens Pass. We crossed bridges with the river underneath us and sped under bridges with the railroad overhead, sometimes occupied by a moving train.

I could feel my tension ease as we left civilization behind. The trees were green. The river was clear as glass, first reflecting the sky, then turning into rapids, then forming deep quiet pools in the eddies of a bank. Franklin snoozed contentedly in the backseat, chin tucked against one armrest, feet pressed against the door on the other side.

A green sign flashed by—STEVENS PASS, ELEVATION 4061—as we raced alongside the ski resort. Summer had turned the snow-covered paths into bare wounds with the zigzag of ski lifts stitching them together. Chava hurtled over the crest and swooped down the other side, like a downhill skier setting a record. Though I'd never admit it, it was always fun being her passenger.

Off in the distance, a thin column of smoke appeared. The plume rose straight up from the dense forest before fading into a gauzy haze and disappearing altogether. A resident probably had a burn pile going—that was how many of the locals disposed of trash or yard waste. It could also be part of a planned burn, designed to clear dangerous underbrush before a spark from a careless camper or a zap of summer lightning lit the mass of tinder. The rest of the sky was clear as far as I could see.

Despite the treacherous and fast-spreading wildfires common out here in the western United States, there were none currently raging in the Cascades. I'd checked into that before we left. There was one burning in Utah, but nothing in our area. Fire season began in summer and could go into October, depending on conditions. Human beings started most early-season wildfires, but luckily that hadn't happened this year. We'd also had record-setting snowfall the previous winter and a cool spring, which helped delay the start.

"What do you see out there? Any signs of Bigfoot?" Chava's voice broke into my thoughts.

"Only the carved wooden one outside the Espresso Chalet," I said, referring to the statue near Index, a tiny community we'd passed just before we crossed the King County line. "But the scenery is beautiful."

"It's something, isn't it?"

"Breathtaking," I said. "Thank you for this."

She smiled and scanned through the stations on the radio again. Driving with Chava meant sampling a wide variety of musical styles. She'd pause to groove with some hip-hop group I'd never heard of, then pop over to a country station, putting her best twang into a duet with Tammy Wynette, before landing on an aria from *Rigoletto*.

At least with the aria, she didn't try to sing harmony.

I began to hum along with the melody of an old Eagles tune. It was going to be a perfect getaway. What could possibly go wrong?

Chapter Two

———•———

THREE HOURS INTO our drive, we arrived at the turnoff to the resort. The Bavarian-themed town of Leavenworth was a mere eight miles up the road. I looked forward to visiting it over the weekend. Based on the Dutch-inspired village of Solvang, California, Leavenworth had been rebuilt in the late sixties, starting with the Chikamin Hotel, now renamed the Edelweiss. The whitewashed exterior was accented with dark wooden timbers and decorated with Bavarian-themed paintings. The hotel proved the scheme successful and the rest of the businesses followed suit. Somehow the renovations managed to be charming, not cheesy. Besides, who didn't love a good bratwurst and beer?

The sign guiding us to our resort was carved from wood and mounted on two tall posts, as if sprung fully formed from trees. The Pacific Northwest theme was evident in the three-dimensional black bears climbing across the top, a mother and two cubs. An arrow pointed us down a long valley between steep-sided peaks. Curving around the west side of the valley floor, the road brought us to a driveway that turned east into the resort, before continuing out of sight. I wondered if anyone else lived on the road, though the canyon looked to end not far away.

The resort was a series of separate buildings. Each one stood on stone foundations, with walls of logs and cedar-shingle roofs. Despite the rustic nature of the materials, the overall effect was grand. The main lodge was stately, with a covered area to park under while you checked in. The summer day was perfect—mid-seventies, blue skies, soft breeze—but a stay here in the winter would most likely include rain and snow.

We parked under the overhang and made our way through the double glass doors to the reception desk. I loved the deer antlers mounted for handles, their texture smooth and warm under my hand. The floors were a rich yellow pine, and an enormous freestanding stone fireplace split the room, open on either side. The scent of wood smoke lingered in the air, conjuring up images of lumberjacks and logging camps. The front section of the main lodge contained soft leather sofas and bentwood chairs, grouped around the space in intimate gatherings despite the public nature of the room. Once you stepped around the fireplace, the reception area came into view, a long counter made of logs sawn in half, sanded, and polished to a high sheen.

"Can I help you?" a cheerful clerk asked as we walked up. "Are you checking in?"

We told her we were and hoped they'd let us into our room, even though it was only one o'clock and check-in wasn't until three.

"Your cabin is all ready," she said, bringing out a map of the grounds. "We have you in a dog-friendly suite." She walked us through the various delights the resort offered: the mineral pools—both indoor and out—the spa, with mani/pedis, massages, and mud wraps, and the restaurants. Breakfast, lunch, and dinner were served, along with happy hour or late-night drinks and snacks.

It wasn't five yet, but I was feeling pretty happy. I thought it might last a lot longer than an hour. Was there such a thing as a "happy weekend"?

"I didn't realize we had a cabin," I said as we went out to move Chava's car to the parking place in front of our accommodations.

"I wanted to surprise you," she said.

We drove to our little home away from home, crossing a bridge over a small stream that cut through the property. Stepping into our "cabin," we found a large front room, which included a fold-out sofa bed for me and a dog bed for Franklin in one corner, a bedroom for Chava, and a full bathroom complete with a Jacuzzi tub.

"It's perfect," I said.

"You're sure you don't mind taking the sofa bed?" she asked. "We could switch tomorrow night."

"I'm sure," I said. "This will suit me just fine."

After unpacking, we took Franklin for a walk around the grounds.

"That's where I'm going to be tomorrow morning," Chava said, pointing to the nine-hole golf course, driving range, and putting green. "Are you sure you don't want to join me for the lesson? I bet I can add you in."

"I'm sure. I'm going on a hike. There's got to be a way to get up on top," I said, pointing to the steep-sided hills around us, "and I intend to find it."

" 'Atta girl," Chava said. "Just don't get lost."

"I'll be fine," I said. "How hard could it be to follow a trail?"

THE FOLLOWING MORNING—BEFORE Chava went to her golf lesson—we dropped Franklin off at doggy daycare. While he got treated to his own day of beauty, we enjoyed the buffet breakfast. This kind of fare could add ten pounds to my almost six-foot frame in a few days if I didn't exercise. Good thing I was going on that hike. Though, given how yummy it was and how relaxed I felt, I wasn't sure I cared.

"Do you want to get together for lunch?" Chava asked, tucking her blonde beehive under a bright-pink scarf. She looked like bubble gum, but I wasn't going to say it aloud. "My lesson will be done by noon."

"I have no idea how long I'll be out," I said, rethinking my harsh fashion observation. After all, the pink went well with her purple eyes, the only feature we had in common. "Will you be able to pick up Franklin?"

He was going to be bathed, blow-dried and poofed out, nails trimmed, and whatever else an expensive doggie spa could do to a canine. Chava had been excited about treating her grand-dog as well as her daughter.

"I promise to pick him up," she said, "though doggie daycare sounds like a lot of fun. We should let him play with the other dogs for a while."

I might not be the only one in this family who never wanted to go home.

We walked out of the restaurant together and I headed over to the main building by myself to get some information on hikes.

It was kind of nice to go off on my own with no one expecting me to show up any time soon.

Of course, that also meant no one would know where to find me if I went missing.

I turned back to tell Chava I wanted her to know what trail I was going up. After all, it made sense to let *someone* know where I'd gone. Even experienced hikers fell or got injured. But she'd already disappeared. I'd have to look out for myself.

Intending to take advantage of the resort's natural beauty and not just the delicious restaurants, I went in search of supplies. I stopped at the gift shop and bought a reusable water bottle. It cost me an arm and a leg, but it had a handy strap to wear like a little purse across one shoulder, with the name of the resort glittering in sparkly red and silver script. If I got lost, it could also be used as a beacon to signal my distress. With a couple protein bars in my pocket, I felt duly outfitted. Finally I asked the sales clerk—Kim, according to her nametag—to suggest an easy walk with a view.

"There are a number of great hikes in the area, but if you'd like a view, I'd recommend the one that starts right across the road from our driveway," Kim said. She explained it went up along a ridge, with a beautiful view of Lake Wenatchee out to the west. "You can't get lost. It's straight up and straight back with no turnoffs."

"That sounds perfect," I said.

"It takes you into the Wenatchee National Forest," she said. "You also cross from national forest to the Lake Wenatchee State Park, with a little bit of private land mixed in. But don't worry, the entire trail is publicly accessible property and you won't be trespassing. Do you have a dog with you?"

"I do," I said with the still newfound pride of dog ownership. "But he's over getting a shave and a haircut this morning." I fought the urge to knock "two bits" out with my knuckles on the countertop. The clerk looked a little young to get the joke.

"Dogs can be on the trail as long as they're leashed. Just make sure he doesn't chase wildlife."

"I'll keep that in mind," I said, wondering if I should have waited until Franklin was done at the groomer. He'd love a walk in the woods with me.

Or maybe he'd prefer hanging out on the bed in our cabin, watching TV and eating gourmet doggy snacks. I paused for a moment at the thought of staying in bed, which sounded kind of nice. After all, I could look out the window to enjoy the scenery …. I talked myself out of being such a lazy slug. Plus, eating gourmet doggy snacks wasn't really my thing.

Noticing the sales clerk had calves of iron, the physique of a long distance runner, and the suntan of someone who spent most of her time outdoors, I said, "It's an easy walk, right?"

"You look like you're in good shape," she said. "You'll be starting at an elevation of a little more than one thousand feet and gaining about fifteen hundred over three miles. Drink lots of water and take your time, and you'll be fine."

Who was I to argue with that? After all, I worked out at the gym. I had muscle tone and endurance. Going slow was fine with me. I certainly didn't intend on racing around in the woods.

"I live at sea level," I said. "Should I worry about the altitude?"

"Some people find they get out of breath quicker at three thousand feet, but altitude sickness rarely impacts anyone at less than eight thousand."

After thanking her for her help, I stepped outside and followed Kim's directions to the trailhead. The sky was blue and the sun was warm, but it was cool in the shade. A lightweight, long-sleeved cotton shirt was tied around my waist. It would only get hotter as noon approached, but I thought I might need protection from the sun—something we had barely seen for months on our side of the mountains. The air carried the earthy scent of dirt and pine needles. The squawk of birds in the trees broke the silence and a dark-blue bird with a black triangular shaped peak on his head flitted down onto a rock near my feet. At the start of the trail, a little wooden kiosk put up by the Forest Service and the Department of Agriculture included a map and a display of the local flora and fauna. It identified the noisemaker as a Steller's jay. It also explained the difference between crows and ravens, told me to look out for poison oak, and not to feed the black bears.

What was I getting myself into? Could poison oak affect me through my jeans? Could a black bear smell a protein bar in my pocket? Pulling my cell out, I started to send a text to Chava to tell her where I was going.

"You're being ridiculous," I said out loud before I'd even brought up her number, just in time for a teenager in running attire to hear me as he passed by.

"What's that?" he asked.

"Just getting off a call," I said, holding up my cellphone

and pretending to hang up. Talking to myself wasn't a habit I advertised to strangers.

He gave me a curious look but started up the trail at a fast jog. I was impressed. Uneven terrain, a steep climb ... the guy was in good shape. Though he was young and might not know what he was in for.

Deciding to play it safe even if I was being silly, I sent Chava a text with a description of my starting point.

It definitely felt good that at least one person on the planet knew where I was. Two, if you counted Kim, the sales clerk in the gift shop.

I was memorable, right?

Tucking my phone and the map of the area in the back pocket of my jeans, I set off up the trail. People hiked in the mountains every day and nothing bad happened to them.

How much trouble could I get into on a bright sunny day, hiking a well-marked, public path with no forks or turnoffs?

IT TOOK TWO hours to reach the top of the ridge. My idea of easy and Kim's idea of easy might be two different things. As I huffed and puffed to a stopping point, I reassured myself that hiking at almost three thousand feet was different than being at sea level even if it wasn't "high" elevation. The view from the top was stunning, though, with the lake stretched out below me. It was the perfect place for a quick break, complete with a nice flat rock where I could sit and enjoy a protein bar.

Lightweight it was, tasty it was not. Cardboard and paste had better flavor.

Penance for this morning's breakfast.

I pulled my cellphone out of my back pocket to check for messages and came up with zip; there wasn't any service up here. The message to Chava still showed a little spinning circle. Useless to try again—I'd be back before she got it. Maybe that's why the kid had given me a funny look when I said I was on a call.

The trail ended at an outcropping of rock not far from where I sat. There were four metal signs glinting in the sun. Putting my phone back in my pocket, I traversed the last fifty feet and found a panorama of the various mountain peaks visible from the vantage point. The metal signs had outlines of the peaks and their names etched into the surface. One sign for each direction: north, south, east, and west. I spent a few minutes identifying mountains.

And let's be honest, I was still recovering from the ascent.

As I looked around, it dawned on me that the runner hadn't passed me on his way back down the trail. He was nowhere to be seen.

The landscape didn't have a lot of undergrowth to block him from my view. It was fairly open between the ponderosa pines. He should be visible. Though some young western hemlocks created denser thickets, there wasn't much to screen him. Look how well I'd integrated what I'd learned at the kiosk. I knew a ponderosa from a hemlock.

He could have gone off the trail and passed me at some point where I couldn't see him or plunged farther into the wilderness. On the other hand, people died every year in our mountains. Just last week, a hiker fell off a cliff on Mt. Si, a popular hike near the little town of North Bend.

Athletic as he'd appeared, the runner was still just a kid. His safety would gnaw at me.

The sun was almost directly overhead, so there were several hours of daylight left. Standing at the lip of the outcropping, I focused my gaze out along the ridge in front of me, then brought my attention closer in, scanning each quadrant one at a time, methodically searching the landscape. Nothing moved, save a few small woodland creatures that might have been chipmunks or maybe hamsters. A lone fisherman sat in a boat far away, out on the lake. Or maybe it was a she. Regardless, it wasn't my teen runner.

I had half a bottle of water and one more protein bar, so I

should be fine for another two hours when I'd be safely back at the resort. Then it would be time for lunch, a meal I planned to indulge in righteously after burning up all these calories. For now, however, I could spend a few minutes trying to spot him and see if he was okay. Just for peace of mind.

Then I looked up.

Big black birds.

Circling.

Were those ravens or crows? It was a good sign they were circling. Ravens ate carrion, right? If something had died, the birds would already be down on the ground. I remembered that from the kiosk.

One by one, they started to drop from the sky.

Well, that couldn't be good.

Chapter Three

---•---

THE BIRDS HAD plummeted to earth not far away. The only route headed in their general direction was a vague track leading off to the north. It clearly wasn't official, but created either unintentionally by careless hikers looking for a nice rock to squat behind or animals on their way into the backcountry. It couldn't hurt to go a little way off the trail; even a townie like me wouldn't get lost that fast. I didn't really think the kid had fallen and couldn't get up, but something was tingling my spidey-sense.

Or maybe I was just lightheaded from lack of oxygen.

Give it half an hour, the little voice inside my head told me. It wouldn't take the whole two hours to go back downhill, so I should still only be out about four hours total, even with a little detour. The weather was perfect for hiking—not quite eighty degrees with bright sunshine. Only a few clouds had appeared on the horizon. I'd neither freeze nor bake with a little extra time outside. And how would I feel if something had happened to the runner, a turned ankle for example, or a kidnapping by Bigfoot? I might be the only person who knew he was up here.

My circle of friends had been left at home, but apparently I'd brought my sense of responsibility for others with me.

On the plus side, I would turn the lovely brown of a well-made cappuccino, proving to my friends back in Bellingham that I had indeed been on vacation on the sunny side of the mountains.

The faint track went straight toward the edge of the forest, then began winding around trees. Although indistinct, the course still showed after I left the open area behind. The world felt very different under the canopy. Out on the exposed ridgeline, a soft but persistent wind blew across my face. Though gentle, it made a shushing sound, like a person learning to whistle. Now, all sound was hushed. Even the raucous blue jays had fallen silent.

Pulling my cell out of my pocket again to check the time, I found that fifteen minutes had flown by. Glad as I was that the clock continued working even when I was out of range for making a call, I wondered how long it would take to run my battery down. Maybe it was time to head back. My missing runner was probably propped up in front of a TV by now, showered and refreshed after his jaunt up the side of a mountain. He had undoubtedly gone off the marked path, despite the big signs reading CAUTION DO NOT STEP OFF THE TRAIL, and passed me heading home.

It was then I noticed the map was no longer in my pocket. It must have fallen out earlier when I pulled out my phone.

Not that I really needed it. The trail was a straight line with no intersections. But it had been nice to have something to look at to put my location into context within the larger landscape. Especially now, after I'd worked so hard to learn the names of all those mountain peaks.

Plus, I didn't want to litter; hopefully I'd find it on my way down.

Another sound came through the trees, breaking the eerie

silence. Definitely not a blue jay. If I didn't know any better, I'd say it was a velociraptor from the movie *Jurassic Park*.

Weren't birds related to dinosaurs?

Meat-eating birds, like … vultures. Did we have vultures in the Cascades? I knew they would eat the flesh of the dead. In Tibetan Sky Burials, corpses were picked clean and the vultures carried souls to heaven.

Visions of the boy being attacked like a scene from an Alfred Hitchcock movie pulled me forward. Unfortunately, it also pulled me right over an exposed tree root hidden under some leaves and pitched me off the edge of a cliff.

Okay, not really a cliff, per se, I said to myself as I lay on my back at the bottom of a small ravine. It wasn't like I had free-fallen twenty feet so much as rolled down a twenty-foot hill.

A hill covered in rocky outcroppings.

Bouncing over the rocks had felt like being pummeled with tiny hammers. It took a few minutes before I could breath normally again, but an assessment of the damage to my body determined nothing was broken or sprained. The rainbow of bruises, however, should be spectacular. My dignity had taken the worst hit. No one had seen me, though, so even that was salvageable. I'd have a good story to regale Chava with when we got together tonight.

I finally sat up. So far so good; everything worked. Then I looked around.

Which hill had I rolled down?

Sunlight came through the trees directly overhead, so there weren't clear shadows to help me get oriented.

I'd tumbled around enough to be dizzy, adding to my confusion.

The landscape gave up no hints at all. No marks in the dirt or broken branches to signal the right way back up. Or rather, lots of marks and broken bits of twigs, but none that looked newly made by a six-foot private investigator rolling over them on her way down.

The good news was my water bottle was intact, as was my cellphone. The bad news was I still had no signal. I wished I'd downloaded a compass back when I'd had a connection.

Something should look familiar, right? If I could scramble my way back up out of this little ravine, I'd either be on the correct side or not and adjust from there.

Panting hard by the time my feet were once more on reasonably level terrain, I really wished I'd stayed in bed. Dessert was definitely on the menu tonight. Maybe two. Starve a fever, feed a cold, but what did you do for a bunch of bruises and extreme physical fatigue? Dessert sounded about right.

Meanwhile, nothing looked familiar on this side of the gulch. The other side didn't look familiar either. It was all just a bunch of trees.

Then I heard it again, the sound of the birds.

Closer.

With nowhere else to go, I might as well continue to look for them. Maybe if I found them on the ground, I could figure out where I'd been standing when I saw them drop from the sky.

Not a great plan, but it gave me a direction and helped keep panic at bay. What started out as an easy hike was devolving into me becoming a statistic, a "city" person lost in the woods.

A few minutes later, a clearing appeared, roughly the length of a baseball field. Someone had a tent set up at the far edge. That was a good sign. The camper could steer me in the direction of the resort. As long as they weren't a follower of Charles Manson or as lost as I was.

Getting closer, I saw that the tent was nothing more than a piece of canvas tied between two trees, held down by rocks, and propped up with sticks. Banjos weren't playing, exactly, but it didn't scream "Silicon-Valley hipster," either.

Movement caught my eye and caution stopped me behind a large ponderosa pine. The hairs on the back of my neck rose.

Birds.

They picked at what looked to be a trash bag torn open, refuse scattered around.

They were bigger than the crows in Bellingham, so these must be the common ravens I'd seen on the kiosk. At least they weren't eating carrion.

Then I noticed something big lying in the field.

A deer?

Whatever it was, it wasn't wearing running shoes, so the kid was okay.

But it was wearing boots, which kind of took the deer possibility off the table.

Had someone had a heart attack or a stroke? Passed out from a bottle of hooch? Or was some more criminal activity going on?

Noises came from the direction of the tent. If the person in the meadow had friends around, why weren't they out here attending to them?

If the person in the tent wasn't a friend, what did that mean for me?

That's when I smelled smoke.

Staying in bed and watching television might have been a better way to spend my first day of vacation.

Even doggy snacks were starting to sound good.

Chapter Four

———•———

Flames shot up from the tent. I was standing in the world's largest tinderbox and a fire had just broken out. Could I put it out? I started to run toward the tent, but the grasses around it began to burn as well. An erratic wind blew the flames around, scattering fire in every direction.

What about the person now behind me in the field?

Were they dead and past help?

Or alive, hurt, and waiting for me to save them?

The ravens took to the air, croaking their raspy calls. I desperately wished I could join them, instead of being stuck down here on the ground.

Sprinting over to the body, I discovered it was a man. I pulled on his arm. If he wasn't too injured to stand, maybe we could both get out of here before the whole place went up in flames.

Dead weight.

He wasn't large, but I didn't think I'd be able to carry him. His face was weathered enough for me to guess mid-forties. His arm was hard, well-muscled. His skin was brown and his hair was black.

He opened his eyes.

"*Cuidado,*" he said.

Latino.

Like my father.

Like half of me.

"*Cuidado*?" I repeated back. Careful? With him? Because he was injured? Or because of the fire? Or was he talking about whomever had been rustling around in the tent? "Can you get up? Can you stand?"

"*Cuidado, mija.*"

My daughter? Was he just saying that because I looked a little like him?

"*Desaparecido.*"

"What?"

"*Desaparecido.*"

Nope, saying the word twice didn't help at all.

"*Secuestrado,*" he said before his eyes rolled back and he convulsed. Trying to hold his head during the seizure, I felt something warm and wet. My hands came away covered in blood.

A wound on the back of his head? Had he been unconscious before I grabbed him?

A hot wind swept across us.

I shook the man again. "*Ayúdame,*" he said, regaining consciousness. Help me. "*Ayúdame a encontrar a mi hija.*"

Help him what? *Hija* I knew, but I couldn't think what *encontrar* meant. Sing? No, that was *cantar*. Wait. Find. Daughter. Was there someone else in this meadow? A child?

I shook him again, "Is your daughter out here with you?" I shouted, but he was out again. I tried to lift him, but barely got him halfway off the ground. The weight was problematic enough, but the awkwardness of lifting an unconscious man made it worse. I tried to pull him over my shoulder in a firefighter carry, but it was like handling one hundred and sixty pounds of shifting sand.

The fire was building not far away. Smoke rolled over me,

stinging my eyes and filling my lungs. I hauled on him and managed to pull him a short distance. The wind had come up, but went around me in circles. I couldn't tell which direction would take me out of the encroaching flames.

"You've got to wake up," I said, bending over him. I yelled in his face while I shook him. "Get up, get up, get up."

His eyes opened and he reached for me. I managed to get him on his feet and we started to move again. The smoke got heavier and the winds continued to buffet us from all around, almost as if we'd stepped into our very own trip to Oz, but our tornado was made of smoke and fire.

We struggled along as fast as we could while the air temperature started to rise. The fire dogged our heels, no matter which way we turned. I tried not to think about the possibility of a child being caught in the inferno behind us.

Tripping over the uneven terrain, the man slipped from my grasp and landed hard. My breath coming in gasps, I could see a line of flames racing toward us. There didn't appear to be any way I could get him out of the way in time.

He roused himself and struggled for a moment. I thought he was trying to stand again, but he was pulling something out of his shirt pocket. "*Ayúdame a encontrar a mi hija.*"

"I don't speak very good Spanish," I said. "I'm sorry."

He handed me something, a small packet of plastic.

"You have to help me," he said in English. "Find my daughter. Help her."

He continued to struggle and I still thought he wanted to stand, but he shoved me away and reached into another pocket. He pushed something heavy into my hand.

"This is all I have for money," he said. I opened my fingers to find a heavy silver crucifix on a beaded chain. A rosary. "Find her."

Shoving the items in my pockets—now was not the time to argue—I got the man back on his feet.

"We've got to go," I said, hauling him with me.

Five minutes later, he fell again, narrowly missing a small jumble of rocks on an otherwise open area. I could barely see, my eyesight tunneling, my labored breathing blocking out all other sound. Leaning over him, he seized again. I held him until the convulsions stopped. He grasped my arm, his strength surprising in its ferocity.

"*Elmaymato*," he said, stringing together words that held no meaning for me. "He has my daughter. Promise me you will find her."

"I promise."

Then he stopped. Stopped speaking. Stopped moving. Stopped breathing. I started CPR, but there was no life left in the man. The flames were coming in my direction. Smoke filled the air again, and that alone could kill me.

"I'm sorry," I said as I laid his head gently on the ground. "*Descansa en paz*," I said. I didn't know if it was appropriate, but rest in peace was the best I could do in his language.

The man was dead. I started to check his pockets for identification, but the heat from the fire became unbearable. Now there was only one action that made sense.

Run.

Chapter Five

———•———

THE REST OF the day and most of the night became a blur of terror. The flames, heat, and smoke sent me scrambling, panicked. Not to mention distraught over the man I'd had to leave behind and wondering exactly what I had promised him in his final moments. But every time I looked back, the heat and flashes of light pushed me forward. Terrified, with little thought to direction, I kept moving. The terrain was so steep, sometimes I had to crawl on my hands and knees. Smoke filled the air, setting off coughing fits and veering me off on a new heading. At other moments, the air would clear and I'd stop, catch my breath, and assess the situation, until a whiff of smoke and shower of cinders started me moving again.

There are probably people in the world who could remain calm in my situation. Not me. My adrenaline-fueled, marathon run through the forest was driven by pure instinct and fear.

Stay ahead of the fire.

That was all that mattered. My entire body shook with the flight aspects of fight, flight, or freeze. I knew I couldn't fight in this situation and freezing wasn't an option. To stop moving would kill me.

Even though it might have been easier to run downhill, I began to feel as if the fire wanted me surging ever upward. The wind continued to increase, and every time I turned downhill, the smoke and threat of immolation propelled me toward some unseen summit. The fire edged ever closer, threatening to consume me along with whatever fuel it could find.

At one point, a deer bolted past, smoke rising from its back where the fire had singed its hair, then vanished over a slight rise ahead of me. The wind helped to force me along, but it meant the fire was moving faster too. I crested the hill just behind the deer and saw a small ravine, the bottom of it stained darker than the surrounding land.

The deer stumbled into the creek, submerging itself, and moving downstream under the weight of rushing water.

A quick glance back showed the advancing flames dodging and flaring, racing forward at a speed I could never match. Though there was now a rocky area with less fuel to burn between the flames and my current position, I couldn't be sure it was enough to stop the inferno in my wake. The heat from the fire had already reached me.

Scrambling and pitching forward, I flung myself into the water. The stream was shallow and I only managed to get the lower half of my body fully submerged. I pulled the cotton shirt tied around my waist up over my head, while frantically trying to scoot farther down into the brook. I hoped the wet fabric would keep me from being burnt to a crisp.

Though my face was underwater, the very top of my head was unprotected. To make matters worse, the breath I took wouldn't last forever, but I couldn't risk rising out of what little protection the creek provided. The waterlogged cotton shirt was draped over my head like a shroud, adding to my sense of suffocation. It didn't help that the air I'd sucked in before my plunge was tinged with smoke and burned my lungs. I felt a flash of pain on the top of my head. Even with my eyes closed and my face submerged, bright light turned my eyelids Day-Glo orange.

My lungs felt ready to burst. I couldn't hold out any longer.

I sat up. From my spot, I could see untouched dirt immediately adjacent the stream, and black smoldering places above. The fire must have jumped the ravine, but the radiant heat had been enough to burn my scalp. Carefully touching my damaged skin, I felt my hair crunch and the pain of the wound, which was blistered and raw. Luckily, the water had protected almost all of me from the heat, so that only the crown of my head was burned. I could breathe okay, and I thought about lying back down in the water until help came. The water sure felt good.

Then I got cold.

Standing on shaky legs, I watched a red line travel away through the trees as fast as the wind could send it. The fire skipped across the land, surviving on the dry grasses under the trees. It wasn't staying around long enough to light the forest. As much damage as it was doing on the ground level, at least it wasn't burning the trees down around my ears. Clearly, the creek in the ditch had protected me and the fire had indeed flashed over. I hadn't known that was possible. I'd always thought fire in the woods ate everything it touched, but parts of the land around me showed no sign of the flames at all, whereas in other places, the grasses still smoldered.

Pain broke through the shock. Though my soggy shirt had shielded my neck and most of my head, the burned portion throbbed.

I lay back down on dry land for a moment, gathering my wits together. It was possible I'd survived the worst. I knew little about forest fires, but if the flames had passed me, I didn't think the fire would double back and get to me again unless the wind shifted. But what if another line followed after? There were still plenty of trees and bigger shrubs for fuel if a hotter, slower fire was creeping up.

Forcing myself upright, I stood and made my way out of the cut. The air was murky, but I could breathe a little easier on higher ground, as if the smoke had settled in the lower-lying area. The best thing to do, it seemed, was to follow the fire that had cleared me. I was working with the theory that behind the burn was the safest place to be. Maybe there was another ring of fire coming my way, but I was doing the best I could under the circumstances. I wasn't going to just sit there all night and wait to die.

Traveling across the black, crunchy ground, I could see where the fire had gone. Noting that the trees around the clearings hadn't burned at all, I thought about striking off through them to get to safety, but feared getting even more lost. At least the drier, more open ground clearly traveled in one direction—up—giving me a better trail. If I could see the lake, I could orient myself. Going into the trees, I dreaded traveling in circles all night long.

Heat came up through the soles of my shoes, but not enough to hurt. It's possible that the pain from the bruises all over my body and the burn on my head had distracted me from new sensations. A flare startled me when a nearby tree stump burst into flames, sending me back into a sprint, but it died out quickly and I learned to ignore the flashes of light that came and went in my peripheral vision.

A rumble reverberated and I stopped, heart pounding so loud I thought at first that had been the noise. Then a flash lit up the sky. High above me, clouds had formed while I'd been dashing across the wilderness.

A thunderstorm.

Would it be enough to douse the fire? Or would a strike of lightning just add to the blaze?

A burst of rain fell, and I bolted under the trees for what meager protection they could give me. Hunkering down between the trunks of two big pines, I waited for locusts and the four evils, or at least the headless horseman, as the world appeared to be charging toward destruction. More lightning lit the sky, which had grown dark from the storm and the late hour.

After what felt like an eternity, the rain stopped. I hobbled out onto a treeless expanse of granite. Stumbling forward, I lay down in the middle of the stony ground, exhausted but relatively safe for the first time in hours. No heat. The flashes of flames no longer visible, I concluded that the storm had passed. The sounds of the wind had been replaced by a sinister silence, and there was no hot orange glow anywhere in the sky.

Now I was really cold.

How cold did I have to be for hypothermia to set in?

Wouldn't that be ironic? Freeze to death after surviving a forest fire. Alanis Morissette could write a new verse for me.

My wet clothes did nothing to protect me from the dropping temperatures. The air temp would probably stay in the forties, but I recognized the danger I was in. Now that I'd stopped moving, the cold was taking over.

No one knew my location. I didn't even know where I was. The fire had burned behind, then over me. I had no food—I'd eaten my last protein bar a few hours ago—and no way to dry out. I'd refilled my water bottle from the stream I'd launched myself into, so at least I could stay hydrated. Now, how to stave off hypothermia?

You could start a fire, said the little voice in my head.

At least my sense of humor hadn't deserted me.

My best bet, it seemed, was to keep walking. Slow and controlled, not the hysterical gallop I'd kept up throughout most of my ordeal.

Then I tried to stand.

Maybe I needed to rest a little longer. Catch my breath.

Good as that sounded, if I didn't get up now, I might not be able to later.

Crawling on my knees to a large rock, I managed to pull myself into a mostly upright position. The thought of taking any more steps was almost more than I could bear. My legs shook, and my quads felt like they might cramp up and never move again. As my adrenaline levels decreased, pain took center stage.

Pictures flashed through my mind.

Chava, the mother I was just starting to get to know as an adult. We were finally figuring out how to be friends.

Franklin was safe down at the resort. I knew Chava would make sure my dog was taken care of, but he was supposed to be with me.

Chance Parker, the homicide detective I'd loved and lost and maybe now found again.

So many reasons to walk out of this forest, not lie down and turn into a smoky popsicle.

"Buck up, girlfriend," I said, channeling the husky Southern drawl of my best friend Iz. I straightened up. "Move it."

I could see her face in front of me, the sweat dripping across her dusky skin as she pushed me at the dojo where we practiced martial arts together. She would never let me live it down if I died out here.

One foot went in front of the other. "I got this, Iz," I said to my insistent hallucination. "I won't fail you now."

Maybe having that circle of friends back home was worth the time and attention relationships required. I'd give anything to see all their faces again.

For the first time in several hours, my luck turned. A road appeared out of the trees. Not much of one—just graded dirt— but still, a road.

I'd like to say I looked up, located the North Star, and made a calculated guess which direction to go, based on the map I'd memorized and my newfound knowledge of the local mountain peaks, but I was so tired it didn't even occur to me I might be walking away from civilization instead of toward it.

My luck held, however, and I'd chosen correctly. The next thing I knew, I came out to the flashing lights of emergency vehicles, various firefighters in full regalia, and someone hustling me into an ambulance.

I heard, "You're going to be all right," just before slipping into unconsciousness.

"*Elmaymato*," I said out loud as darkness swam in front of my eyes. "Don't forget. *Elmaymato.*"

A man's final words. It had to mean something.

Chapter Six

———◆———

I AWOKE WITH a start. The smell of smoke and burnt hair spiked my heart rate. Blipping sounds coincided with the jolt my cardiovascular system had sustained and my feet, covered in a white blanket, swam into view. I was in a hospital bed. Various electrodes, IV bags, and monitors were attached to my extremities. Scenes from the night before started to surface. An ambulance ride.   emergency room. X-rays and an oxygen mask.

The smell wasn't my imagination. My hair, my skin, my very cells appeared to be permeated with the particulates of last night's conflagration.

At least I hoped it was last night; surely I hadn't been out for more than a day.

Hearing my name, I turned to the left and found two faces peering at me, concern etched in their features.

"Eduardo?" I croaked out. "What are you doing here?"

"Your father drove in while you were missing," Chava said.

My father—mastermind of criminal enterprises and cleaner for the mob.

I didn't ask how he'd known I was in trouble. His recent

interest in my well-being bordered on somewhere between touching and terrifying since he always seemed to know where I was.

"It's nice to see you," I said.

"You too, *mija*. How is it you always seem to be in so much danger?"

He did tend to arrive while I was skirting death.

"I'll work on that," I said. "What happened?" I waved my arm around, making the wires dance.

"What's the last thing you remember?" Chava asked.

"Coughing a lot in the emergency room. I don't remember being moved up here."

"Luckily you don't have a head injury," Chava said. "But the doctor told us your memory might be spotty because of the exhaustion and other trauma you sustained. Do you remember being out in the woods?"

"I do. I was looking for a teenage boy. But, there was a fire. Then a storm. Then there were firemen."

"*Sí*, you were brought here in an ambulance," Eduardo said. I must have looked blank because he clarified. "To the hospital in Wenatchee." His accent made "Wenatchee" sound exotic.

"Ah. Wenatchee. Right." Wenatchee sat on the Columbia River about twenty miles east of Leavenworth. I didn't want to admit I'd forgotten what forest I'd been wandering around in. Wenatchee National Forest. The resort and spa with Chava. Got it. I must have been brought down out of the mountains to the bigger town, where there would be at least one major hospital.

"In addition to the bruises all over your body, you suffered exhaustion, dehydration, hypothermia, smoke inhalation, and a small second-degree burn," Chava said, ticking off my various maladies with vigor. "How did you get so bruised up?"

I thought a moment. What exactly had happened yesterday?

"I fell down a hill."

Chava dropped her head into her hands. "I thought you were going for a nice, peaceful walk."

"Where's Franklin?" I asked. It was hot outside. I couldn't believe Chava would have left him in the car all this time.

"Debbie Buse drove over from Bellingham and got a dog-friendly room."

"She did that for us?"

"Of course she did," Chava said. "You could have died out there. I called her as soon as you were on your way to the hospital. I knew I couldn't leave him in the car or at the resort for very long alone."

"What about her business?" I asked.

"Her kids are watching the bookstore. She left Gracie Allen with them, but she's got Indy with her. I'm sure those two have about wrecked her room by now." Chava said this last bit with affection. Gracie Allen was an elderly beagle. Indy was a Goldendoodle who liked to wrestle with my mammoth canine. The two of them together could create quite a stir.

"Did we at least pay for her room?" I asked.

"It's all taken care of," Eduardo said, touching my arm. "Don't worry about *tu perro* or your friend."

Concern for Franklin had gotten me half out of bed, and I realized I was tangled up with a plastic tube in my nose.

"What the hell is this?"

"Oxygen," Chava said. "Leave it—"

The rest of yesterday's events came rushing back to me and I cut her off. "I need to talk to the police."

"Was someone murdered?" Eduardo asked. "Or did someone try to kill you?"

Chava and I both looked at him in shocked silence.

He really did know everything.

"Someone else died," I said. "But what makes you think the guy I found was murdered?"

"What guy are we talking about?" Chava asked, looking back and forth between us. "What do you mean you were looking for a teenage boy?"

"Why else would you keep saying '*él me mató*,' " Eduardo

asked. "It doesn't make sense to me you would say this in Spanish. I think someone else said this to you."

"I don't know what that means," I said, remembering the mantra I'd been saying when oblivion overtook me in the ambulance.

"He killed me," Eduardo said.

Then I remembered the rest of what the man said.

"His daughter," I said. "She's missing."

"Missing?" Chava said. "In the fire? Is she the teenager?"

The man didn't seem worried about his child being in the fire. He didn't say to get her out of the meadow. He said to find her.

"No. Not the teenager," I said. "And it wasn't the fire he was worried about."

Then I remembered the stuff he'd handed me.

"Where are my things? I need to see what was in the—"

"Plastic?" Eduardo asked, holding up the object and the heavy silver rosary.

"We've been wondering what these are," Chava said. "I'd never seen them before."

Inside the plastic, which turned out to be one of those photo holders like you'd have in a wallet, were pictures of a lovely young woman at various ages, the most recent putting her in her early twenties. Pulling the most current photo out, I turned it over and found, *Te amo Papi, Gabriela* written in script on the back. I love you, Daddy. I went through the rest of the photos, but there were no other notes on the backs.

"Where did these things come from?" Eduardo asked.

I explained about the runner who had disappeared from the trail. How I'd planned to spend a few minutes looking for him, but instead I'd come across the man in the meadow. How I'd tried to get him to safety after the fire broke out, and listened to his claim that his daughter was missing.

"This must be his daughter," I said. "But why the rosary?"

"This is antique," Eduardo said, taking it from me and

looking closely at the design. "Probably from Mexico. I'm sure it is old and very valuable. It may be the only possession of value he could travel with, so he brought it with him to barter or pawn."

It's the only thing of value I have, he'd said just before handing it to me.

Find my daughter, he'd said. Then he'd paid me. Was I now on a case for a missing girl?

I'd never worked for a dead man before.

Chapter Seven

———•———

A NURSE HUSTLED into my room. She nodded to my parents and walked over to a computer I hadn't noticed before, on a table in the corner of my room.

"Nice to see you're awake, Eddie," she said. "My name is Tanesha. I've been looking after you today."

"Tanesha came on at seven this morning," Chava said. "She's been in every hour to check on you."

"What time is it?" I asked.

"It's four," Tanesha said, clicking away on the computer. "I'm just going to update your charts."

"Four? As in p.m.?"

"You've slept all day," Chava said.

"Your oxygen looks good," Tanesha continued. "How are you feeling?"

"Thirsty."

"I should think," she said with a laugh. Leaning over a bedside table, she poured water from a pink plastic pitcher into a white plastic cup. She tore the plastic off a bendy straw before sticking it in and handing it over to me. I felt about five years old. Except, I really liked the bendy straw and the nurse was big and warm and matronly, making me feel protected in a way Chava couldn't quite pull off, no matter how good her intentions.

After taking a long sip, I handed it back.

"Can you breathe deeply for me?" Tanesha asked, setting the cup back on the hospital table next to my bed.

The coughing felt like it might never end.

"That's it," the nurse said, handing me a wad of tissues. "You're okay," she crooned in a reassuring voice. "I know it feels awful, but you've got to get all that out of your lungs."

The tissues came away covered in black gook that made me feel like I'd expelled the contents of an old hibachi.

"That's disgusting," I said, not wanting to hand the dirty tissues over, but Tanesha took it without batting an eye.

"Better to get it all up and out," she said, tossing the tissues away and peeling off her gloves.

"Guess I took in a lot of smoke," I said, hearing how gruff I sounded. Had I turned my vocal chords permanently into bacon?

"It sounds worse than it is," Tanesha said. "The good news is your lungs aren't permanently damaged. You're going to cough for a few days, but you should be fine."

Was there bad news to go along with the good?

"So I can get out of here?" I asked.

"You're not *that* fine," the nurse said. "Let's start with seeing how you do with keeping water down."

"Just water?" I asked.

"Yes. We have to make sure you can keep down liquids, then solid food. We've got you on intravenous antibiotics through an IV. You also had a dose of Lactated Ringer's to get your electrolytes up, which are fine now. You've got a small but nasty burn on your head. We don't want to risk infection. Because of the potential damage your lungs received breathing in smoke and heat, you're also at risk for pneumonia." Her voice was matter-of-fact as she laid out my apparently dire condition.

Had I managed to escape hypothermia and a forest fire only to die in the hospital from complications? And what the hell was a Lactated Ringer's? So many questions. Like how did Eduardo get here so fast?

"Now what?" I asked.

"Now, we make sure you can breathe without oxygen and keep down food as well." As she spoke, she unhooked the tube from my nose. "It took warmed IVs to get your body temperature back up to normal. There's no reason for you to be rushing out of this nice warm bed."

She had a point.

"The doctor will come talk to you on her rounds. She saw you this morning, but I don't think you remember that."

"Not really," I admitted.

"That's okay," Tanesha said. "You don't have a concussion, but you experienced other trauma; it's all right if you have a few holes."

I didn't like the sound of that, but Tanesha continued talking about the doctor.

"She needs to determine if you're healthy enough to go home. We also want to see where your pain level is. We had you on morphine in your IV, but we can switch you over to oral pain meds now that you're conscious."

"I'm doing okay," I said, though I wasn't sure what was worse, the bruises or the burn on my scalp. Both were competing for my attention.

"You just let me know when you're ready for something else. The morphine you've been on will continue wearing off."

After taking the rest of my vitals—normal—and checking out the burn on top my head—icky—the nurse left us alone again. She promised I'd get to eat dinner soon, which had me salivating. I hadn't consumed real food since our buffet breakfast the day before. I had more than worked that off, along with those protein bars. Hopefully dinner would include Jell-O and ice cream. I wasn't sure what else my throat could handle. Tanesha also said I could take a shower. I'd do that as soon as I had a few answers to my questions.

Turning back to Chava and Eduardo, I picked up the thread of our earlier conversation.

"We have to get me out of here. I've got to talk to the police."

"You aren't going anywhere," Chava said. "Not until the doctor comes and sees you and says it's okay."

"But Chava, a man died out there and a woman is missing. Plus, I still don't know if that teenager is all right."

"The only person I've heard reported missing in the fire was you; I'm sure that boy is fine. The man you found will be just as dead tomorrow. There's nothing the police are going to do tonight. They aren't going to charge up that mountain into a forest fire and start taking fingerprints. I'm sure the firefighters found him. As for this woman, you said you don't think she was caught in the fire?"

"I don't. He would have been panicked about getting her out of immediate danger. It wasn't that. I think she's been missing for at least a few days."

"I'm not sure that's *your* problem," Chava said.

My mother—the amateur sleuth—didn't want to break me out of the hospital to go locate a corpse and a missing person?

"She's an adult," Chava said. "Maybe she just left home."

"I have to agree with your mother," Eduardo said. "You're our priority and you need to rest."

Since when was I my father's priority? He hadn't been a part of my life when I was a child and had only resurfaced back in December. Was he making up for lost time? Or did he have some other agenda I hadn't figured out yet?

Looking back and forth between the two of them, I could see it was a losing battle. They had control of the car keys, my wallet, and my clothes. Currently I had nothing on but one of those silly gowns they give you in places like this, tied in the back and flared out to reveal your naked backside if you walked too fast. Plus, it was covered in little ducks. Who would take me seriously dressed like this? I couldn't even reach the bedside phone without dislodging a few wires, and what would I say if I did call 911?

"What does *desaparecido* mean?" I asked.

"Missing," Eduardo said. "That could mean a lot of things."

"How about *secuestrado*?"

"Say that again." Eduardo's expression changed to one of thoughtfulness.

"*Secuestrado*. That's the other word he used. What does it mean?

Chava and I both turned to Eduardo. He paused a long moment, and I started to prompt him when he waved me off.

"Abducted."

"Well," I said. "Does that change anything?"

Chapter Eight

———•———

CHAVA AND EDUARDO exchanged a glance. I finally had their full attention about Gabriela.

"Now do you believe me when I say I need to talk to the authorities?"

"Okay," Chava said. "I'll call the police and have them send someone over to take your statement. But that's going to have to do for now. You are not leaving this hospital against doctor's orders."

"Fine," I said, "but better make it the Chelan County Sheriff. The events didn't happen in the Wenatchee city limits, and Leavenworth is so small, I doubt they have their own police force."

Chava nodded and poked around on her smartphone to find the non-emergency line for the Chelan County Sheriff's Department. "And don't ask for the front desk or information," I said before she connected. "Find a specific detective online and ask for them by name. Otherwise I'll just end up talking to a deputy. We want to go straight to a detective."

Chava navigated through various prompts on her phone before she connected with a living, breathing person. She outlined the story and said, "Okay," before hanging up. "A Detective Campbell is coming over to take your statement," she said.

"Good," I said. "Let's use a cellphone and take a photo of the most recent picture of Gabriela before they get here. They'll take it with them and I want a copy."

"What about the rosary?" Chava asked.

That was a good question. How much attention would the authorities really give this case? I didn't know the man's name, the woman's last name, or where she might have disappeared. For all I knew, she'd gone missing in Mexico, if that was even where she was from. We didn't have much to help them start a missing person's case or even prove one existed.

"Let's hang on to that for now," I said and watched Eduardo tuck it into an overnight bag at his feet. He was nodding as if that met with his approval. "I don't want to hand over our only clue if they aren't going to consider her a kidnap victim."

While we waited for the sheriff's detective, my parents caught me up on their side of events, each contributing to the story. Chava had come looking for me at noon, to see if I was back and wanted lunch. Unable to find me, she assumed I was still out on my hike, but left a message for me on my cellphone as well as a note in our room while she went to get Franklin.

"When you hadn't come back by five o'clock," Eduardo said, "your mother—she began to get worried."

"Then I found out there was a forest fire not far away," Chava said, picking up where Eduardo left off. "I asked around about where you might have taken a walk and the clerk in the gift shop remembered you."

See? I was memorable.

"She told me what hike you'd planned to take."

Chava paused and Eduardo took over again.

"Chava," Eduardo said with a nod toward my mother, "she called the local authorities and said you might be caught in the fire, but they did not take her as seriously as she thought they should."

Chava's eyes narrowed in annoyance at the authorities as she continued the story, "The fire was a long way from the trail you were *supposed* to be on. Still, when you didn't come back down, I just knew that's where you were. I have a sense about these things, you know."

Mother's intuition? I'd never thought of Chava that way, but who was I to tell her what she felt?

Seeing the two of them overlapping their conversation like an old married couple gave me the heebie-jeebies. It was as if I'd gone to sleep in one reality and woken up in another. I'd fallen into a Blake Crouch novel.

"How did you get pulled into this?" I asked Eduardo. Had Chava really called my father just because she thought I might be getting burned up on the side of a mountain?

Eduardo smiled, which always gave me a shiver. I wondered how many people had seen that right before he sent them off to their final reward. "*Fatherly* instinct," he said. "I tried to call you too. I wanted to see if we were still on for next week's Spanish lesson. When you didn't call back, I got concerned. I may have called your mother …."

How was it I suddenly had two parents anxious about my welfare? I'd been on my own so long it was hard to wrap my head around the new normal.

"I'm glad you're here," I said. It was the simplest answer.

"You were found while I was still on Highway 2, so I came straight to the hospital here in Wenatchee."

"Are you going to stay a few days?" I asked.

"I think perhaps I will," he said. "Like you, I believe the detective will take a report and it will sit on his desk. What would he be able to do to find this woman? Perhaps we should look into it together and see that this man is returned to his family, wherever they may be."

I wondered for a moment why this might matter to Eduardo. Was he thinking of people he had "disappeared" over the years? Perhaps he felt regret in ways I couldn't imagine.

That thought sent guilt shooting through me. Could I have done more for the man I'd found?

"*Mija*, you could do nothing to save him." Apparently my father could also read my mind, further proof we thought too much alike. "But perhaps you can do something now, so his death doesn't go unreported. It will matter to someone."

He had a point, but it didn't make me feel any better. Maybe if I'd tried a little harder, I could have gotten the man up. Perhaps he could have come out of the fire with me, under his own steam. If only I'd had more time ... I could have looked for some identification; then at least we'd know who he was.

I closed my eyes to picture him. I could see his face, down to a tiny scar under his right eye. I remembered his convulsions and the wound bleeding on the back of his head. He had died before the fire reached him. Of that I was sure. No way could I have carried him out of the woods.

But still, I felt a responsibility to his family and friends to make sure they knew what happened to him. And he had hired me to find his daughter, even if he didn't know he was talking to a private investigator. It was his dying wish. He'd even paid me. If he'd been alive, I would have taken his case. It wasn't his fault he couldn't fill me in on the details.

What had he been doing at that campsite? He didn't strike me as a camper. If memory served, his tent had been nothing more than canvas patched with duct tape. His shoes were work boots, not hiking boots. He looked like a day laborer, not a man on vacation, down to the straw hat, which had fallen on the ground next to him. Details from that moment were coming back to me. As was the image of the man's face. I just hoped it wouldn't start to haunt me.

I had to hope his body wasn't destroyed in the fire. If there was no ID on him, perhaps the authorities could figure out his identity through fingerprints or dental records. As awful as it was, maybe the fire would keep wildlife from getting to him too soon. Would the area still be hot? Hopefully not so hot that he'd completely disappeared. Would he even have fingers left to fingerprint? An image of a dead man from a recent case of mine rose in my head. *Please don't be another fingerless corpse*—a person shouldn't face that more than once in her lifetime.

Before my thoughts could get too morbid, a hospital assistant arrived with my dinner on a tray.

I've never been so happy to see green Jell-O and chocolate ice cream. Even the soup was pretty good, though having just outrun death, I ate dessert first.

Chava and Eduardo had apparently been taking turns going down to the cafeteria while I'd been asleep. Eduardo decided to make himself scarce and go have dinner while the sheriff's detective spoke to me.

I can't say I blamed him, nor did I want to explain to the detective who my father was. It wasn't long after he left that a knock sounded at the door. Though the door itself was open, a curtain was pulled across it, so I couldn't see who stood there.

"Come in," Chava called out.

A woman who looked to be in her early forties pushed through the curtain. She reminded me of Chance Parker's partner Kate Jarek back in Bellingham. She had that same no-nonsense vibe I appreciated in Kate. As she seated herself next to my bed, she introduced herself as Detective Campbell.

"So," the detective said. "You want to report a missing person?"

"Yes," I said, realizing how tricky this was going to be. I had no idea who Gabriela really was. But maybe the authorities already knew about a missing woman with that first name and I would just be giving them another piece of the puzzle. "As reported to me by a man just before he died."

That got her attention.

Chapter Nine

——◆——

NOT KNOWING WHAT else to do, I launched into my story. The detective listened with minimal interruption. First, I explained my concerns about the teenage boy and why I'd gone off the trail to begin with. Then I told her about finding the man and how he'd told me his daughter had been abducted. How I'd had to leave him behind, presumably dead. I'd found the road, the firefighters, and then woken up here.

I was spinning quite the tale. How much would the detective believe?

"So what you're saying," she said after I'd come to the end, "is that a man, who could be local or visiting from anywhere, including another country, may be somewhere within several smoldering acres, and most likely dead." She looked at me to confirm her assessment of my story.

"Yes," I said.

"And you think he's not only dead, but he was murdered," she said.

"Yes. He said, 'He killed me.' "

"In Spanish."

"Yes."

"A language you aren't fluent in."

"I know what he said." I realized how stubborn I sounded. "I speak enough Spanish to know that." It didn't feel useful to tell the nice detective that my father—who worked as a fixer for the mafia—had actually done the translation secondhand. My story was tenuous enough as it was.

I tried not to wither under Detective Campbell's unflinching gaze. "But, before he died, this man in the woods told you his daughter had been abducted."

"Yes. He started by using *desaparecido*, which means disappeared, but he changed that to *secuestrado*, which means—"

"Abducted. Yes. I know."

After a beat, she said, "Okay. We have a few separate issues here—the teenager, the man, and his daughter. Let's start with the man you found in the meadow." She pulled up a Google map on a tablet she carried and asked me to locate where I'd left him.

When I failed at that, we'd tried retracing my steps from the resort, out to where I'd been when I found the man, but all I knew for certain was the trail I'd gone up across the road from the resort. After I left the trail, it was speculation. A few minutes later, we gave up.

"Okay, we'll come back to that," Detective Campbell said, putting her tablet away. "The second issue is the boy you saw from the resort, and lastly we have this woman," she held up the photo packet of Gabriela, now in an evidence baggie, "who may have been abducted."

There was so little to go on—the detective wouldn't be able to do much to follow-up. Maybe file a report, but nothing that would get any attention. She couldn't know if a crime had actually happened, though I had no doubt she would go looking for the body in the woods. It was possible his head wound would provide evidence of suspicious circumstances. If he'd been hit with something manmade, for example, it would point to a homicide.

"As far as a teenager lost in the woods is concerned, no one was reported missing this weekend except you. It's unlikely a teenage boy would be lost up here with no one looking for him. You said he didn't look like a runaway. He can't be staying at the resort without a parent or another adult. It's possible he drove up to make that hike, but there's no overnight parking, so his car would have been reported."

The detective tapped her pen against her notebook. She didn't look too thrilled by my tale.

"So what happens now?" Chava asked.

Detective Campbell stopped tapping and chewed on her bottom lip instead. I'm sure she was thinking about all the other active cases she was currently working on.

"I'll double-check no one left a car parked overnight nearby, just in case your runner came up alone, and I'll check with the resort to see if they can identify him. The fire department should know where the fire started. If the tent you saw catch fire *was* the point of ignition, that should give us the location where you found the man. We'll go in and see if we can find his body."

Good plans on her part. It wasn't like there was much else she could do.

"You report you aren't sure which direction you went after leaving the meadow, and you also aren't sure if he was actually in the path of the fire?"

"I might be able to retrace our steps if I went up there," I said. "But when I left him, the air was full of smoke. I thought the fire was coming our way, but whether he was actually caught in the flames, I don't know."

"But you're confident he was deceased."

"He wasn't breathing and I couldn't find a pulse. He had convulsions several times before he finally collapsed. I started CPR, but that failed to revive him."

Detective Campbell nodded, though I could see she wasn't fully convinced. "How long were you with him after you believe he died?"

"It was fast," I said. "I could see flames, so I ran."

"Okay. I'll check in with the fire department, but if they'd found a body, I'm sure I would have already been notified."

"You'll find him," I said. "They just haven't been to the right spot yet." I wondered what kind of shape he'd be in. "What about his daughter?"

"I'll start by going through missing person's reports. It's possible someone's already looking for her, though her face isn't familiar and I don't recall anyone matching her description reported as missing."

"Gabriela," I said, to remind her we had a name from the back of the photo.

"Yes, Gabriela," Detective Campbell said. "I don't recall a report on a missing woman with that name."

Maybe the man had been in touch with the authorities in another county. Or another country, for that matter. This was looking more and more difficult to pursue through conventional means.

"And before you ask," she said, "yes, I will contact the surrounding counties."

So many loose ends. My mystery man, his daughter, the teenager.

"I'm sure the boy you saw is fine," the detective said, resting a reassuring hand on my arm. "He would have been reported to us if he were missing. I would have been contacted immediately. We all knew about you," she reminded me.

"Will you keep me in the loop?" I'd already explained about being a private investigator from Bellingham, so she had to know my curiosity wouldn't let up.

"Would you be willing to sit down with a sketch artist," she asked, "to get an image of the man?" That didn't answer my question, but it was better than nothing.

"I'd be happy to."

Detective Campbell got on her cell, and we heard her talking to someone about setting me up with a sketch artist. She made me an appointment for the following afternoon. I told her I anticipated being out of the hospital before then.

"Just call if you need to reschedule," she said, handing me a business card and getting up to leave. Soon after she exited, Eduardo slipped back into the room, which made me think he'd been watching.

"What do you think?" Eduardo asked.

"She's probably right about my teenage runner, but I think we'd better start looking for Gabriela," I said. "Unless she was reported to the authorities by a friend or family member, what can anyone really do? Detective Campbell no doubt has several open cases with more information to go on than a photo, a first name, and only the possibility of a crime and only maybe in her district."

"What's our first move?" Chava asked.

"Tomorrow we talk to the firefighters," I said. "If they've got the fire out and know where it started, I might be able to determine which direction I went when I walked out of there with my guy. We can go and figure out where his body ended up. If it's not in the area the fire burned, I doubt anyone else will find him; it's not like we were on a trail. Maybe if we locate him, Detective Campbell can figure out who he was, and what caused his head wound."

Eduardo had brought me more Jell-O, which I dove into. Apparently my appetite was fine.

After eating, I managed to clean myself up. The nurse had left me a shower cap and reminded me to keep my head out of the water, but getting the grime and dried sweat off sure felt good. I left the door to the bathroom cracked and sat on the plastic stool, using the hand-held wand. Every couple of minutes, Chava called out, "Are you okay in there?" I yelled back that I was fine. I'm not sure what she thought would happen, but it was better than having her join me in the bathroom.

Finishing up, I donned a clean hospital gown and settled into bed. My hair smelled like smoke, but I felt a whole lot better.

"Here," Chava said, getting up, "let me help you." She began to move the pillows around. "Anything else? Do you want any pain medication?"

"Maybe just a little more water," I said.

Chava filled my cup, got me a fresh sippy straw, and helped me with the remote for the bed.

Nice to be someone's kid and have both a mother and a father waiting on me. Weird, but nice.

I fell asleep to the sound of the TV, my parents' voices murmuring words I couldn't hear, and curiosity about what I'd learn from the firefighters. Was the teenager all right? Would I be able to locate the man's body?

Where should I start looking for his daughter?

It looked like I really was working for a dead man.

Chapter Ten

———•———

THE NEXT MORNING, I awoke feeling much better. I had vague recollections of the doctor coming in to check on me, but I hadn't stirred when the nurse came through to take my vitals again. Chava told me about it. "He took your temperature and listened to your lungs. You didn't even move."

"I can't wait to get out of here."

"How are you feeling?" Chava asked. "Do you think you're ready to be released?"

I was.

"The teenager," I said. "Did you call the resort? I know the detective thinks he's fine, but I want to be sure." Chava had promised last night to see what she could find out.

"Yes, Eddie," Chava said. "I followed up. The resort wouldn't give me any information about another guest. But, they said they will ask his permission to contact you with the information that he's safe, which I think was their way of saying they know who he is and he's fine. It's all we can do for now. I have also been monitoring the news, and you're the only person reported caught up in the fire. They don't say your name, but 'unnamed woman found safe' can't be anyone but you."

That made me feel a little better. If a teenager was missing, social media and the local news would be blowing up. I was also glad the media hadn't released my name.

"How *are* you feeling," Eduardo asked, "now that you are caught up on your sleep?"

"Good enough," I said. "Besides, I have to go over to the sheriff's station and meet with the sketch artist. Not to mention that hospitals are the most likely place for a person to get sick and die."

I looked at my father as I said that, and the memory of an event six months ago slipped across my mind. Eduardo had visited a hospital, and a very bad guy didn't survive his surgery. We had just been reunited, my father and I, and I wasn't totally sure what had transpired. And didn't ask.

Eduardo patted my leg in reassurance. Maybe the same memory had gone through his mind.

The doctor came through on her rounds and determined I was out of the woods.

"You will need to take it easy," she said. "We have some silver sulfadiazine cream for the burn on your scalp, and if you feel lightheaded or have any trouble breathing or start to cough more, I want you to come back in immediately."

"I promise, Doc," I said, hoping I'd seen the last of the hospital.

We sat around a couple more hours before Chava finally went out to track down my discharge papers. Tanesha, who was back on duty, came in and went over them with me. I verified that I had all my personal items, glad my wallet and cellphone had made it out of the mountains with me. I had snapped a few pictures prior to the fire. Maybe it would help me figure out where I'd been. Or at least be a reminder of the good part of my hike.

The cotton shirt I'd tied around my waist had survived, but there were pinholes burned into it, and it would never be any color but "soot," so we stuffed it into the wastebasket in my room. The rest of my clothes had been cut off in the ambulance.

Last night after my shower, Chava had done what she could with my hair. She'd also purchased a pair of sweats and a sweatshirt for me in the hospital gift shop and had picked up socks and underwear from a Target store nearby.

Inspecting my shoes, I found the soles misshapen. Chava had gone down to the pharmacy, so it was just my father and me. "They melted in the fire," Eduardo said, his eyes following my gaze. "Probably when you walked across the charred ground."

"Let's not tell Chava about that," I said, and he nodded. There are some things a mother doesn't need to know. I slipped them on. They felt okay despite the fire damage. Then I called Detective Campbell and confirmed I was heading over to meet with the sketch artist.

A volunteer rolled me out of the room. "Hospital policy," he said when I told him I could walk out on my own. "You can get up when we're outside."

We rolled into the crowded elevator, and I stared at everyone's backsides as we went down the three floors. I'd had enough of the chair by the time we arrived at the ground floor, grateful I could leave it behind. As we left the air-conditioned hospital, the heat slapped me in the face. Wenatchee was a good ten degrees hotter than the resort, which sat higher in the mountains. The surrounding hills, jagged shapes of rocks jutting from dry, grass-covered peaks, showed how dangerous fire could be if this area had a spark. When Chava pulled up to the curb, I was never so glad to see her bright red Mazda in my life.

"Don't you have a car here too, Eduardo?" I asked, assuming my father had driven over from Bellingham.

"I do. I will follow you after we get you settled in with Chava."

The two of them got me wrangled into the front seat. I wasn't that bruised up, but who was I to keep them from being helpful? They could both use some practice in parenting.

"Have they figured out what started the fire?" I asked Chava as we waited for Eduardo to show up behind us, which he did, in a dark-blue Jeep Cherokee.

"If they do, I haven't heard anything on the news yet," Chava said as she pulled away from the curb, eyes on Eduardo in the rearview mirror. "But I'm sure it's still under investigation so they aren't releasing information. Plus, I don't think it was very dangerous, except for you. It wasn't back on the news much after you were found."

Seemed like a pretty dangerous fire to me. But I guess these things are relative.

"Do you know where you're going?" I asked.

"I know the directions to the sheriff's station," Chava said. "It's very close by. You can fulfill your responsibility with the sketch artist; then we can get you back to the resort."

I looked over at my mother, who usually jumped at the prospect of investigating a suspicious death. Surely by this afternoon she'd thought about it enough to want to get involved. Especially since I wasn't going to drop dead in my hospital room.

"After the sketch artist, we're going to go talk to the firefighters," I reminded her. "I have a missing girl—possibly abducted—to find. I promised her father."

Chava said nothing.

"Don't you want to spearhead the investigation?" I teased her.

"You could have died in those mountains," Chava said, her eyes riveted to the road in front of her, hands tight on the wheel. "I just want to go back to the resort and let you recover."

"I'm okay now," I said, patting my mother on the shoulder. There was a long moment of silence in the car. "Chava, I have a responsibility to that man. And his daughter. He's my client."

"He's dead."

How could I explain to Chava that witnessing his death made me feel responsible for him?

"Her mother is probably worried about her too. Just like you worried about me."

Even that didn't get through to her.

"He paid me."

Chava continued driving, but her hands finally unclenched from the tight grip she had on the steering wheel.

"Well, since you put it that way," she said. "I know how much you need my help with things like this." Now that was the Chava I knew and loved. "I'm sure we'll do a better job than the local sheriff."

"Why would you say that?" I asked. Chava had great respect for our friends at the Bellingham Police Department, so her words took me by surprise.

"Hick town like Wenatchee?" Chava said under her breath. "They probably still have hitching posts outside their jail … complete with horses tied to them."

Wenatchee wasn't Las Vegas, but I didn't think Chava's assessment would turn out to be true. It was a small community compared to the cities spread out along the I-5 corridor west of the Cascades, or Las Vegas, for that matter, but that didn't mean their detectives weren't capable of running solid investigations. Gesturing over the broad valley, I mentioned that Wenatchee was hardly a one-horse town. The population was spread out on either side of the Columbia River.

"Detective Campbell seemed on the ball to me," I said when I got no response.

"Maybe," Chava said. "Maybe not."

"We're about to find out," I said as we made our final turn toward the station. "Maybe they've already found the man I had to leave behind." It sure would help if they knew who he was.

Chapter Eleven

WE ARRIVED AT the Chelan County Sheriff's station—where nary a hitching post nor horse could be seen. The complex was larger than I'd expected and housed the courthouse and some other governmental offices.

After pulling into the parking lot, we all stood for a moment looking at the front doors. With my mother's reputation as a card counter in Vegas and my father's connection to organized crime, having them join me felt like a bad idea. Maybe no one would ask for their IDs, but I didn't really want either of them chatting with the local authorities. Plus, I wasn't sure I wanted my mother butting into any conversation I had with the sketch artist. Not to mention, it might take a while, and patience away from the poker table wasn't one of her virtues.

"Maybe I should go in by myself."

"That might be a good idea," Eduardo said. And for once, Chava didn't argue.

"Eduardo and I can go get him settled at the resort, then come back down here in one car," Chava said.

"*Buena idea*," Eduardo said. "We'll drop off Chava's car and be back in the area in an hour or so."

"Or maybe we'll drop off yours," Chava said to him. She turned to me, "Call us when you're done."

I couldn't wait to see who won that fight. I was still chuckling about it as I walked in to the front of the station. I told the receptionist who I was, and a few minutes later, a short, dark-haired officer came out from the back. She didn't look like she was much over twenty-five, but she exuded a calm confidence I found appealing.

"Eddie Shoes?" she asked, holding out her hand to shake. "I'm Deputy Amy Tan."

"Like the author?" I said before I could stop myself. She had to get that all the time. But if she was tired of the question she didn't let it show.

"Yep. No relation," she said without missing a beat. "Have you ever worked with a sketch artist before?"

I told her I hadn't, and she outlined the process as we walked through the locked door into the heart of the station. I followed her to a small meeting room, the walls mostly windows looking out at the rest of the station. A laptop was perched at the far end of a long table. She explained that she would bring up a generic face after getting some basic information from me; then we would start to fine-tune the image with all the details I could remember. The program she used had thousands of individual features to choose from. Eyes of different shapes and colors, haircuts and facial hair—she could even include scars and put in tattoos or other distinguishing marks.

"So you don't do these with a pencil and an eraser anymore?" I asked as I settled in next to her where I could see her screen.

"We find the computer program works a lot better. But I'm still a pretty good artist off the computer," she said with a smile.

She asked about the gender, race, and estimated age of the person I saw, and brought up a Latino face. While I could see similarities, there were a lot of things that needed modifying to make him look like the man from the meadow.

An hour and a half later, I was staring at a very close facsimile to the man I believed had been murdered, or at least left to die in the fire.

"That's him," I said, stopping myself from reaching out to the screen. "That's him exactly." Down to the tiny, crescent-shaped scar I'd noticed under his right eye.

"Okay, great. I'm going to let you look at that for just a moment while I have a quick chat with Detective Campbell. Look away from the screen, let yourself relax, and then look at it again to see if there's anything else you want to change. Sometimes looking away for a while can help."

It was a relief after staring at his face for so long. His eyes were starting to feel accusing, even if leaving him behind hadn't been a choice. Deputy Tan stepped out into the hall and stood nearby on a cellphone, no doubt letting Detective Campbell know we were about finished. Getting up, I glanced out the windows of the interrogation room. Despite being in a room visible to the rest of the sheriff's station, I could not easily be seen. Deputy Tan had only left a few of the blinds open. She hadn't wanted the light from the outside rooms to spill on to the computer screen.

No way would they let me have a copy of the sketch I'd created, but I did have my cellphone with me. As quickly as possible, I snapped a few pictures of the screen, finishing up just before Detective Campbell came around the corner to chat with Deputy Tan.

I couldn't hear what they were discussing, but it had to be about more than just the fact that we'd finished the sketch. Both women looked my way with expressions that displayed a combination of curiosity, concern, and suspicion. The conversation ended with a quick nod by Deputy Tan and Detective Campbell turning on her heel and disappearing back the way she came.

"Okay. Any other changes?" Deputy Tan asked as she came back into the room.

"Nope. I think this is a very close likeness."

"You have an exceptional memory," she said. "Most people don't remember such specific details."

She undoubtedly meant the scar, the attached earlobes, the difference in size between his left and right eye.

"I'm a private investigator," I said. "I would assume I'm better at remembering details than the average citizen." Amy Tan didn't look surprised at the revelation of my day job. "Were you just asking Detective Campbell if I could be trusted?"

First, she looked surprised, then she laughed. "You caught me. I wanted to make sure Detective Campbell knew you might be a little *too* good at this. She told me about your job."

Any officer would be suspicious of a witness who was overly confident in their memory. Most people make terrible eyewitnesses. Even a few minutes after seeing another person, an eyewitness will forget the color of clothing, whether the individual had long or short hair, the estimated height or weight. Police officers, however, and anyone in law enforcement or private investigations like me, were usually more observant by nature. Additional training helped us to remember details. We filed them away like a mini computer, almost without thinking about it and even under stress.

"Believe me, I'm not making anything up. I only told you details I'm confident in."

Deputy Tan nodded, and her expression returned to a neutral cop face. "Thank you for your help in this matter. I'll walk you out."

"I'd like to talk to Detective Campbell before I leave," I said. "Can you call her for me?"

"She just left the building," Deputy Tan said, without elaborating further. I wasn't going to learn anything else from her.

She walked with me through the door, which required a key card to enter, and shook my hand once we reached the public lobby.

"Have a great day," she said with a smile before disappearing back into the bowels of the building.

Stepping into the sunshine, I started to get out my cell to call Chava, when I noticed her car parked in the shade of a maple tree at one side of the parking lot. Chava must have won the battle about whose car to leave at the resort. Walking toward them, I contemplated the near impossibility of the situation. I wasn't sure where I had left the man after he died. I wasn't totally sure the fire started at the campsite. It was possible the fire had started elsewhere and engulfed the tent, taking all evidence of a campsite with it, and I'd only inferred it started there. The man might have been injured from an accident, a physical ailment, or a deliberate act of violence. And all I knew about his daughter's situation was that he thought she'd been abducted.

The detective had mentioned yesterday that my mystery man could have had some kind of camp stove or candle burning in the tent. With the shear number of raccoons, squirrels, coyotes, and other animals running around in the woods, it didn't have to be a person I heard rustling around inside.

"How did the sketching go?" Chava asked as I arrived at her car. She'd stubbed out her cigarette as soon as she noticed me, but I decided not to give her a hard time about it. After all, she'd had several hours of near panic, thinking her only daughter was getting burned up in a forest fire.

Wordlessly, I held up the screen of my cellphone. Chava and Eduardo bent over the image as if they might recognize him too.

"I wonder how long it will take for the sheriff's department to get some people out there to investigate," Chava said after a moment of memorizing the man's face. Chava didn't need any special training; she had the professional poker player's instinct for reading faces and remembering tics.

"No idea," I said. "Detective Campbell has to follow up on a report of a body. She's going to want to get out there today, to see if she can find him, but it will depend on whether the fire department says it's safe for her to be at the scene."

"We should go to the location of the fire," Eduardo said.

We? Now both my parents were using that pesky little word. Though, as I didn't have my car or even my dog with me, maybe Eduardo and Chava were the next best things.

"We're going to go see the firefighters. Maybe they will tell us where the fire started. That would give us a place to visit."

What could be simpler?

Chapter Twelve

———•———

As WE GOT ready to climb into Chava's Mazda, I was further amused to watch a wordless power struggle between my parents about who was going to drive. Eduardo held out his hand for the keys, which Chava pointedly ignored. He stood at least a foot taller than she did, however, neatly blocking the driver's side door.

Hands on hips, she glared at him as only Chava can do. He gracefully accepted defeat and slipped into the back. He had to realize he wasn't going to win that battle, no matter how macho he might be. After all, they'd already come back in her car. He wasn't going to gain ground now.

Eduardo found the address for the Chelan County Fire Department on his smartphone. It wasn't far away, and he directed Chava there from his spot in the backseat. We figured it would either be the location my saviors had come from or they could tell us which location to visit instead. When Eduardo said, "Turn right on Easy Street," Chava laughed out loud; then she saw the street sign. The firefighters really did live on Easy Street.

We arrived to find the bay doors open and firefighters

moving around the bright-yellow trucks. Chava parked in the lot adjacent to the station.

Walking up, we could see the firefighters appeared to be restocking their vehicles and doing maintenance on their equipment. I remembered clutching the heavy uniform of a firefighter as my legs gave out. Bits and pieces of memory kept coming back to me, just as the nurse at the hospital said they would.

The firefighter had half walked and half carried me, lifting me into the back of the mustard-yellow ambulance. I remembered thinking, *What a strange color*. It stood out, even in the dark. His face was hidden behind his mask, so I never saw who got me on the truck. Then an EMT rushed to my side, strapped an oxygen mask over my face, and reassured me I was safe. I was sure I'd been muttering my Spanish mantra and not making a lot of sense. What must everyone have thought, seeing me reel out of the backcountry, wet, covered in dirt and soot, a big burned spot on my head?

My parents hung back, an action I didn't know either one would do under any circumstances, allowing me to make the first contact.

One of the firefighters—a white, buff-looking twenty-something with tousled brown hair and a serious five o'clock shadow—eyed me as I walked up to the open bay door.

"Can I help you?" he asked, taking in my rough appearance. Maybe I should have gotten some better clothes and covered my bandaged head with a hat.

"You guys saved my life Friday night," I said. "Or at least I think it was someone from here. I wanted to say thank you in person." This introduction had the added bonus of being true and might get me more information than just showing up to grill them about the fire.

"Are you the woman who showed up near the Langston place?" he asked.

"That was me," I said. "At least I assume so. I don't know

where I was, but I doubt there were a lot of us running amok out there."

"Just you," he said. "Yeah, that was this station. Are you okay? You sound a little raspy. Are you sure you should be on your feet?" He looked genuinely concerned as he continued to assess my disheveled state.

"I'm okay. Nothing a little time won't cure. I just got out of the hospital, and before we headed back up to the resort where we're staying, I wanted to drop by and say thanks."

"That's very kind of you," he said. "I'll make sure everyone knows."

Chava and Eduardo had been creeping closer while I spoke to the firefighter. Now they stepped up to join the conversation.

"I'm her mother," Chava said, putting her hand out for a shake. "I wanted to thank you all in person too. Am I shaking the hand of the man who got my daughter into the ambulance?"

"That was Jake," the young guy said. "Let me go get him." He turned and headed through an interior door into the firehouse.

Another firefighter who had been listening in on our conversation walked over while we waited.

"Would you like to sit down?" he asked. He was older than the guy I'd been speaking to, lines crinkling at the corners of his bright-blue eyes. His tan stopped just above his eyebrows, the pale white skin on top proof he usually wore a hat. "That was quite an ordeal. You do look a little rough."

"You have no idea," I said, while I let him lead me over to a bench. "At one point I lay in a creek while flames whooshed over my head." My heart jumped just thinking about that moment. "That's how I ended up with this burn." I pointed toward the gauze bandage on my scalp.

"Are you serious?" another firefighter asked as he came around the side of the fire truck, hearing my words. "That must have stopped your heart."

Next thing I knew, men of varying ages and one young woman surrounded me, asking what had happened in the forest. I left out the dead man, but explained about getting lost in the first place. I'd just started describing my run from the fire when the door to the station house swung open and the young guy returned with another firefighter right behind him. The new guy was a short tank of a man, somewhere in his forties or early fifties. He was as solid as an oak tree and almost the same shade of brown. A surprisingly boyish charm appeared as a smile split his face. I immediately smiled back.

"Hi, I'm Chava, Eddie's mother." Chava stepped forward. "We're so grateful to you for saving my daughter's life."

"I appreciate that, but I was just doing my job," the man said, shaking our hands. "I'm Jake." Reaching Chava first, he found himself in a bear hug with a short Jewish mother.

Then Jake shook my father's hand, no doubt relieved Eduardo wasn't going to hug him too.

"Thanks for getting me down to the hospital," I said.

Jake shook my hand, eying my bandaged head. "I just put you in the ambulance," he said. "The EMTs did the rest."

"I'm still glad you were there."

We stood around for an awkward moment. What was the best tack to take here? I wanted information, but I wasn't sure how much the firefighter would want to share. How could I find out where the fire started and what he knew about my dead man?

Chapter Thirteen

———•———

I MANAGED TO pick my story back up, with Jake listening intently. When I came to the part about falling out of the forest into a sea of flashing lights, I turned to him.

"The rest is a blank. You probably know more than I do."

Jake filled in the holes about getting me into the ambulance. "I was so surprised," he said. "We'd heard a hiker had gone missing near the resort, which is why we had the ambulance on standby, but we never really thought you'd travel that far. Most of the fire was contained by the time you found us. Thanks to the wind dying down and the rainfall."

"So is the fire fully out now?" I asked, thinking about the likelihood we could go up and poke around.

"It is," he said.

"Was it hard to put out?" I knew nothing about fighting fires, and now that I'd been in one, I was even more impressed by the men and women who went into them on purpose.

"It wasn't a big fire," Jake said. "But it was unpredictable. We fought it from all flanks, but it traveled in an erratic pattern, so we were spread out over a long thin section of forest."

"Why so erratic?" Chava asked.

"Wildland fires can burn in a lot of different ways, based on fuel, weather, and topography," he said. "A big fire can cover hundreds or even hundreds of thousands of acres and engulf trees and anything else in its path. But that wasn't what this one did."

"Lucky for my daughter," Chava said.

"That's the truth," Jake said. "Although this wasn't a big fire, it was burning fast and low. It was what we call a running fire, never turning into a crown fire. In fact, in a lot of places, the grasses just burned across the top, hardly reaching the ground. But it was really windy, and the area there has a lot of ravines and creek beds. The wind can blow cinders up over sections of land and start another fire. So it wasn't a nice neat circle."

I thought about all the people who had been nearby. Men and women I never saw. How close had I been to a firefighter, when I thought I'd been alone in the woods?

"How many of you were out there?" I asked.

"We had about fifty guys working, but the crews were fairly far apart. You may have run right past someone and never known it with all the smoke and the darkness coming on."

Not to mention the sheer terror I'd felt at the time.

"Since I traveled for so long after that," I said, not mentioning how scared I'd been, "I must have turned away from the fire, and farther from you, before I came out on that fire road."

"Forest Service road," Jake said. "Not fire road. The Forest Service puts them in. They allow us to get our equipment up into the state and national forest when we need to."

"I'm just glad the road was there," Chava said. "That's what my daughter followed out to civilization. Who knows how long she might have been lost in the woods if she hadn't."

"I'm curious about how far I went," I said, taking the opening Jake and Chava had given me. "Can you show me on a map?"

"Sure," he said, "come on over here." While he walked to a giant wall map posted on the far side of the station bay, the other firefighters patted me on the back, said they were glad I was all right, and drifted back to their various chores. Chava, Eduardo, and I followed Jake to see what we could learn.

"Here's the place where you're staying." Jake put his finger on a spot on the map. "We had our staging area here." He pointed to a place just up the road from the resort. There was a section of white inside a larger section of pale green. I leaned in to read the fine print. The green area was labeled Okanagan-Wenatchee National Forest, with Langston Ranch written inside the white patch. "Then, see this?" he said, as his finger traced a thin dotted line. "That's the Forest Service road. You found us about a mile up from the Langston place."

"This isn't national forest?" I asked, pointing to the white spot on the map.

"Private. The family has been there since before the national forest was established. But they are at the end of the maintained road and we knew we could park our equipment there."

"We're so lucky that's where you were," Chava said. "I can't imagine what might have happened if Eddie hadn't found you when she did. Even though she wasn't far from the resort, I don't know that she'd have ever found her way back in the dark."

"You were pretty far gone," Jake said, his face serious. "How are you feeling now?"

"Much better," I said, touching the bandage on my scalp, "but I know how bad I look. I don't think this new hairstyle is working for me. Our next stop is to get me a hat."

"We've got just the thing for you," Jake said, crossing over to a locker.

Returning to the map, I followed my route with one finger. I started at the trailhead near the resort and went up the ridge. I spread my fingers across the area where the burn had taken place. It was roughly the same width as my palm. "How many miles is that?" I asked as Jake walked back over, carrying a plastic bag.

"If you'd gone in a straight line, not quite ten, but I'd guess you went farther—it's so rugged."

More than ten miles? I usually got my exercise in the gym. Jogging around town wasn't my idea of fun. My sprint across rough, uneven terrain, chased by fire and fearing for my life, was farther than I'd ever traveled on foot at one time.

"No wonder I was tired," I said as Jake pulled three baseball hats out of the bag.

"Courtesy of the Chelan County Fire Department," he said, handing one to each of us.

"Thank you, that's so kind," Chava said as she popped one on her head, covering her uncharacteristically un-styled hair. Chava usually wore a heavily structured beehive, held in place with a liberal application of Aqua Net. It finally dawned on me that my parents had been up for over two days at the hospital and must be tired too. They'd taken catnaps in my room, but hadn't left my side.

"*Gracias*," Eduardo said as he put his on as well. I wondered how often my father wore a baseball cap. He was, after all, a stylish man. With it on, he still looked dangerous, just incognito. Maybe this was how he looked when he didn't want to be noticed. He was good at fading into the background.

I struggled to slip the hat over my bandaged head.

"You look pretty good for someone who outran a wildland fire," Jake said, laughing as he helped me place the hat over my damaged head. "Except for the hair."

"Too bad I still smell like a campfire."

"That will go away in time," Jake said. "I promise."

"Can you show us where the fire started?" my father asked.

"That would be here," he said, locating another spot on the map. Clearly, I had added miles to my flight, first racing away from the flames, then staggering around in the wrong direction before coming out on the Forest Service road.

"So I started my hike here," I said, putting my finger back on the trail I'd taken from near the resort. "And somehow ended up there." I pointed to the spot Jake identified as the fire's point of origin.

"Wait," the firefighter said, taking a step back and sizing me up. "Are you saying you started the fire?"

"No, n-n-no," I stuttered. The last thing I wanted was anyone thinking I was a deranged firebug. "But I was there when it started. Or at least, I think I was."

"You'd better go back to the beginning," Jake said. Given the look I was now getting from him, I didn't have much of a choice.

Chapter Fourteen

———•———

JAKE LISTENED INTENTLY while I filled him in on the rest of my story, leaving out the *él me mató* and how I thought the man in the meadow had been murdered. I did tell him it looked like the man had fallen and hit his head or had some kind of medical emergency, and that I hadn't been able to get him out of the fire with me.

"He had another seizure and didn't respond to my CPR," I said. "I'm sure he was dead when I left him."

"We found what we thought was evidence of a campsite," Jake said. "There were some burnt scraps of canvas, probably the tent you described, and some utensils and other items, but there was no evidence of anyone being caught anywhere in that fire."

"Could the fire have been hot enough to burn a man up completely?" Chava asked.

"No way," he said. "The fires we fight can get up to fifteen hundred degrees, but that's about max. It takes a sustained fire of two thousand degrees to cremate a body, and even then, there's something left. Trust me. There just wasn't enough fuel for it to reach those kinds of temperatures, and he wouldn't have been in it long enough. If there was a body, we would have found him or at least residue where he had been."

I didn't want to think too much about what kind of residue a burnt body would leave behind.

"Maybe you never visited the spot where I left him," I said, though doubt crept in. Could I have been wrong about his demise?

"We went over the entire area that burned," Jake said. "We can't declare a fire is out until we've done that. If you left him in the path of the fire, we'd have found him."

He sounded sincere, and he certainly knew his business. Maybe the fire veered away from the man, and the firefighters never crossed his path.

"You are right about one thing," Jake said, when I didn't respond. "Our best guess is whoever camped there was the cause. Either by accident or design, someone started the fire, then ran."

Great. No one believed that a man had died up there.

"It's not that I don't believe you helped *someone*," Jake said— my thoughts must have shown on my face—"but maybe he wasn't as injured as you assumed. You ran; maybe he got up and ran in the other direction."

There was no way that man got up and ran anywhere. Even before his heart had stopped, he couldn't walk by himself.

"Or he had another person with him, someone you didn't see, and they got him out in time," Jake said. He was just being kind, even if he was trying to placate me. But he hadn't been there. First, if someone else had been there, why didn't they help when I was struggling to move the guy? Second, I knew that man was dead when I left. I hadn't abandoned a living, breathing person ... had I?

"Why didn't he reappear somewhere?" I asked. "He'd have needed medical attention too. Where would he have gone besides Central Washington Hospital? That's where I was taken."

"Maybe he did. Have you checked with them to see if anyone matching your guy's description came in with injuries? The hospital won't give you patient information, but they can tell you if someone you describe *isn't* there."

It hadn't occurred to me to ask at the hospital because I assumed the guy was dead. But maybe he'd survived and there wasn't a mystery here after all. Or the only mystery was about his missing daughter, and I could get more information from him about her disappearance. Chava already had her phone out and was calling back to see if anyone like him had come into the emergency room.

We all waited while she did, listening to her half of the conversation. She clarified she wasn't asking for a specific patient name or status.

"The nurse was adamant they wouldn't have told me anything else," Chava said after she ended her call, "but they could confirm no one matching that description has come in."

"At least we know he didn't go there," I said.

"He could have gone to another facility," Chava said. "We should call the other emergency rooms in the area."

"That's where they would have taken him," Jake said.

"Maybe he didn't die, but he also didn't seek help," Eduardo said.

"Because he wasn't hurt as badly as I thought?" I asked.

"Because he isn't in this country legally."

There was that. He might have been afraid he'd be asked for a green card or proof of citizenship. Looking at Jake, I had the sense he was gauging if he should share additional information with me.

"You sound like you plan to follow up on this yourself," he said.

"Maybe I should tell you what my day job is in Bellingham," I said, watching his reaction. I hoped my being a private investigator would make me appear more worthy of his confidence. I hadn't mentioned it to begin with because I wanted to get a sense of him first.

I filled him in on my history, including that I'd done missing person's cases in the past and knew how to avoid stepping on the toes of local law enforcement.

"I just left the sheriff's department here," I said, fighting the urge to cross my fingers behind my back. "The lead detective knows I'm doing some investigating."

I just hoped no one would ask if Detective Campbell thought that was a good idea.

Apparently my plan worked.

"The ranch we used as a staging area is the last one on that maintained road, but it's not the last private property in the area," Jake said. "These acres here," he pointed toward the map again, and I noticed a second white patch with no label next to the Langston Ranch, "this is also private property. But the group is a little odd."

"Odd like what? A commune?" Chava asked.

"More like odd in a survivalist kind of way," he said. "We don't know much about them, but we did check on them when the fire looked to be heading in their direction before the wind died and the rain fell."

"Did they let you on the ranch?" Eduardo asked.

"I wouldn't call it a ranch exactly. It's more of a compound," the firefighter said. "They do have a herd of cattle and we saw a few horses. They also grow fruit trees, but they have a couple buildings I don't think are used for animals or food storage."

"Did you see those when you got on their land?" I asked.

"We never got that far," Jake said. "We got stopped at their gate … by a guy with a rifle. We explained we were just there to make sure they were prepared if the fire moved their way, but they didn't want us there."

"They can just say no to firefighters?" Chava asked. "You don't have the authority to overrule the owner?"

"They had adequate defensible space," Jake said. "Firebreaks around their buildings. No trees overhanging the structures. They clearly had access to water. It's not our job to force anyone to take our help."

"Are they Latino?" my father asked. "Like the man my daughter found?"

"I think the folks in charge are white," Jake said. "I talked to two white guys in a truck, but there were workers on the farm who might be immigrants, legal or otherwise. I'm not really sure how many people were on the property."

"Why would one of their workers be staying in a tent so far away?" I asked. "Camping for the weekend doesn't really make sense."

"It's true. My people don't camp," Eduardo said.

I couldn't tell if he was making a joke.

"Maybe he's a friend or relative of someone there?" Jake said. "Or planning to ask for work and wanted to size the place up first? It's just the closest group of migrant workers I thought of. There are plenty of ranches and farms that use immigrant labor in our area, along with the restaurants and hotels. Maybe he's connected to someone who works at the resort?"

Lots of places to ask around about my enigmatic dead guy, for I was still convinced he didn't make it out of that forest alive. And what about his daughter? Was she someone who lived here full-time? Or was she a migrant worker, with only loose ties to the region?

"I know you believe you would have found him," I said to the firefighter, "but I don't believe he left under his own steam. And if he had friends with him, why would they have let me try to get him out of there all by myself for so long?"

Jake looked at me with something between doubt and concern.

"We went over the entire fire zone, mopping up," Jake said. "Believe me, there was no body anywhere out there. Unless you left him pretty far outside the area that burned, he's not there."

"Is it safe now? To go up and walk around? In case my daughter wants to see for herself?" Chava asked.

Jake sighed. I figured he wasn't too thrilled by that idea, but he also couldn't stop me. "We do think the fire is out—we've done our third inspection—but keep in mind that material can smolder underground and flare back up again. It's not completely safe."

"But you believe it's fully out, right?" I asked. "Otherwise you'd still be up there."

"Are you really that sure the man died?" he asked. It was the first time in the conversation I felt like I'd pierced through the man's conviction and planted a seed of doubt.

I thought a moment. Was I that sure? In my head, I now had doubts, but in my heart, I knew. That man had died up there. And someone had killed him. And I was the only person invested in finding out who he was and what had been done to him.

"No, I'm sure you're right. I was scared, injured already from my fall down into the ravine, disoriented, exhausted. He must not have been as hurt as I thought."

Jake didn't look convinced I'd changed my mind. "You're still thinking about going up there," he said, making it a statement, not a question.

"I'm curious about what it looks like," I said. "If it's safe, and only a mile up the Forest Service road, I would like to see where I survived my very own disaster. But maybe I'll give it a few days until I've recovered a little more."

"Okay," he said. "I can see that. Just make sure if you do decide to go, you wear good shoes, take extra water, and this time, don't get lost. And if you smell smoke, call us immediately."

"Wouldn't that just be residual?" I asked.

"The saying, 'Where there's smoke, there's fire'?" Jake looked at each of us. We nodded our understanding. "Take that very seriously."

"I think perhaps my daughter doesn't need to revisit the area any time soon," Eduardo said.

"It would be best just to go back to the resort and get some rest," Jake said.

"Thank you for putting the fire out," I said, as it didn't appear there was anything else to learn from him. "Without that, who knows what might have happened to me?"

We said our goodbyes and got back into Chava's Mazda.

"Now that we know where the fire was," I said, "we can go back up there and take a look ourselves."

"I assumed you'd want to," Eduardo said. "I just wanted to reassure him you wouldn't."

"When do you want to go?" Chava asked. I guess her amateur sleuth side had come out of hiding now that I was on the road to recovery.

"I suggest tomorrow morning," Eduardo said, his gaze on me. "We could all use a break from hospitals and fire stations."

"Good idea," Chava said. "We can go back to the resort now and have some real food for a change."

"And get some sleep," I said, realizing how fatigued I was. My head had a swimming sensation, as if the car bobbed on the road like a tiny boat. Lying back against the seat, I noticed all the bumps and bruises I'd gotten from my tumble down the ravine. I coughed a few times, earning a glance of concern from Chava. Apparently she was still a little worried. "I'm good," I said.

"We should call the other emergency rooms and clinics in the area," Chava said. "Just in case someone did take him to East Wenatchee or another little town."

"At your service," Eduardo said, pulling out his smartphone. Chava and I listened to his side of the conversation as he called the other clinics in the area. No one reported a man matching his description coming in over the last couple of days.

"Are we worried about the guy's body being disturbed by wildlife?" I asked, as an image of carrion-eating ravens tearing into him rose up in my mind.

"I think one more night won't matter," Eduardo said. "Besides, it's getting dark. We aren't going to find *Fulano* easily anyway."

"*Fulano?*" I repeated the unfamiliar word.

"You would say 'John Doe' in English," Eduardo said.

"We'll hunt for your *fulano* in the morning," Chava said.

We went over a bump, and my entire body hurt.

They didn't have to suggest that to me twice.

Tomorrow would be plenty soon enough to find *el hombre muerto.*

Chapter Fifteen

———•———

B ACK AT THE resort, Chava and I immediately went to see Debbie Buse, while Eduardo headed to his room. Debbie had gotten one of the dog-friendly rooms in the main lodge building, and I was soon reunited with Franklin. He did a lot of dancing and woofing, while Debbie's dog Indy added to the excitement. Franklin finally calmed down, pressing his nose against the bandage on my head as I sat on the floor.

"I really am okay, buddy," I said to him as he finally relaxed with his head in my lap.

"Are you sure?" Debbie asked. She sat at the table in the corner with Chava, watching me with sharp eyes.

"I'm sure. I'm so grateful you came over and took care of Franklin."

"We both are," Chava said, reaching out to pat her arm. When Chava had first come into my life in such a permanent way, I'd worried about the dynamic between my friend and my mother. Debbie was naturally maternal, something Chava had never been, and I sensed an instant dislike between them. But I'd discovered each was just anxious about giving the other the wrong impression. Chava didn't want Debbie to think poorly of her mothering skills, and Debbie didn't want Chava to see her as an interloper. Through a common love of cooking, Franklin, and me, the two were finally starting to become friends.

"Once I knew you were okay, I actually began to enjoy myself," Debbie said. "It's beautiful here, and I can't remember the last time I had a weekend off. I'm thinking about staying a few extra days. My kids are encouraging me to have a real vacation. Do you plan to recuperate here? Or head back to Bellingham?"

We didn't give Debbie all the details, but sketched out what had happened in the forest. Finally I explained we would be staying a few days to investigate.

"That settles it," she said. "You may not be able to take Franklin with you everywhere your investigation leads. I'll stay here and take care of the dogs."

Who was I to argue with that? It was great to have people on my side after all.

Chava and I took our leave of Debbie and Indy and headed back to our own cabin. Walking up, I noticed the drapes were closed. Something prickled on the back of my neck, but I wasn't sure why.

"Did you close the drapes?" I asked.

"No, why?"

"I'm sure it's nothing."

The front door was locked, and as we stepped into the cabin, Franklin growled low in his throat. The front room was dark with the drapes closed, and for a moment I thought something moved in the bedroom. I pushed Chava behind me and flicked the lights on, letting Franklin off his leash at the same time.

"What are you—"

"Shhhh …" I cut off Chava while I rushed into the bedroom. The window by the bed was open—the sheers tented outward, as if someone had gone out as we came in.

I rushed back past Chava and ran around to the back of the cabin, Franklin on my heels. No one was visible, but the woods weren't far away, and it was possible an intruder had time to escape before I came out. Franklin sat down at my feet. I looked at him and he cocked his head sideways as if to say he also wasn't sure what he'd seen.

Chava had come up behind me while I scanned the woods. "What was that about?"

"I thought I heard someone or saw someone or something."

"You think someone broke in?"

Turning around, I walked over to look at the ground under the bedroom window. It was grassy, and the earth was hard underneath. I leaned over and peered at it sideways. There might be impressions of footprints in the grass, but I couldn't really tell. Franklin sniffed halfheartedly, then lifted his leg to pee.

"Let's see if anything is missing," I said, laughing at my dog. Was he trying to say I was imagining things? Or showing distaste for an intruder?

We went back into the cabin, but nothing was gone.

"Did you leave this window open when you left?" I asked Chava.

Chava stood for a moment in the bedroom, staring at the window as if it could give her the answer.

"I'm just not sure," she said. "I was so worried. Then, after I found out you were on the way to the hospital …. It's all such a blur. I might have."

The drapes in the front room could have been closed by the maid service. Chava could have left the window open. It could all be explained. But I still had the feeling someone had gone through our things.

"Should I be worried?" Chava asked. I looked at her face. She'd had enough worry for one weekend.

"No. I'm sure I'm being paranoid," I said. "I probably saw the curtains move when I opened the door. You left the window open, and the housekeepers closed the drapes. Nothing to worry about at all."

* * *

LATER THAT NIGHT found me alone in our cabin. We had confirmed with the resort that we could stay for at least a week. The resort even gave us a discounted rate for the near death experience I'd endured, which was very nice of them, considering that I'd gone off the trail after being warned not to. I'd swung by the gift shop to let Kim know I was all right. In her relief, she didn't give me a hard time for breaking the rules and almost getting myself killed.

Chava had missed out on some of the fabulous amenities of the resort, so I'd encouraged her to go enjoy the hot pools and dry sauna, which were open until ten o'clock. We'd grabbed some food on the way back from Wenatchee, so my immediate needs were taken care of. She *had* been sleeping in a chair for the last couple of nights.

"Don't think I haven't noticed you're walking around like you're ninety," I said. "You'll feel a lot better if you go spend some time relaxing in hot mineral water."

"What if you need something?" she asked.

"I'll call room service."

"What if you stop breathing?"

"I'll tap SOS out on the window. Someone will hear me."

Chava gave me her look.

"I'll be fine, Mom," I said, figuring I'd butter her up.

"Don't *Mom* me, I have the right to worry about you for at least another twenty-four hours. And what if someone really did break in while we were gone?"

"I'll call Eduardo. He can come keep me company."

That seemed to concern her as much as leaving me alone, but she didn't want to argue about it with me in such a fragile state. I should be almost consumed by wildfire more often.

Before leaving, she'd gently rubbed her fingers through my hair, carefully missing the burnt section, covered in new white bandages. Changing them turned my stomach and even Chava had looked a little green as she helped me. "I'll restyle your hair again when we get home. No one will be able to see the bald parts after the bandages come off." Chava, with a lot of support from my best friend Iz, had talked me in to a cute, but spiky 'do, which she maintained herself. I'd had to admit they were both right. It was very chic.

Despite her worries about my continued recovery, she apparently realized I wasn't going to drop dead in the next fifteen minutes. She didn't wait until Eduardo arrived to leave the cabin. This allowed me to have a quiet moment to myself for the first time in days. Horrified to discover that even my eyebrows were singed, I was still looking in the mirror when Eduardo knocked on the door.

"*Buenos noches, mija,*" he said as I ushered him in. He was carrying a paper bag and looking around for a place to sit. I think we realized at the same time that this situation was a little awkward, and I almost suggested we move to the bar over in the main lodge, though I felt too exhausted to leave the room. I would have admitted that I just wanted to go to sleep, but I rarely had time alone with my father. I didn't want to miss out on the opportunity. Even when we'd gotten together over the last couple of months, it was usually somewhere public, as if we were both afraid of a situation where we might say something that would make us vulnerable. What might I learn from him in such intimate surroundings? While I was contemplating all of this, Eduardo pulled out a chair from the table and sat down. I sat down across from him, and we both tried to find something to say.

"I brought you this," he said, pulling two Styrofoam cups out of the bag. "I think you like chocolate."

The milkshake felt great on my throat. "Thank you. It's perfect," I said. I wondered how many days in a row I could eat ice cream before feeling guilty about it.

"These chairs are not the most comfortable, are they?" Eduardo said.

"I have to say, the bruises on my backside aren't making this whole adventure any easier," I said, getting up and moving over to the sofa bed. "Give me a hand, would you?"

Eduardo came over, and we pulled out the sofa bed. Franklin watched from his spot in the corner, though I knew from experience he would work his way up into bed with me before morning. Making sure I was comfortable, Eduardo propped me up with extra pillows. He was very different than Chava in his ministrations. Perfunctory, but his touch was gentle. It was a side of Eduardo I hadn't seen very often, though he'd once given me a beautiful gift for my dog, so the softer aspects of his personality were there in the right context.

"Sit here with me," I said, patting the spot next to me on the bed.

"*¿Estás seguro?*"

"I'm sure. I can't make you suffer through that chair."

Eduardo came over with his own milkshake and we sat like two birds on a wire against the sofa back. It was easier, not looking at each other. My father and I were still uneasy about where we stood in each other's eyes. Or at least I knew I was, and it felt like we were in the same boat. I wondered what he wanted from me, given how uncertain I was about what I wanted from him.

We sipped in silence for a while, though I'd also discovered silence with my father wasn't a bad thing. He could sit quiet for long moments without it becoming uncomfortable. I liked that he didn't feel we always had to fill the space.

"Tell me about my grandfather," I said, surprised at the words as they came out of my mouth. He knew I meant Chava's dad. My father had worked for him, which is how my parents met.

"*¿Qué quieres saber?*"

What did I want to know? My grandfather had been an older man when he'd had Chava. He'd survived Germany in World War II as a boy, then immigrated to the U.S., where he'd met my grandmother in Spokane. According to Chava, her mother's family had been against the marriage. They were Ashkenazi

Jews and my grandfather Sephardic. My grandparents gave up their community for each other, so Chava grew up without a connection to a synagogue or her extended family.

"I don't know much about my history," I said. "Chava doesn't talk about her parents. I remember her father, but not a lot. You worked for him, right?"

"*Sí.* He was a very ... self-contained man."

"What does that mean?"

"You know what he endured, no?"

"Sort of. I know he almost died at the camp."

"*En verdad, fue más que eso.*" Eduardo paused while I figured out what he'd said. *True, but it was more than that.* He started again after I nodded. "Your grandfather and I, we spent a lot of time together, you know, we had a ... friendship of a sort. When I worked for him. He helped me with my English. He knew what it was to be a stranger in a strange land. He had no one to talk to, not really. Your grandmother was a lovely woman, but she didn't want to know the horrors he'd endured, and he didn't want to tell her about them."

"I forgot you knew my grandmother too."

"Not well."

It felt like a door closed, so I returned the conversation to my grandfather. Eduardo appeared more amenable to sharing information about him. I'd stopped trying to learn anything about Chava's parents from her at a young age. Both were dead before I was out of elementary school. So now, I'd take what I could get.

"I know almost nothing about his experiences," I said. "I just know he was in Bergen-Belsen before he was saved by the Americans."

"That's true, but he spent time in Auschwitz first."

"He did?"

"Yes. That's where he got the tattoo. You remember?"

The blue ink, faded into his skin, becoming a blur.

I nodded.

"When the war was almost over, the Germans tried to keep their prisoners from the Allies. They were marched to other camps by the thousands. Many died on the journey."

"I had no idea."

Eduardo shrugged. "He had no reason to share that story with his daughter. He told me because I shared my experiences of coming across the border. Not the same, but still … we understood some things about each other. I doubt Chava knows much of her father's history. It's not that she doesn't want to tell you."

I turned to look at Eduardo, realizing he might be the only link to my family on both sides. Maybe Chava was interested in other people's names because she knew nothing about her own.

"And he couldn't talk to other Jews," I said, "because the community in Spokane was Ashkenazi and he wasn't, right?"

"That's what Chava believes?"

"It's what she said. At that time theirs was considered an interfaith marriage. Isn't that true?"

Eduardo sipped, his eyes trained on the wall across from where we sat. The room was dim, intimate. The only light came from a standing lamp in the corner. I felt closer to my father than I ever had, listening to him tell me of my own history, providing a window into what made me who I am. I'd read articles about the scientific study into fear passed down through DNA. If my grandfather endured such horrors, maybe some of that fear had come to Chava and on to me. Maybe that explained my difficulty in building strong ties with people. A deep-rooted belief in catastrophe claiming people you love— that safety lies in not loving in the first place.

"It's true your father had Sephardic blood in him. But that was on his mother's side. His father—your great-grandfather— was German. A Lutheran."

I sputtered, ice cream coming out my nose. That made me what, a quarter German? I was a Mexican, an Ashkenazi and Sephardic Jew and … German?

"How is that even possible?" I asked, taking a tissue from the box Eduardo handed me.

"They met before the war, before the rise of the Nazis, before the camps. They were married and had your grandfather. Then your grandfather and his mother had to wear the stars before they were taken together to Auschwitz. His mother died on arrival, but he was put to work and survived." Eduardo shrugged again. "The world is never as simple as we'd like."

"What happened to *his* father?"

"That I don't know."

Had he survived? Or was he killed for marrying a Jew?

"You really think Chava doesn't know the truth?"

Eduardo nodded. "I think she believes what she tells you. I just think she's got it wrong."

All the things we think we know only to learn we don't .... I knew little about my history, but I'd always thought I had those facts right.

How accurate was Eduardo's information?

I'd always been solitary, a person comfortable without roots, but recently, I'd let my guard down and let some people in. I had a best friend in Iz and others I trusted, like Debbie Buse. And now Eduardo. That was enough, right? Did it matter if what I thought about my history wasn't true?

"Well," I said after digesting what he'd said to me. "At least I know I'm Mexican on your side."

A look passed across Eduardo's face.

"Wait. We *are* Mexican, right?"

Before he could answer, Chava swept into the room.

"You are not going to believe what I learned while I was out and about," she said.

And the spell was broken.

Chapter Sixteen

CHAVA DIDN'T APPEAR to notice that anything more serious than drinking milkshakes was going on. She grabbed one of the chairs next to the table and pulled it up to the sofa bed. Her face was slightly flushed and her eyes shone with excitement.

"So what's up?" I asked.

"People here at the resort have already learned you were the woman missing in the fire," she explained. "A few people came over and asked what happened."

"While you were sitting in the hot springs?" I asked. That seemed a little weird.

"I might have gone to the bar instead," Chava said. It was then I noticed she was totally dry.

"As if you'd be having a casual drink if I'd been barbecued out there," I said.

Eduardo poked me in the ribs with his elbow, but I could see a smile at the corner of his mouth. It was kind of fun to have him on my side.

"Not the point," Chava said. "The point is I had the opportunity to talk to people, including some who work here."

She pulled a copy of the drawing the sketch artist made out of her pocket, along with a copy of the photo of Gabriela. Before leaving Wenatchee, we'd made several copies of both off my cellphone at a FedEx Print and Ship store. "So I showed these around, to see if anyone recognized them."

I didn't know she'd taken the photocopies with her.

"Did you tell people I think this guy was murdered? Or that Gabriela has been abducted?"

And why did people already know about me?

"No, nothing like that. I just said we were concerned about their safety."

"And …? Did anyone recognize either of them?" Had someone been poking around in our cabin because they already knew I'd found the dead guy? Maybe the person who set the fire?

"No." Chava was acting as if she'd said something important. I glanced at Eduardo in case I was missing something, but he looked just as confused.

"What are you two drinking?" Chava said, eyeing the cups in our hands.

"Mine is vanilla," Eduardo said. "I'm willing to share." He held up the cup and gestured toward the kitchenette.

She crossed over to the cupboard and got a glass to pour it in. Leave it to Chava to tantalize us this way. Sometimes she and I engaged in a test of wills to see who could outlast the other, her wanting me to ask her to finish a story and me pretending I didn't care. I'm not sure how we got started in that little competition, but it was deeply ingrained in our dynamic.

Chava poured half of Eduardo's milkshake into her glass and came back over to sit in her chair. Taking a sip, she said, "Thank you, Eduardo," and raised her glass in a toast.

"*De nada,*" he said, taking his cup back from her. Apparently we all knew how to play this silly game.

I sighed.

"There must be more to the story," I said. It seemed a small concession. Besides, I was curious.

"No one recognized either of them, but one person had something very interesting to say about the crew that lives in that commune or compound or whatever it is at the end of the road."

This could be helpful.

"And what is it they said?" I prompted her. I'd already handed Chava the win on this little battle; another prompt or two didn't matter.

"Apparently they showed up a few years ago. The property had been for sale for a while."

"What was it originally?" Eduardo asked.

"It had been used as pasture for cattle and an orchard, fruit trees of some kind. They still have those, and workers that care for them, but that's not all that's interesting."

Eduardo and I waited as Chava took another sip.

"You should hear all the rumors about what those people are really doing there," Chava finally said after we'd waited long enough. "No one believes they are just running a farm. The list is long: religious cult, drug manufacturers, a group of people who left either an Amish or a Mennonite community and want a more modern lifestyle. Some people even think they have a gold mine somewhere up in the hills."

"A gold mine—that would be interesting," I said. "So what's the consensus?"

"There really isn't a consensus, but there is one thing everyone agrees with. They did install a number of sheds, which they don't use for the animals. They also put in a series of solar panels and a wind turbine, and sunk at least one major well."

"So they are generating more power and water than they should need," Eduardo said. "They are up to something."

Chava sipped at her milkshake. "Tomorrow we reconnoiter the compound, right?" she said, smacking her lips in delight. "After we investigate the original scene of the crime."

Chava had clearly recovered from fearing for my life. At least this time, there wouldn't be a fire involved.

Right?

Chapter Seventeen

———•———

THE FOLLOWING MORNING, we drove up the road to the Langston Ranch, where we would park to make the trek up to the fire area. I sat in back with Franklin, relinquishing my spot in the front to Eduardo in order to sit with my dog. The length of the valley was deceptive, and it took us longer than I expected. The night of the fire, I'd been in no condition to look around even if it hadn't been dark and I hadn't been in the back of an ambulance. Now, in the bright light of a clear day, I could see how beautiful it was. The valley was bright green under the blue June sky.

The ranch had white wooden fences, a vast expanse of pasture with a massive house and a barn next to it, and a few vehicles and horse trailers parked nearby. Another barn sat at the top of a rise. Two big posts flanked the driveway, topped with a large sign over the private drive. The sign was emblazoned with the ranch name and FOUNDATION QUARTER HORSES etched in, which made me wonder where the other three quarters went.

Chava pulled over just before the END COUNTY MAINTAINED ROAD sign. The verges were wide, and the bright-white gravel glowed in the sun. Getting out of the car, we stood a moment and watched horses grazing under a peaceful sky. Far off in the distance, a man mounted on a black and white horse ambled across the horizon and disappeared into the far reaches of the property. A pickup truck was parked not far away, but the hood was cool, so we knew it had been there awhile. Maybe someone else was curious about where the fire had been. I doubted a homicidal firebug had returned to the scene of the crime.

"Ready?" I asked, swinging my backpack over my shoulder and clipping the leash on Franklin.

"Ready," Chava said, hoisting her backpack on. It was filled with water bottles, a few energy bars—I'd warned her they were like eating hard-packed dirt, but she wanted to try one anyway—and a light jacket.

"Ready," Eduardo said.

Walking three abreast, we headed up the Forest Service road, marked by a brown sign, F.S. 3520. Jake had warned us the road had a washout not far from the Langston Ranch, which was why they'd parked at the ranch and not closer to the fire.

At first, nothing looked familiar, as my memories from the end of the trek were still a little vague. But then we arrived at the section of road Jake mentioned. A gully crossed the Forest Service road, big enough to swallow a car. It was easy to see the fire trucks wouldn't have been able to navigate the gap. A memory surfaced.

"I do remember this," I said. "I almost fell in and I'm not sure I could have gotten back out."

"Glad you didn't, *mija*," Eduardo said and we started back up again.

Memories of trudging down the road came back to me. By this point, I'd been exhausted, but determined to get out of the forest to safety. We trekked another fifteen minutes, not nearly as far as I'd been on it three nights ago. Then the road moved into a part of the forest where the fire damage was easier to see.

I found a spot to leave the road, and we began walking cross country. Traveling through the burned section felt surreal. The ground didn't smoke anymore, but the ghost of the fire followed us in the puffs of black dust kicked up by our feet. The scorched earth crackled under our weight. The images of fire rushing up returned me to the panicked hours I'd spent running across this landscape, convinced I wouldn't survive. I'd thought I would die out here in this wilderness. My heart started to pound. I stopped and pressed my hands just above my knees, taking deep breaths to still my rising panic.

Franklin whined and pressed his nose against my chest.

"Are you all right?" Chava asked, turning at the sound of Franklin's distress.

Eduardo watched while I gathered myself. I couldn't read the expression on his face, but something about it made me pull myself together. Maybe I did have something to prove.

"I'm fine," I said. "Let's keep going."

Jake had told us they knew the meadow was the point of origin because the firefighters ascertained the parameters of the fire. Then, knowing which way the wind was blowing, they could determine the direction the fire had traveled.

"You find the far edge, work yourself a little way in, and look for obvious signs of an ignition point," Jake had said. "That's when we found the bits of canvas and what we thought was a campsite, which made us believe it was the origin."

"Don't you have to figure out if it was arson?" I'd asked, curious as to why he wasn't more interested in the man I'd seen and what role he might have played in the fire.

"Not our job," he explained. "We're just the manpower for the Forest Service. They're in charge of investigating."

I hadn't realized there was a separation of duties.

"We just send in the team and put the fire out," Jake said. "We describe what we observe, but after that, it's up to them."

The trees around us remained untouched by the fire. The ground had a zigzag pattern of black and brown, depending on the vagaries of the wind and whatever else made a fire hungry for one section of land and not another.

"I always thought that when an area burned, nothing survived," I said to my parents, amazed how random some of the destruction appeared to be. "This isn't what it felt like when I was running through it."

"What did it feel like?" Chava asked.

"Like the whole world was on fire. This seems so much smaller than I thought. There are so many untouched places."

"It was your whole world," Eduardo said, "when you were in it."

He had a point.

"I could use some water," I said, not wanting my parents to know how much my lungs burned or the extent of my fatigue.

"Here," Eduardo said. "Turn around and I'll get your water out."

He unzipped my bag and dug around, pulling out my fancy bottle. "Are you hungry too?"

"Sure, I could use one of those energy bars."

It dawned on me I was procrastinating. Now that I was up here, part of me didn't want to go back to the meadow. I didn't want to find *Fulano*, proof I'd failed to save a man's life. I'd been the only person who could help him, and I'd left him there to be consumed.

"I can eat and walk at the same time," I said, after drinking from my bottle and handing it back to Eduardo. He handed me a chocolate/peanut butter power bar and zipped my bag back up. Turning around, I caught a glance between my folks.

"What?" I asked. "What's going on?"

"We're just ... you went so far," Chava said.

"And the fire destroyed so much," Eduardo said. "It may look small to you, but it does not look small to us."

"The firefighters also said it was a small fire," I said, reminding them of our conversation the day before.

"Not when your daughter is running around in the middle of it," Chava said, closing up her own water bottle.

Eduardo touched her on the arm and I caught a moment of tenderness between them I didn't expect.

Not having a response and wanting to avoid witnessing any more private exchanges, I started back up through the charred and blackened landscape, Franklin at my side. It felt a lot safer with an enormous dog next to me.

We soon arrived at the meadow. I recognized the spot, even though the entire area had been reduced to mostly burnt ground. Stepping out into the middle, I determined where the tent had been. The ground was dug up, no doubt from the firefighters making sure the fire was completely out, but I was confident it was the right place. Once that was firmly in mind, I walked over to where I'd found *Fulano*.

Blackened earth. Marks from the firefighters' shovels. Untouched grass and piles of rocks. Had a man been attacked here? Franklin sniffed and pawed at the earth, letting out another whine, but it was more contemplative than concerned. My dog had a fascinating repertoire of sounds.

A voice came out of the woods, "So, I guess this means you *did* decide to come back up and see where it happened."

Franklin let out a bark, and I looked up to see Jake standing not far from where the tent had been.

"That is the biggest dog I've ever seen," he said, walking toward me, hand out, the back tilted toward Franklin. "I hope his name isn't Cujo."

"What are you doing here?" I asked as Eduardo and Chava came over to join us. "And no, his name is Franklin."

Jake crouched down, and Franklin gave his hand a sniff and a lick. "You were so sure about that man being here. It stayed with me. I know we didn't miss anything, but I had the day off so I figured I'd come up and look around. I hike a lot anyway, so why not here?" Jake gave Franklin a rub between the ears, and my dog reciprocated with a lick on the cheek.

"That was your truck down near the Langston Ranch," I said.

Jake nodded and stood back up. "I went back over the area.

There is no evidence of a body in the fire. Trust me, I know the signs."

"We have no doubt you are right," Eduardo said, "but now that we are here, we will just look for ourselves. Perhaps Eddie can determine where she left him. If nothing else, it will give my daughter some peace."

Jake glanced at me and I could see something change in his face. He looked at me with empathy.

"You survived something terrifying," he said.

"Yep," I said, though he hadn't really asked a question, "and I just keep seeing his face."

Jake nodded and stood silently, waiting while the rest of us did our thing. I checked to see what my parents were doing. They both walked slowly around the meadow. Chava carried a stick and poked at various lumps of turf. It wasn't clear what she was looking for, but she gave the impression she had a plan. Eduardo skirted the meadow, peering into the trees as if someone might be hiding out there, waiting for us to turn our backs.

When I started walking again, Jake trailed behind me, a shadow to my investigation.

"This is where I found him," I said, standing where the man had lain. Chava turned at the sound of my voice, eyeing the ground at my feet. Looking around, I noticed a pattern across the meadow. It looked like chevrons. I pointed it out to Jake and he laughed.

"What's funny?" I asked.

"There's a type of wind event that makes that pattern." He stood next to me and swept his arm out toward the uneven burnt patterns visible in the grasses. "When the wind hits certain ridges or bumps, it changes directions. It can become almost like a ball rolling across an area. Picture a ball with fire on only one side: it burns the ground only once in a revolution. Can you imagine that?"

I nodded. "I still don't understand what's funny."

"Those are called eddy winds."

"Okay." I felt myself smile. "You're right. That's kind of funny."

Jake's expression sobered. "I wasn't laughing at the situation," he said, putting his hand on my shoulder in reassurance. Something about him reminded me of my mentor Benjamin Cooper, strong and capable. I trusted him. "I know what you endured was awful. Fire is unpredictable, and you can't fully understand how dangerous it is until you're in one."

It was nice to have him tell me that. He understood my experience from a personal perspective. My parents could only guess.

Chava and Eduardo came over to where we stood.

"Do you know which direction you went?" Chava asked. "After you got the man on his feet?"

I pointed into the wilderness at one end of the meadow.

"Lead the way," Eduardo said, and the three of them fell in behind Franklin and me, my father taking up the rear. I noticed he kept looking back as if someone might be following.

What did he know that I didn't?

Chapter Eighteen

———•———

STRIKING OUT ACROSS the terrain I'd half dragged, half carried the semi-conscious man a few days ago turned my anxiety into motivation. I hadn't saved the man's life, but I had tried. And I was now the only person committed to finding his missing daughter. The police might eventually agree there had been an abduction, but I knew it now.

"Slow down," Chava laughed as I began to speed away from them. "What's gotten into you?"

"I know I'm headed the right way," I said, but I did slow my pace. Franklin matched me step for step, nose twitching as we went.

Continuing across the landscape, I saw the evidence of the fire crisscrossing our path, further proof of the inconsistent route the flames had taken. Then, for several minutes, we traveled across unburned ground. "I guess the fire wasn't as close to us as I thought," I said, as we finally arrived at the location where I had left the man behind. The ground was rocky, and I could see the small cluster of rocks I'd noticed when I'd been there before. It was distinct enough to make me confident I had the right place.

"Smoke can be deceptive," Jake said. "It may have been heading your way, but the wind shifted at the last minute."

"Now I could use a drink," Chava said, dropping her backpack and rooting around for her water bottle. Eduardo and I did the same, but Jake wandered off, and I could see him looking closely at the ground a short distance away. Franklin put his nose down to where I'd pointed.

"Smell anything, buddy?" I asked my dog, but he just looked at me as if to say, *Of course, I smell many things. What's your point?*

"There's evidence of the fire just past that stand of trees," Jake said as he walked back over to us, gesturing toward a group of ponderosa pines. "We would have been over there, but not come this far. You're correct. If the man was here, we wouldn't have found him."

"So, where is he?" Chava asked.

We all scanned the land around us as if a body might appear if we concentrated hard enough.

"Maybe he wasn't hurt as badly as you thought," Chava said. "He might have run out of here without ever going for medical help. Especially if he started the fire, he'd be afraid of getting into trouble."

I shrugged. I didn't think the man started the fire. He'd been halfway across the meadow when it broke out. Though maybe he knew who did.

"Are you sure this is the right place?" Chava sounded skeptical. "You were disoriented, scared. Everything looks the same out here."

"I'm sure," I said, confident in my memory. Franklin had kept his nose down to the ground for quite a while. Now he scratched at the rocky surface. "I think Franklin's picking up something," I said. Though I knew it could be the scent of an animal. Franklin sat down, staring off in the distance.

"Perhaps we should look this way," Eduardo said, and started down a ravine, calling Franklin to join him. I unclipped his leash and my dog stepped up to Eduardo's side.

"What are you looking for?" Chava called after him as he disappeared.

"*El hombre muerto*," he said, and the rest of us followed. Even Chava knew the Spanish word for dead.

Fifteen minutes later, Franklin let out a howl and dropped to the ground.

"How on earth did you know he'd be here?" Chava asked as we stood looking down at the corpse. Edging closer, we could see a body wedged into a rocky section of ground.

Franklin stayed in the position I'd come to learn meant he'd located a corpse: ears forward, tail flat to the ground. No doubt in my mind we'd found *Fulano*. Though I couldn't see the man's face, his hair was black and the clothes were as I remembered them. Besides, how many dead people could be stashed around these mountains?

"Eddie says she leaves the man—this, I believe," Eduardo said in answer to Chava's question. "She says we are in the right place and I see what Franklin does. The man is no longer there. Either he walked away or someone moved him. If he walked away, he could be anywhere. If someone moved him, to hide him perhaps, they might follow the path of least resistance. But dead bodies are heavier than people expect. I look where Franklin is pointing. I see the ravine. It goes downhill. Here he is."

"That's pretty smart," Jake said, looking at my father with newfound respect.

Eduardo shrugged, "It's what I would do if I had to hide a body."

Jake's expression showed the slightest flicker of fear.

"He's just kidding," Chava said, elbowing my father in the side.

Eduardo looked at Chava with barely concealed amusement. "Of course. It's what I *would* do, should I do things like that. Sometimes my English is not so clear."

I thought his English was just fine, but now wasn't the time to point that out.

"I don't understand," I said, clipping Franklin's leash back on. "Why would someone put him here in this ravine?"

"Maybe he tried to escape the fire on his own, but only got this far before his head wound finally killed him," Chava said.

Possible, but doubtful.

"I've got to call Detective Campbell," I said. "She'll want to know what we've found."

"We'll have to get back down to our vehicles," Jake said. "We don't have any cell service here. But for now, let's all get out of here before we ruin any evidence that might have been left behind." Jake had stayed farther up the hill, above the corpse. He could see the body and knew no amount of CPR was going to revive him.

I started to reach into the man's pockets to check for identification.

"I don't think we should touch anything," Jake said with an authority in his voice I wasn't going to ignore.

We started up the steep, rocky ravine back toward the flat, granite expanse above. Eduardo dropped back behind us, and a quick glance around caught him pocketing something.

It was so much easier having one of my parents around to break the law so I didn't have to. I couldn't wait to discover what he'd found.

Back up at the top, Chava asked Jake if he thought the police would arrive by helicopter.

"No. I think they'll hike in like we did.

"That's going to take a while. What's to keep something from happening to him between now and then?" I asked.

Jake looked troubled. "I hadn't thought about that. The smell will undoubtedly draw wildlife. I'm surprised it hasn't already. Franklin apparently caught his scent."

"Will the recent fire keep animals away?" Chava asked. "Even though it didn't burn here?"

"No," Jake said, "it won't."

The man's face rose in my mind alongside the thought of animals feeding on his remains. I swallowed hard.

Eduardo spoke up. "I could stay with the deceased until the police arrive."

Jake paused. This wasn't really his problem, but he was the "official" on the scene. He looked at us for a moment, clearly unsure what to do next.

"I can stay too," Chava said. "You and Eddie go back down to the cars and call in what we've found."

"It might be a long time before anyone can get here," he said. "It could get dark, and these afternoon thunderstorms come up awful fast."

"I have been uncomfortable before," Eduardo said. "We have food, water, and it won't get so cold it will hurt us." He looked at my mother, the amusement back in his eyes. "Chava and I have many years of catching up to do. We won't be bored."

"I can wait down there for the detective," I said to Jake. "This isn't really your problem." I held out my hand to Chava. "Let me have the keys to the car."

"I'll stay with you," Jake said. "I've come this far. Plus, they'll want a statement from me too." I took the keys from Chava, but he was right. The authorities would want statements from all of us.

Half an hour later, Jake and I were back down at the vehicles. I got Franklin's water bowl out of the car and poured him a drink, then got out my cellphone to call Detective Campbell. I hadn't even gotten through to the sheriff's station, however, when Chava and Eduardo appeared on the trail.

"What are you doing here?" I asked as they walked up. "Why aren't you protecting *Fulano*?"

"We got back to where we left the body," Chava said, her voice breathless from a combination of exertion and excitement, "but he was gone."

Chapter Nineteen

———•———

"WHAT DO YOU mean, *gone*?"

"I mean," Chava said, trying to tamp down her excitement with Jake watching, "that your father and I got back to the ravine, and your *fulano* had disappeared."

I looked at Eduardo. "Seriously?"

"I believe the expression is 'into thin air,' no?" Eduardo's face showed no expression. Could he have done something to the body? Why would he? I wished I could talk to my parents without an audience, but Jake's presence kept me from asking anything that would get either one of them in hot water.

"Any signs of an animal dragging the body away?" I asked. I could hear the hitch in my voice.

"No," Eduardo said, "and we searched the immediate area. We found nothing."

"Okay. Well, I still have to call Detective Campbell," I said. It wasn't like I could ask Jake to forget about seeing a corpse while I went back up and searched for clues.

"What are you going to tell her?" Chava asked.

That was a good question.

My cell was still in my hand. I'd already brought Detective

Campbell's number up. Clicking on the call button, I took a deep breath. She answered after just a few rings, and I explained the situation. She kept her voice neutral, but I could tell she wasn't happy.

"I'll get there as soon as I can," she said. "One of you is going to have to take me back up to the scene."

"I'm happy to do that," I said.

"I think I'll take the firefighter," she said, as she hung up the phone. I would too, under the circumstances.

Putting my cell back in my pocket, I told Jake what she'd said. "I don't think she wants me to take her back up there."

Jake sighed, rubbing his face with his hands. "Great. I can't say for sure what you two," he gestured toward my parents, "might have done after I left."

"You think *we* moved the body?" Chava asked with an audible edge of indignation. "And what, hid him for later?"

"I don't know. It's more likely an animal hauled him off. You say you didn't see any signs, but that doesn't mean it didn't happen. Besides, I'm only taking your word for it he disappeared so quickly."

Chava's voice rose. "If we wanted to come back to the scene of a crime and hide a murder victim, we certainly wouldn't have pointed him out to you in the first place."

"People do strange things," Jake said. "Maybe you all were up to something and it got out of hand. You felt guilty, so you decided to find out if he was really dead. Actually finding him was a surprise."

Tuning out their conversation, I turned away. I didn't really think Jake believed we'd killed the guy, gone to the sheriff's office to report him, then come up here and found him, just to lose him again. I was more curious about what Eduardo was doing. His instincts concerning acts of violence were much finer honed than mine. He'd walked away from the parked cars and was looking up the road toward the shadowy compound next door to the Langston Ranch.

"Strike one against us with Detective Campbell," I said, though I didn't think my father was too concerned about the opinion of the local authorities.

He shrugged, eyes still pinned on the outfit up the road.

"What are you thinking?" I asked him.

"This man, he disappeared too fast for someone to have carried him away on foot. If an animal had done it, I would have seen signs, no matter what the firefighter might think. Plus, I believe Franklin would have been anxious, if a mountain lion or a pack of coyotes had been nearby. We heard nothing. So he also wasn't removed on an off-road motorcycle or vehicle. I'm thinking perhaps someone came in on a horse."

"Wouldn't you have seen hoof prints? Or heard something?"

"Not necessarily. It was stony where the body was. Someone could have come in close, gotten off the horse, put the body on the horse, and ridden away during the time we walked out of the ravine and before we decided to go back. Chava and I were gone for at least fifteen minutes. A man on a horse could have gotten a long ways away."

Or a woman, I thought, but I wasn't going to point that out to Eduardo just now. Gender equality in the criminal world wasn't something he thought about, and fixing that wasn't my responsibility.

"You're thinking the off-grid survivalist camp might be just the place for that someone to have come from."

Eduardo shrugged. "We know they have a few horses. I have learned it's best not to make assumptions, but logic would dictate that's the place to start."

My father, the Latino Mr. Spock.

"Yep," I said.

"You were already planning on talking to them, weren't you?" Eduardo asked.

"Yep."

Eduardo smiled. "I should not underestimate you."

"It is my day job," I said. "Even if my investigations don't usually involve kidnap victims and dead men."

"So, next we go and visit them?"

"I'd like to figure out a way to do a little reconnaissance." I said. "Much as I don't want to climb around in these hills again, maybe we can hike in behind them to try and get a feel for what they're doing there. If they're growing marijuana or processing cocaine, I don't really want to stumble around on their property and get shot."

"I suppose Detective Campbell will go there as well," Eduardo said. "We don't want to bump into the authorities either, since we will say we plan to leave the investigation to her."

"She will want to talk to them, but if it were me, I wouldn't talk to the authorities. There's nothing she can do to force them."

There was no probable cause for a crime having been committed by the folks at the compound. There was no body to process. The place the man might have been attacked had been burned. We had only my word as to what the guy said, and the four of us were the only ones to have seen his body.

"Do you think they would talk to you?" I asked.

"You mean if there are Latinos on the property?"

"*Sí*," I said, with a smile. "I'm thinking you might open doors a white woman in a uniform could not."

"You have a good point, *mija*." Eduardo fell silent for a long moment. Then he gave me that sly smile of his. "I think I have an idea." He began texting on his phone, back turned away from me.

Regardless of what my father had planned, it was going to have to wait until after we spoke to Detective Campbell. She knew we were all here, so it would look strange if my father disappeared before she arrived.

"First, we hear what the detective has to say," I said. "Then we go do our own investigation. Sound right?"

"*Sí*," my father said. "*Buena idea*." He barely looked up from his cell. What was he planning? And how much trouble could it get me into?

Chapter Twenty

———◆———

DETECTIVE CAMPBELL ARRIVED with her partner, a stocky man who reminded me a little of a wine barrel with legs. They took our statements, then headed up the trail with Jake as a guide, expecting us to return to the resort. She wasn't exactly angry, but we had come up here behind her back. Though I'd told her I'd be monitoring what happened, I don't think she anticipated me returning so fast to poke around. Still, it wasn't as if we'd crossed a line of crime-scene tape. I tried pointing out that she wouldn't even have proof a crime had taken place if we hadn't found the body today and had it stolen out from under us. She reminded *me* she had promised to investigate, and I shouldn't assume that wasn't happening just because they hadn't arrived on my schedule.

"I *was* coming up here," Detective Campbell said. "I took your report seriously. We would most likely have found him ourselves."

The implication being she wouldn't have let him slip through her fingers.

I tried to look contrite. It took all my restraint not to point out that she wouldn't have found the body if she'd come up later, since he'd already be gone.

"You are here as a private citizen," she said as we finished up our conversation, "which means I can't stop you from asking questions, but I can arrest you if I think you're tampering with evidence or hindering our investigation."

She had a point. She couldn't stop me from asking questions. I knew enough about the law to understand what was and what wasn't going to cross into illegal behavior. Besides, as far as I was concerned, he was my client. Even if I didn't know his name and he was already dead.

There was the little complication of whatever my father had removed from the body, but I'd decided to ask him about it after the detective left so I wouldn't have to lie about it now.

"In fact, just to make myself clear," she said, giving me a look I hoped never to see again, "I'm going to serve you with a trespass."

Uh-oh. That couldn't be good.

The detective walked around to the back of her SUV, the Chelan County Sheriff logo painted on the side. She popped open the tailgate with a touch of her foot under the bumper and gave me another withering look when I told her that was really cool. I guess complimenting her on her ride wasn't going to get me back into her good graces. No gold star for Eddie Shoes. She dug around through a plastic file box full of papers and came up with a form.

"I'm giving you official notice that you are not allowed back in this area—which, need I remind you, is now a crime scene— for one year."

She filled out the form and handed it over to me. "Do I need to give one to you two as well?" she asked, pinning both my parents with her electric gaze.

"No, ma'am," Chava said, without even crossing her fingers behind her back.

"We will stay with our daughter at all times," Eduardo said, with his predatory smile. His comment earned him a long look from Detective Campbell. He hadn't actually said he wouldn't return to the scene of the crime.

"You're Eddie's father?" she asked instead. "We didn't meet at the hospital."

"That's correct," he said.

When Detective Campbell had taken our contact information down at the start of her interview, I'd expected Eduardo to be uncomfortable about it. But he'd just whipped out a Washington state driver's license and rattled off a Bellingham address as if he'd lived there for years. He also used the name Eduardo Zapata, which made me wonder if he worked for the mafia under a different name and kept his original name "clean."

Or was Eduardo Zapata even his real name?

Regardless of whatever vibe Eduardo was putting out, Detective Campbell made some sort of decision and pushed another button, which automatically closed her tailgate with a quiet clunk. I bit back another compliment about her car.

Detective Campbell did share with us that she had contacted other authorities, including the US Forest Service, which had an investigative arm. Because there was a question about if and where a crime might have taken place, she had let the other agencies know an investigation was ongoing. First, to ask around about a missing Gabriela. Second, to see if anyone had reported a missing man matching my police sketch—she would have sent out copies of both pictures to everyone. Now she'd have to call them back and tell them a private eye had been tromping around in the potential crime scene along with her parents and an enormous dog. Also, that the supposed victim had disappeared.

"Did you ever get confirmation on the whereabouts of that teenage boy?" I asked as we finished up our interview.

Detective Campbell shook her head. "You don't give up, do you?"

"No," I said. "I'm just concerned about his welfare." It was what had gotten me into this mess, after all. The cryptic message from the resort wasn't totally comforting.

"We identified the boy you saw running on the trail. He's fine. Don't ask me to tell you anything else."

"Thank you," I said. "I appreciate that."

There was a pause and I realized Detective Campbell expected me to ask more questions. Apparently I'd surprised her with my thanks.

Jake and the two detectives got ready to head back up the Forest Service road. Eduardo and I got back into Chava's car. Franklin was already sound asleep and barely moved as I squeezed into the backseat with him, sliding his head onto my lap.

"We aren't just leaving, are we?" Chava asked.

"We must move the car," Eduardo said casually, as if he evaded law enforcement's eyes on a daily basis, which of course he did, or had, as his current occupation showed signs of being a little up in the air. Had he retired? Or was he just taking some personal days?

"Where are we going?" Chava asked as she hopped into the driver's seat.

"Before we do anything else," I said, looking up the Forest Service road and confirming Jake and the two detectives were out of sight, "what was it you found in *Fulano's* pockets?"

"His pockets?" Chava said, turning to look at Eduardo. "You searched him?"

Most people would be slightly horrified at frisking a corpse, but by her tone, Chava was impressed. Or sorry she hadn't done it herself.

"Ah, you see me do this," Eduardo said with that half smile. "Something very interesting. Let me show you." He dug around in his pocket and handed an object over to me.

"Is this what I think it is?" I asked.

"That would depend on what you think it is," Eduardo said.

"Let me see that." Chava took it out of my hand and inspected it closely before turning back to me. "What would your *fulano* be doing with this?"

Chapter Twenty-One

———•———

THE THREE OF US sat for a moment while Eduardo tucked the Purple Heart back into his pocket. Did the military medal for being wounded on the battlefield belong to *Fulano*?

"Where do you think he got it?" I asked my father. I'd seen one once before, when I was helping to clean my mentor's things out of our office after he committed suicide. The sight of it—a symbol of sacrifice—filled me with sadness.

"And why didn't he give it to you along with the rosary as something of value?" Chava asked us both.

We sat for a moment thinking about what this new piece of information told us.

"We have no way of knowing if he was wounded in action or if it came from someone else," I said. "I think we have to proceed with what we already talked about." I said this last bit to Eduardo and caught Chava's glance out of the corner of my eye.

"What was it you two talked about?" she asked, sounding vaguely annoyed she hadn't been privy to our conversation.

"We need a better look at the place up the road," I said.

"I agree," my father said. "We need to know more about *el recinto*,"

"*El recinto*?" I asked, not recognizing the term.

"*Sí*, enclosure ... military compound."

I filed that one away for later use.

"Head to the resort," he said to Chava.

"Isn't that the wrong direction?" Chava asked. "The compound, or *el recinto* or whatever it is, is back the other way."

"No," he said. "Eddie and I, we agreed, we need to reconnoiter. If we want a better look at a large area of land, without anyone knowing we are doing so, we don't want to drive onto it, we want to fly over it."

Now why hadn't I thought of that?

But what was Eduardo going to do? Commandeer a plane?

WE GOT BACK to the resort and discovered Eduardo planned to go on his errand alone. Chava tried to talk him into taking us with him, but she didn't get any traction.

"I won't be gone long," he said, getting out of Chava's car and heading toward his Jeep, parked in the lot behind the main building. "Why don't you two have lunch?" My stomach growled and Chava gave in.

We met up with Debbie for lunch, and she agreed to take Franklin for the rest of the day. "Don't you worry about a thing," she said, sighing in contentment. The boys napped at our feet, under the table on the outdoor patio where dogs were allowed. "Franklin will be fine. Just do me a favor and be careful."

After we finished eating, we walked back to Debbie's room and said goodbye to her and both dogs; then Chava and I went back to our cabin to wait.

It was going on three o'clock in the afternoon and the sun was dipping to the west, but we still had several hours of daylight left when Eduardo pulled up in front of our cabin. When we went out to find out what he'd gone after, he motioned us to get into the Jeep with him.

Chava hopped into the front seat, relegating me to the back. I guess my elevated status as a forest fire survivor was over.

"So?" Chava asked as soon as we were both inside. "Do we have a helicopter? A plane? A glider?"

Eduardo eyed Chava. "Where is it I would hide these things? In my pocket, perhaps?"

Were my parents flirting? Had my father just made a joke? After the revelations about my ancestry last night, and now the view of these two together, my world felt uncertain indeed. Chava hadn't even demanded he turn the driving over to her.

"We could be on our way to an airstrip," Chava said, buckling up her seatbelt as Eduardo turned out of the driveway, back in the direction of the Langston Ranch and *el recinto*. Before we got to the Langston Ranch, however, we turned off onto another dirt road I hadn't noticed this morning. Rutted and overgrown, it looked rarely used, and even in the four-wheel-drive Jeep, it was rough going. Though it wasn't that far in distance, with the rockiness of its surface it took us a good twenty minutes to travel to the end.

"I hope your little errand was worthwhile, along with this drive," I said. "Where exactly are we?"

"We have skirted one side of the Langston Ranch. The compound will be ahead of us about two miles." My father glanced at me in the rearview mirror. "You are used to doing everything by yourself, *mija*." True, though I might change my methods depending on what Eduardo had come up with for our investigation. "Trust me, the errand was worth it, as was the drive."

"How did you know this road was here?" Chava asked.

"My friend who I asked this favor. We used his computer and looked at satellite images of the area."

"See anything interesting?" I asked.

"Perhaps," my father said, "but we will see more soon."

My father got out of the Jeep, and Chava and I scrambled out behind him. Walking around to the rear, he popped open the rear hatch with the button on the key. Chava and I both elbowed past each other in our curiosity to see what he'd collected.

"A drone?" I said. "That's brilliant."

My father began to unload the equipment. "Please carry this," he said, handing me the remote control.

"And this," he said, handing Chava a plain manila folder. Then he lifted the drone out of its case. It was much bigger than any I'd ever seen before, and it took some effort for my father to lift. Its black frame, multiple rotors, large camera lens, and various wires made it look like a prop from a sci-fi movie.

"Chava, you have some photos there," Eduardo said. "Can you pull them out, please?"

Chava withdrew several aerial shots from the manila folder and laid them on the hood of the Jeep. Picking them up, Eduardo looked around where we were parked and eyed the setting sun. Then he pulled out his cellphone and clicked on an app.

"What are you doing?" I asked.

"Double-checking our route. We'll have to walk without a road or a trail from here."

Leaning over his shoulder, I saw he had a compass on his smartphone. I had to remember to download one of those, just in case I got lost again any time soon. Though I didn't have plans to travel on my own in the near future. For the first time in my life, safety in numbers felt like a real thing.

"Okay, we're ready to go," he said. "We are trespassing on the Langston Ranch, so we don't want to be seen. Quietly now. Voices carry in landscape like this. There are no city noises to drown them out."

Chava fell in behind Eduardo, carrying the photos, now returned to their envelope. I took up the rear, carrying the remote control. All of us wore the backpacks we'd prepared for this morning's hike, so we had our water bottles, which we'd refilled at the resort. I'd fought the urge to carry a fire extinguisher and settled for an extra power bar. I was not getting lost again and starving in the woods.

After climbing through a barbed-wire fence, Eduardo moved silently through the trees. Luckily, they were fairly dense, blocking us from the view of anyone at the Langston Ranch or *el recinto*. Chava could walk quietly on her panther paws, but I seemed to find every downed twig to snap under my feet and every dry leaf to crinkle and crunch. I don't think anyone nearby would have taken my crashing around for a herd of deer, unless the local deer were drunk or wearing clown shoes. Luckily, we didn't come across anyone else during our trek—or at least, no one we saw—so I hoped for the best.

We didn't have to get too close to any of the Langston Ranch buildings, but stayed far away under the cover of the trees. We could see a large outdoor arena made of white fencing, with what looked like barrels and orange plastic cones set up inside. There were also some smaller pens made of pipes rather than fence boards. I could see a woman inside one of them with a horse circling around her. She had a long white stick with a bright yellow flag on the end, which she waved at the animal. He seemed to know what she wanted him to do. To me it looked like magic.

Much of their property was open grazing land for their horses, but they'd left the tree line intact at the edges. Moving at a good clip, we traveled the distance from our car to *el recinto* before five o'clock. Though the ridgeline of the mountains to the west would make sundown earlier by at least an hour, we still had a few hours of daylight left.

Eduardo stopped ahead of us, raising his right arm, hand fisted in an obvious signal for "stop." Chava edged up behind him, peering around his taller frame. I moved up behind her, able to look over her head. We would have looked like a multi-ethnic totem pole if anyone had been there to see us.

We were once again at a barbed-wire fence.

Roughly the length of a football field away, past a small

stand of trees, a few buildings stood surrounded by a chain-link fence. No people were visible from our spot. A small herd of cattle had gathered in front. They looked content, chewing their cuds and dozing.

Eduardo signaled me to hand him the remote, and for us to stay put. He'd already told us he wanted to get as close to the compound as he could, to maximize flying time over the buildings before the battery ran out. He made his way about twenty yards farther than where we stopped, before disappearing from sight. A few minutes later, I heard the low buzz of the drone, but even that sound faded immediately and I couldn't see the thing flying above us.

Chava and I stood for a few minutes, but nothing happened. The world was quiet around us, and I could feel the fatigue from my ordeal sneaking up on me again. I sat down, resting my back against a tree, carefully extricating my water bottle from the pack.

My sparkly bottle from the gift shop was a little worse for wear after having tumbled down a rocky hillside, but I was keeping it as a symbol of my survival. Pulling my cellphone out, I was surprised to find I had a strong signal on my phone. I clicked through a few emails—nothing that couldn't wait until I was back in Bellingham.

Chava soon joined me against the tree. Debbie had sent a photo of my dog Franklin sound asleep with Indy on the bed in her room. The dogs slept in a pile together. My heart soared at the sight of his fuzzy face. Chava peeked over my shoulder. "Good to see our boy is doing well." Chava got her own cell out and checked her signal. "Do you think the compound has a cell tower somewhere on the property? I wouldn't expect these to work out here."

"Maybe Eduardo will find it with his drone," I said. We both spent the time connecting with the outside world, which from here felt far away.

* * *

FORTY MINUTES LATER, Eduardo reappeared, carrying the drone. "Time to go, *mija*," he whispered. Chava and I got up and we brushed ourselves off.

I started to ask what he'd discovered, but he put his fingers to his lips and motioned for us to fall in behind him as he led us back to the car. By the time we arrived at the Jeep, the sun was sinking behind the mountain peaks. Eduardo quickly loaded the drone back into the Cherokee.

"Where to now?" Chava asked.

"Back to the resort so we can look at the photographs," he said.

"Do you think you got anything that will tell us what that crew is up to?" I asked.

"I do," he said.

Who was I to argue with a man who could show up at a moment's notice with a fancy drone?

Chapter Twenty-Two

———•———

BACK AT THE resort, Chava went into our cabin, Eduardo headed to his room to grab his laptop, and I went over to Debbie's to collect Franklin and update her on our progress. By the time I got back with the dog, Eduardo had commandeered the table, plugged in the laptop, and turned off the overhead light. Next, he inserted the memory card from the drone into the computer and began clicking through files.

"What's a drone like that worth?" I asked out of idle curiosity as his fingers flew across the keyboard.

"About thirty thousand dollars."

Chava, who'd fetched a glass of water from the sink in the kitchenette, promptly sprayed a mouthful across the counter.

"And you're leaving it in the back of the Jeep?" she said, glancing out the window. "You can't even see your car from here."

Eduardo cocked his head and looked at her for a long moment. I'd come to learn that look meant he was assessing how much information to reveal.

"There is a GPS location device on the drone. If someone

should be foolish enough to steal it from me, I will track them down and retrieve it."

No doubt also making that particular individual sorry for stealing from Eduardo Zapata.

"Why is it so expensive?" I asked. "I thought you could buy a drone for less than two grand."

"Because of this," he said, tilting the computer screen in my direction.

I walked over a little closer, gently moving Chava aside. The photos he brought up were crystal clear. I could make out the license plates of cars and the faces of people caught by the camera lens.

"These are incredible. But didn't those guys notice a drone hovering over their heads to snap these pics?" I asked.

"The drone was several hundred feet in the air," Eduardo said. "And almost completely silent—that's the other thing the money buys you."

I'd noticed how quiet it was when it took off.

"Can we trace these license plates?" Chava asked, pointing her finger at the computer screen.

Eduardo gave her another look, but this time with that sly half smile of his.

"I don't think that's going to be a problem," I said to Chava before turning back to Eduardo. "You were able to fly a long time. What else did you see?"

"*Sí*, the drone, it has about thirty-five minutes of flying time. Many, many pictures. Thousands. But how useful they will be, I won't know until we look through them."

Chava and I leaned over his shoulders for a few minutes, but soon realized we were in for a long stretch of clicking through photos, most of which looked a lot alike. Eduardo was right; there were advantages to having someone else help with the workload. Maybe I should take on an assistant when I got back to Bellingham.

To get licensed as a PI in Washington State, you had to show three years of private investigation experience, typically under the wing of a licensed private eye. I'd worked for my mentor Benjamin Cooper—that's how I'd gotten my hours in. Could I be to someone else what Coop had been to me?

Was that something I wanted?

Chava sighed and flopped down on the chair in the corner, which was much more comfortable than the ones at the table where Eduardo sat. I felt restless. They didn't really need me for this.

"I'm going to go take a little walk," I said. "Stretch my legs."

Chava had gotten a deck of cards out of her pocket and was practicing a card trick; prestidigitation was another one of her gifts. It went well with being a card counter.

Eduardo was focused on his computer screen. Neither parent looked up as I hooked Franklin on his leash and headed out the door. Hopefully, by the time I returned, the photos would have yielded something valuable.

Surely a thirty-thousand-dollar drone could promise that.

Walking around behind the cabin, I went out into the woods a ways. I was curious about any trails or obvious signs of someone hanging out back there. While I still wasn't sure if someone had searched through our room, having come in and out of Chava's bedroom window, I was curious if there was any evidence of a watcher in the woods.

The moon had started to rise, shining bright just above the top of the ridgeline, but the woods were dark. I pulled my penlight out but didn't turn it on. There weren't any obvious trails through the stand of pines, but several faint tracks, most likely left by deer, patterned the ground ahead of me. With none of them looking more traveled than the others, I chose one at random and began to make my way through the trees.

It didn't take long for me to realize how many sounds existed in a "silent" wood. Wind whispered through the treetops, like a mother as she comforted her child. Animals, out hunting or being hunted, scrambled through the bushes. At one point, a loud crash came through off to my left, and I clicked on the flashlight, catching a white tail with a black tip on a large deer as it disappeared into the undergrowth.

Franklin was alert, but not anxious. He appeared to be enjoying our sojourn into the wilderness. We continued on for another fifteen minutes after the flight of the big deer, when I came upon a dirt path. A NO TRESPASSING sign was nailed to a tree on the far side. It looked like I'd reached the edge of the resort property. I doubted anyone would notice me creeping around, so I wandered down the trail, the resort slipping away behind me on my left. If my internal compass was working, I was heading north.

Another five minutes and I felt I'd done enough time out in the hinterlands. It wasn't like I even knew what I was looking for. I stood still a moment. The moon was bright enough to illuminate the track, as the clearing allowed a slice of light to come down through the forest. No sooner had I stopped when the unmistakable sound of a rattlesnake broke the quiet.

Was there really a snake out at this time of night? It was cool now the sun was down, in the forties or fifties. It didn't make sense for a reptile to be out. Franklin didn't move either, nor did he make a sound.

The rattle came again.

Snakes were unlikely to strike unless they felt threatened. Where was the sound coming from? It was hard to tell. Should I stay where I was? Or go back the way we'd come. I didn't want to jeopardize Franklin, though he'd probably be better at avoiding a rattler than I was. The sound of something heavy moving in the woods set my heart racing even faster. What was really out there in the dark? I wouldn't hear a snake slithering along, would I? It would strike so fast, I'd never hear it coming. It rattled to warn, but it struck in silence. It certainly wouldn't sound like a person in boots, which is what I thought I heard now.

"Is someone there?" I asked, feeling foolish talking to a

snake, but my feet felt rooted to the ground and I didn't know what else to do.

Nothing.

Was that good or bad?

Chapter Twenty-Three

A FTER AN ETERNITY, I decided I had to do something. I couldn't just stand there all night. Slowly, I took one step and then another, heading back down the trail. Every so often, I'd stop, listening. Franklin stayed with me, occasionally turning back, ears pricked forward.

A few minutes later, the NO TRESPASSING sign I'd seen when I came out of the woods appeared as a white square off to my left, too dark now to read the words. Picking up the pace, I clicked on my flashlight and plunged back into the trees, following the animal track I'd been on earlier. Not long after, I launched out of the trees behind the cabin again. My heart pounded in my ears, and not just from the exertion of stumbling through the woods. I'd felt watched. It was probably just adrenaline, triggered by a primeval fear of snakes, but the noise I'd heard of something moving made me think something or someone else was out there.

I stood a moment to calm my breathing and listen to the night sounds. All had gone still. The wind had stopped. No animals moved. If anyone or anything had followed us through the woods, they were far better at blending into the wilderness than I would ever be.

Moving around to the front of the cabin, I decided not to mention what had happened to my parents. I'd almost died in a fire. If I told them I'd just come across a rattlesnake, they might never let me outside again. I chalked up the sound in the woods to either my imagination or another deer.

When I reentered the front room, Chava and Eduardo were in the exact same spots as when I left. Franklin wandered over to his dog bowl and slurped loudly, while Chava held up my cellphone.

"Iz has been trying to reach you," she said. "I thought about answering and letting her know you didn't have your phone, but I figured you'd be back soon."

I looked at the screen and noticed a couple missed calls from my best friend.

"I'll call her now." I started to ring Iz back when I noticed my parents, staring.

"What?" I asked. "It's just Iz. Why the looks?"

"Are you going to tell her about your ordeal?" Chava asked.

"Probably, why?"

Eduardo and Chava both looked tense and the cabin felt very small.

"I think I'll step back outside," I said.

"No, no, don't worry about us," Chava said. "We won't make a sound."

But they would hear every word.

"I could use a decaf latte anyway," I said. My canine had plopped down on his dog bed and was rolling around with his feet in the air, making happy noises. "I'll leave Franklin with you two," I said as I slipped back out the door.

The main building had a couple of decks that looked out over magnificent scenery. Scenery I hadn't had time to fully appreciate, especially since it had tried to kill me a few days ago. I got myself a decaf latte from the coffee stand on the ground floor and made my way over to a quiet corner on the porch farthest from the lobby entrance. Checking the time, I saw it was not quite eleven o'clock. Iz would still be up. Parking myself in a surprisingly comfortable wooden rocking chair, I hit the redial button.

"Hey, girl," she said after two rings. "Are you having fun out there in the wilderness?"

"Well, sort of," I said. "It's gotten a little complicated."

"Uh-huh," she said, her Southern twang amplifying as her emotions rose. "I thought that might be true when the Chelan County Sheriff's Department called the station to check up on you."

Oh crap.

"I guess I should explain."

"That would be a good idea."

I filled Iz in on all the recent events. Because Iz worked for the Bellingham Police Department, she'd fielded the call from Detective Campbell when she called in to ask about my work as a private investigator. I'd mentioned to Detective Campbell I'd worked a few cases that intersected with the BPD, so I guess she'd followed up to find out if I'd been telling the truth.

"Who did she talk to?"

"Kate Jarek," Iz said. Chance's partner. At least Chance was out of the office for a few days and Detective Campbell didn't talk to him.

"Do you know what Kate said about me?"

"Not entirely, but what I did manage to overhear sounded pretty routine. She said you had been helpful in some previous investigations."

That could have been a lot worse.

"Are you sure you're all right?" This time, Iz's voice carried real concern.

"I feel better than I sound," I said, knowing I was still croaking from the smoke damage. Then I chuckled, remembering how visions of her had been part of what kept me going.

"Want to let me in on the joke?" she asked.

I described my hallucinatory image of her prodding me on through the cold, dark night, until I found my savior in the form of a firefighter from the Chelan County Fire Department.

"Glad to know I helped," Iz said. "It's true, if you'd died out there, I would have had to kill you."

We both laughed again and I was relieved she wasn't upset I hadn't gotten in touch with her sooner. She had just worried about my welfare. One of these days I'd trust that a true friend cares more about your welfare than occasional bad behavior.

"So what are you going to do about the guy you found, then lost again?" she asked.

I'd been careful what I relayed to Iz regarding the investigation my parents and I were engaged in. She couldn't help me from Bellingham, and telling her we'd been surveilling potential suspects with a very expensive drone Eduardo probably borrowed from a Seattle mobster didn't feel like useful information to pass on.

"Let the local authorities do their job, I suppose." I kept my voice light, thinking that would make me more believable.

Iz let out a snort. "Yeah, right. Just keep in mind I can't easily get over there to bail you out of jail if you get into trouble nosing around where you don't belong."

"Who, me? I'm a bastion of self-restraint."

Iz snickered again. "Maybe, but you've got Chava with you."

She had a point there.

"So what's going on in B'ham?" I asked to change the subject. "Anything exciting?"

Iz went on to tell me what she'd been up to while I'd been incommunicado. She sounded a little tense, though I couldn't put my finger on why. There was no reason for me to think she had lied about not being upset with me, so something else must be bothering her. Then she fell quiet, which she definitely didn't do very often. Iz was as talkative as I could be taciturn, part of why we got along so well. She was the yin to my yang.

"Something bugging you, Iz?" I asked.

"We had another police shooting," she said. "Down in Seattle. Another black man."

And just like that the color divide slipped between us. I rarely thought about the fact my best friend was black and I was a very light brown and usually thought of myself as white. At times like this, I realized I couldn't fully understand how she felt.

"I'm sorry," I said, unsure what else to say. We were standing on dangerous ground. I wanted to be supportive, but I wasn't sure how.

"There's going to be a march here in Bellingham," she said. "A show of solidarity."

It dawned on me the complexity of the situation for her. She was employed by the police department. I know she respected the people she worked with, the ones who put their lives on the line every day. We had black officers in the BPD. Where did they stand in all of this? Where did I?

"Are you thinking of marching?" I asked.

"Yes," she said.

"I'll worry about you."

"I'll be all right."

But we both knew that wasn't necessarily true.

"What day?" I asked.

"Saturday."

"Okay. We'll talk before then. And after, when everything is over and you're safe."

"When will you be home?" she asked.

"Soon," I said, though I wasn't completely sure about that. The image of the Purple Heart rose in my mind. Had the man been a veteran? Or did that belong to someone else? I felt I needed to see this through, find out who the dead man was and what happened to his daughter. Perhaps in part because the world felt so fractured. Black against white, brown against black, white against both. And here I was, stuck in the middle, with a foot in every camp. Maybe part of why this incident mattered so much to me was because deep down I believed the death of a Latino migrant worker, if that's who he was, or the abduction of his daughter, mattered just a little bit less to our society than a wealthy white man's would have.

Maybe I understood Iz's dilemma better than I thought.

"I'll be glad when you're back," Iz said. "Life feels fragile. I want all my peeps home, where I can keep an eye on them."

I couldn't argue with that.

"I'm safe," I said, "and I'll be home soon."

I just hoped I was telling her the truth.

Chapter Twenty-Four

———◆———

RUSHING BACK TO the cabin didn't feel important. It wasn't like we were going to solve the mystery of *Fulano* with a single image, no matter how good the camera in the drone was. I had my doubts we'd find evidence of the missing woman, unless the drone could see through walls.

The resort had few lights on this side of the buildings, just enough of a glow to safely navigate the furniture on the porch. From my vantage point, I could see thousands of stars overhead, twinkling in the night sky.

The air, still redolent with the smell of earth and pine needles baked by the afternoon sun, pricked at my skin as the heat dissipated. Behind me, I could hear the sounds of the vacationers and staff from the resort. Laughter through an open window. The clinking of glasses and silverware from the restaurant with outdoor seating. Someone had killed a man not far from here, but why?

My thoughts turned to the reasons people committed murder. Greed, fear, and anger often played a role. People killed for money. People killed to protect themselves or someone they loved.

I'd also learned from Chance the causes of homicides often correlated to geography. He always kept an open mind going into an investigation, but location impacted his thought process. Dense urban settings made gang violence or drugs likely. Upscale neighborhoods drew burglaries gone wrong. Murders in rural settings were often domestic violence, though crimes related to drugs, especially opioids, were becoming more common.

This was the first time, however, I'd ever come across a murder in an area like this. The statistics of demographics and geography didn't fit out here like they might have back in Bellingham or more conventional neighborhoods.

It was unlikely the man in the meadow had a lot of money, so robbery was probably not the motive. And who would even know he was there to rob? Unless it was someone camping with him. He was off in the woods, so he didn't appear to be a direct threat to anyone. Was his death connected to his daughter's abduction? Was he killed to cover up another crime?

Maybe he was a courier from Latin America. Or his daughter was. But again, why would he be out in the woods?

If he was involved with smuggling, maybe he had contraband in the tent. Perhaps whoever I heard crashing around there was looking for drugs. But again, why would he be so far from his buyers or sellers or partners in crime?

Unless that really had been a raccoon.

My phone buzzed, the sound it made when a text came in. I looked down to see my father's number.

Something you should see.

Apparently Eduardo's drone photos had paid off.

Chapter Twenty-Five

—·—

WALKING BACK TO the cabin, I saw something flash out of the corner of my eye. A green light, moving across the landscape. The resort was darkest away from the main building, with only a few scattered path lights pointed down to mark the way.

Someone with a fancy green laser sight on their weapon? If that was true, I didn't stand much of a chance to get out of the way if they started shooting. Had someone been watching in the woods tonight? The person who moved *Fulano's* body?

"I know you're there," I said into the dark night. "Why don't you come out where I can see you?" I heard a rustling in the bushes. Definitely not a snake this time. My heart pounded again. I waited a few minutes longer. The light reappeared, moving toward me like a cat stalking a mouse. Finally I understood why a hunted animal froze. Which way should I run?

The light came to rest on the path a few feet in front of me.

Was it a warning? To let me know someone was watching. And they could take a shot any time they wanted. A scare tactic to get me to leave?

The light flicked off.

Rooted to the spot, I waited until my heart returned to my chest and I could move forward again.

Could it be some kind of joke? A kid playing a prank? I should tell Eduardo and Chava what happened. But, what could I really tell them? With no other sign that I was being watched, I continued on my way. Taken one by one, these incidents wouldn't make me think twice. Maybe someone in our cabin, maybe someone in the woods, maybe someone watching me now …. But taken together, they told me I was being followed. And warned off.

Deciding to keep this latest creepy event to myself—out of habit as much as anything else—I arrived back at the cabin, to find Chava and Eduardo both hunched over his laptop.

"What 'cha got?" I asked, rubbing Franklin's head as he came over to greet me. I shook off my feeling of unease, telling myself Franklin would bark if anyone tried to get into the cabin.

"*Mire esta, mija*," he said, gesturing toward the computer.

Crossing over to the table, Chava stepped back enough to let me get a view of the screen. The photographs Eduardo had pulled out consisted primarily of images of cows. Big cows, small cows, black cows, black and white cows. They were standing around, lying around, and occasionally walking around, doing cow things.

It wasn't clear what I was supposed to be getting from the pics other than an education in bovine behavior.

"What you are seeing," Eduardo said as he continued to click through a series of photographs, "is the area around the main buildings on the property."

An area currently filled with cows.

And the occasional horse.

"I'm sorry," I said, "I don't get it. Are we interested in their livestock?"

"See anything else?" Chava asked. I could tell by her satisfied expression that she did.

I looked again, but this time I focused on the background, not the cattle.

"Wait," I said, pointing toward a squarish object I hadn't noticed before, nestled in high grass. "What's that?"

Eduardo clicked onto a photo he had pulled out of the thousands he'd taken. It was a close-up of the boxlike thingamajig.

"A vent?" I said, hazarding a guess from what I could see in the close-up. "What does that have to do with cattle?"

"Nothing," Eduardo said, "but it has everything to do with rooms underground."

What happened next wasn't too surprising. Chava proclaimed loudly that we should race back to the compound and sneak around, looking for the entrance to the underground rooms she expected to find filled with arms or child slaves or some other illicit shipment of goods.

"It could be where Gabriela is being held," she said, reminding me of the job I'd taken on—as if I'd forgotten.

Eduardo suggested we continue with surveillance and try to isolate potential witnesses in the workers who might be willing to talk to us. Or we could follow them and see what we could learn. He also left the door open to using less savory methods for encouraging one of those individuals to talk.

"If we show our hand and let them know we're looking for Gabriela, and they are holding her, they might kill her and get rid of the body," he said to Chava. "Barging in on them without a plan might make everything worse."

I could see his point.

The two went back and forth for a while, Chava's voice the louder of the two, but Eduardo never wavered. Finally, my mother turned and looked at me.

"You've been awfully quiet over there. What do you think?" she asked, putting me in the middle. I'd retreated to the sofa, where I sat with Franklin stretched out with his head in my lap.

"Neither of you is going to like it," I said.

"You don't know that," my father said.

"I haven't finished thinking it through," I said.

"That's okay," Chava said. "Just tell us what's on your mind."

"I was thinking, we could deliver these photographs to Detective Campbell. I'm sure she doesn't know there are hidden rooms underneath the compound. Maybe she can get a warrant to search the premises."

"A warrant based on what?" Eduardo asked. "There's no connection between your dead man and this property."

"That's why I said I hadn't finished thinking this through. It just seems like it might be time to bring in the authorities. If Gabriela is still alive and being held against her will, I don't want to jeopardize her safety by doing something stupid."

I'd already failed her father. I didn't want to fail her too. Or put all of us in danger if someone was out there, trying to scare me off.

"The authorities?" Eduardo's spoke with just a touch of disdain. "We both know finding Gabriela isn't high on their list of things to do. They don't even believe she's been abducted at this point. Or at least … I think we both know that."

My conversation with Iz zipped through my mind. Eduardo understood the difficulty of being Latino in our culture much better than I did. I only occasionally experienced overt racism. I didn't have an accent or the last name Zapata. But Eduardo was also involved in criminal activity. Were his feelings about the authorities based on his actions, their actions, or some complex combination of the two?

It also didn't mean he was right about Detective Campbell.

"We don't know what Detective Campbell's priorities are," I said. My voice was cold even to my own ears. "She came out to the crime scene awful fast when we called her."

Eduardo's eyes took on a hard look and I wondered if I'd crossed a line I would later regret. But he couldn't expect me to agree with him on everything, especially when I had friends in law enforcement. He knew about Chance and Iz. He had to understand my feelings about the people involved in keeping the average citizen safe.

Chava looked ticked off too. I had implied that her suggestion about hurrying over to *el recinto* was stupid. Now I had alienated both my parents.

The three of us fell into silence, each lost in thought.

"We must get an answer about our *fulano's* identity," Eduardo finally said. It sounded like a bit of a white flag. "If we could draw a line between him and *el recinto*," he tapped on the image of the vent, "then perhaps that would be enough for a warrant. Or at least a legitimate reason for the sheriff to ask permission to search the buildings without one."

"And if they say no, it will at least put them on the sheriff department's radar," Chava said.

"If they aren't already," I said. Neither parent responded to that. "Okay, then," I said.

"What does 'okay then' mean?" Chava asked.

"It means that tomorrow we should drive back up to the compound and ask if they've ever seen this man." I tapped the copy of the computer-generated sketch of *Fulano*, which sat next to the computer.

"You can't believe they are going to tell you if they killed this guy or not," Chava said.

"Of course not. But I'm good at sensing when someone is lying. One way or the other we'll know if we're looking in the right direction."

"Won't that do exactly what you don't want … jeopardize Gabriela?" Chava asked.

"If they don't know her, they can't connect her to him. We aren't telling them we're looking for her. We have to start somewhere."

Eduardo nodded, the half smile back on his face as he packed up his laptop. "Excellent, *mija*. I agree with your thoughts on this." I breathed out a sigh of relief. Eduardo had put his metaphorical six-shooter back in its holster and decided not to see me as the enemy. "Tomorrow we go into the teeth of the lion," he said.

I didn't like my idea quite as much when he put it that way.

Eduardo said good night and I stood in the doorway for a long moment after he left. The nearby woods were still, but again, I sensed somebody watching me. Or was that just because I'd had those three strange events back to back?

"Everything all right?" Chava asked when I didn't shut the door right away.

"Yes, fine," I said, closing and locking the door behind me. "Just enjoying how peaceful it is here."

If only I could shake the feeling someone was hiding in the dark. Maybe I should have told Eduardo. And asked him to get me a gun.

Chapter Twenty-Six

———◆———

THE MORNING WAS sunny and clear. Chava and I managed to change the bandage on my burn again. The wound was continuing to heal, and she said she didn't see any sign of infection, but the green in her face told me it still looked pretty bad. Chava had a strong stomach for physical traumas except when they involved her daughter.

After a delicious breakfast where I put away enough food to satisfy a linebacker for the Seattle Seahawks, we piled into the Mazda. The drive to *el recinto* took us half an hour, slowed down by the dirt road after the end of the county-maintained section. It was not quite ten o'clock by the time we reached our destination. This time I sat in the front with Chava driving. We'd left Franklin with Debbie.

We parked in front of the main gate. When we'd discussed our approach this morning, I stated we were going with direct. I got out of the car and walked up to the gate, waving my arm.

"What are you doing?" Chava asked.

"Getting their attention," I said, pointing to a camera mounted on a tree. We had discussed using a cover story for

today's interview, but I thought we should go with the truth.
Or at least part of the truth, shaped to fit our needs.

"What is it you Americans say?" Eduardo said with a laugh.
"Go big or go home?"

Chava hadn't looked so convinced—she'd voted for sneaking
around—but she'd kept quiet in the face of two against one.

Whatever else happened, we were about to go big, then
maybe go home, because the sound of a vehicle coming our
way broke the silence of the morning.

A truck came into view. It was white and nondescript,
driven by a big, twenty-something white guy with a military
haircut and dark glasses. A second man hulked in the seat next
to him—same hair, same shades, same build. They looked like
the men Eduardo had photographed with the drone, though
beefy white guys all look the same to me. They pulled up about
twenty feet from the front gate and sat for a moment, watching
us. The men did not move or exchange looks, just sat. Two
rifles were mounted on a rack across the window behind them.

It was a strange impasse. We couldn't get past the gate or the
fence, which was at least six feet tall, or talk to the men from
this far away with their windows up. So we all just waited.

In the background, I could hear the lowing of cattle. A light
breeze ruffled through the tall grasses and the trees on the
edges of the property. From where we stood, the buildings
were barely visible, just the top ridges of a few metal roofs.

The two men in the truck never spoke, or if they did, they
were able to do it without their lips moving. They did finally get
out, simultaneously, as if having counted to a pre-determined
number first. Both wore guns strapped to their hips.

"They're armed," Chava said, keeping her voice low.

"That's legal with a license," Eduardo said. "It's the concealed
weapons I worry about."

Was Eduardo armed? I wasn't sure I wanted to know.

The two men walked up to the gate, the man from the
passenger seat one step behind and slightly off to his partner's
right.

"Can we help you?" the driver asked. I took him to be higher up the food chain in whatever hierarchy served this outpost.

"We hope so," I said, standing with my hands resting easy at my sides. Something told me not to make any quick gestures around these two.

"Help you with what?" the passenger asked. A look of annoyance crossed the driver's face and my intuition said the other guy wasn't supposed to speak unless spoken to. The driver sent a glare the passenger's way, and the other man flinched. I filed that away for later; maybe the passenger was a weak link. Chava and Eduardo let me have the floor.

"We are trying to identify someone," I said. "We have a picture we'd like to show you."

"Identify someone?" the driver said.

"Yes."

"And you all are what, the three musketeers?"

We were a bit of a strange trio—me in my Chelan County Fire Department hat, Chava in one of her beloved velour leisure suits—I think its color is called "mushroom"—hair shellacked back into its usual blonde beehive, and Eduardo with his air of danger. Though maybe that's just how I saw him because I knew what he did for a living. To the rest of the world he might just look like a businessman.

"My name is Eddie Shoes," I said. "And you are …?"

"I'm not sure that's any of your business."

"Is there a problem here?" I said. "I'm just asking for a little help."

That seemed to confuse the two men. I'm not sure why they thought we had shown up on their doorstep, but clearly this conversation wasn't going the way they expected.

"Sure," the driver said. "Let me see your picture."

I stepped close enough to the gate to hand the photo through. The leader of the duo came forward, while gesturing for the other man to hang back.

The driver studied the sketch for a moment before shaking his head. "No, sorry, I've never seen this man before."

"You're sure?"

"I never forget a face." Based on how he was studying the three of us, I believed him.

The man held the photo out to return to me, but instead of taking the picture back, I nodded toward the second man. "Perhaps your friend might recognize him?"

The driver signaled the passenger with a lift of his chin. He stepped up to take the sketch.

It was always possible we were talking to one of the men who hit *Fulano* over the head, followed us out of the fire, and came back later to take his body away.

The second man took his time with the picture, but finally shook his head as he handed it back to the driver.

"Sorry, can't help you," he said.

"Perhaps we can show it to the others who work here?" Eduardo broke his silence, though he remained standing near the car.

"What makes you think there's others who work here?"

"Back in Mexico, I was a rancher. I know how many men it takes to work a large piece of land and care for … cattle." The slight hesitation in Eduardo's sentence spoke volumes.

The man looked over Eduardo with narrowed eyes. I wasn't sure he believed my father ever spent any time on a ranch.

"Angus?" Eduardo said with a nod toward a group of cows standing on a hill not too far away. "Beef cattle, no?"

"Yeah," the driver said, "Angus." His tone didn't soften, but his body language relaxed a little.

I wondered how Eduardo knew anything about cows. Maybe he really had grown up on a ranch. Or maybe he just liked a good steak.

"Is that all?" the driver asked.

"I'd like to leave the picture with you," I said. "You can ask the others who work here if they've ever seen him. We'll come back later and check."

I expected the driver to refuse, but he folded the picture in half and stuck it into his back pocket. "I'll do that."

I thanked them and the three of us got back into the car. The two men continued to stand at the gate while Chava pulled out in a perfect three-point turn.

"So what did that teach us?" Chava asked as we drove back down the road.

"We have learned many things," Eduardo said before I could speak.

"Such as …" Chava said.

"We have confirmed they do more than raise cattle," he said.

"How did we confirm that?" I knew nothing about cattle, so while I surmised something else was going on, I wondered what Eduardo had seen.

"Because those two men work security, not with the animals, and no one has that kind of muscle for a cattle ranch."

"How do we know they don't also work with the animals?" Chava asked.

"Those cows weren't Angus; they were Belted Galloways. Did you see the white band around their bellies?"

Chava and I nodded.

"Anyone who works around cattle knows an Angus from a Belted Galloway," Eduardo said.

I turned around in the passenger seat to look at Eduardo. I could see curiosity in his eyes.

"What else did we learn, *mija*?" he asked, as if wondering if we'd seen the same things.

"They didn't recognize the man," I said.

"Why do you say that?" Chava asked.

"They expected to," I said, and Eduardo nodded in agreement. "You could see it in the tenseness of their bodies when we handed the picture over. But the man in our picture wasn't who they thought it would be. They telegraphed relief."

Eduardo nodded as I spoke, agreeing with my assessment. "They know someone is missing, but not *Fulano*."

"They were also overly antagonistic," I said, "as if they expected trouble from us and wanted to come out swinging."

"*Sí*, I agree," Eduardo said. "They were surprised we weren't demanding to come inside or ask them more questions."

We had arrived back in front of the Langston Ranch and were out of sight from the armed guards at the compound. Chava pulled over while we talked and figured out our next move.

"Do you think they were expecting a photo of Gabriela?" Chava asked.

"That's my thought," I said. "I can't imagine there's a third missing person around here."

"Notice anything else?" Eduardo directed his question at me.

"The police haven't been there with the sketch yet," I said.

"Now you're just guessing," Chava said.

"No, she's right," Eduardo said. "If the police had brought the sketch yesterday, they would have indicated, even without intending to, they'd seen the man before. But instead, his face was a surprise. They weren't lying when they said they'd never seen him before, even in a drawing."

"Okay," Chava said, "I can see that."

"They might also be ex-military," I said, thinking about the Purple Heart we'd found. "But what's most interesting," I continued as I watched the Langston horses running around in the field next to the road, "is what they didn't say."

"What didn't they say?" Chava asked.

"They never asked anything about the man," I said. "Not what he did or why we were looking for him."

"Because they don't care if something happened to him," Chava said.

"Or they had reason to believe someone might show up asking about a missing person, like Gabriela, and they were so relieved we weren't asking about her, they didn't ask for details about ours," I said, thinking out loud.

"So now the question is whether they are the people who abducted Gabriela, right?" Chava asked.

That was the question, but how would we find the answer?

Chapter Twenty-Seven

———•———

THE HORSES OUT in the Langston field were a variety of colors and sizes. One especially large tan horse with a white mane and tail came over to check out what we were doing, parked in front of his home.

"That's a pretty horse," Chava said as he leaned over the fence and nibbled the grass on the other side. "He's so big."

"Palomino," Eduardo said. "And yes, that's a very big Quarter Horse. A confident animal too. He's not nervous about us at all. See how calm he is?" The horse lifted his head and chewed, watching us with bright eyes. "His ears are up," Eduardo continued, "and his tail is still."

"You know about horses too?" I asked, wondering why my criminal father knew a palomino from a Pomeranian.

Not to mention a Belted Galloway from an Angus.

"Sí," he said softly, "I have always preferred their company to that of men."

Wasn't that interesting. Of course, given the characters my father usually hung out with, I'd probably feel the same way. An image of Franklin's giant, shaggy face rose up in my mind. "I feel the same way about my dog," I said.

"And your mother," Chava said.

"And my mother," I said, patting her on the head. While she pulled down the mirror on the visor and checked to make sure I hadn't damaged her 'do, which she'd carefully reconstructed this morning in our bathroom using half a can of Aqua Net, my thoughts went back to *Fulano* and his missing daughter.

"What's our next move?" Chava asked, molding her hair back into shape.

Eduardo and I began speaking at the same time. At first Eduardo looked annoyed. I guessed he wasn't used to working with a group any more than I was. I held my breath. In all honesty, I didn't know this man, this cleaner for the mob. Just because I was his daughter, it didn't mean he was going to change his spots just for my benefit. I'd been thinking of him as an ally, but was he really?

"Go ahead, *mija*. You were saying?" I wondered what it cost him to defer to another, even to me.

"We should talk to the folks here at the Langston Ranch," I said. "They might know something about the crew up the road. They do share a property line."

"To the ranch!" Chava said, snapping the visor back in place, her hair once again perfect. Either she was unaware of the undercurrents between Eduardo and me, or she chose to ignore them. Knowing how observant Chava could be, I guessed the latter.

She drove under the entry sign, and the big palomino raced along the fence as if showing us the way. We reached the end of the fence, and he looked like he might jump, but he veered off and raced away at a gallop. We'd arrived in front of the large farmhouse, so I guess his duty to us was done.

A moment after we pulled up, a young woman came out, clapping a straw cowboy hat over her dark-brown hair. It looked like the woman I'd seen yesterday in the pen with the horse.

As we got out of the car, I expected a "howdy folks," and a

country drawl, but she just smiled and asked if she could help us with something. Eduardo glanced at me with a slight nod of his head, signaling I should do the talking. I appreciated his confidence. I introduced myself as a private investigator and explained Chava and Eduardo were my associates.

"Reyna," she said, introducing herself. "I've never met a real life PI before. I've only ever seen them on TV."

"I hear that a lot," I said.

Usually that comment would be followed by asking if I carried a gun, but in this neck of the woods, that wouldn't be unusual regardless of one's profession.

"We're hoping you can help us locate someone," I said, deciding to go with as close to the truth as I could.

"Someone's missing?" she asked, taking a step closer to us. She didn't appear the least bit suspicious or nervous about this odd trio showing up on her doorstep. Even though I was about a foot taller than she was and Eduardo looked like … well, a hit man for the mob. Of course Chava in her leisure suit probably made us look less intimidating—the Joe Pesci of our little trio.

"Can we show you a picture?" I asked.

"Sure."

Chava handed over a copy of the police sketch and the young woman took a long look. "Is he in some kind of trouble?" she asked, never taking her eyes from the sketch.

"No. But he may have gotten caught in the fire that burned across the road from you." I decided that was better than saying we knew he was dead but had disappeared right out from under our noses. I clamped down on my imagination when an image of him rising like a zombie out of the ravine floated up in my mind. That was one scenario I hadn't considered yet.

"Oh, that's terrible," she said, looking up from the picture in her hand. "I heard a woman was lost out there, but I thought she was the only one."

"That was me," I said.

"You?" she said, shock registering on her face.

"The one and only," I doffed my CCFD hat and tilted my burned head down so she could see the gauze bandaging.

"That must be painful," she said, concern in her voice. "Are you all right?"

"It hurts," I said. "But I'm lucky; that's the worst I endured. This man," I tapped the sketch momentarily forgotten in her hand, "may not have been so lucky."

"That's so sad," she said under her breath as she turned her attention back to the sketch. A moment later she held the drawing back out. "I'm sorry, I don't recognize him."

"Maybe someone else might? You have other people here on the ranch?"

"Just a few," she said. "We're a small family outfit. My father is the owner, but he's gone for the day. We also have a couple of men who live on the property and help care for the animals. Plus Luis."

"Who's Luis?" I asked, noticing he'd been given a name as if he were special or perhaps the others were interchangeable for her.

"Luis Rivas," she said. "He's the other trainer. My father was injured in a car accident a few years ago, so he doesn't ride any more. Luis and I do all the training under saddle."

"Is it possible your father or Luis or one of your other workers knows this man?"

"It's possible. Luis is with my dad. They're delivering a horse to Ellensburg and won't be back until late tonight. Guillermo and Alejandro are fixing a fence at the far end of the property. They'll be back about six o'clock to help me feed."

"Have Guillermo and Alejandro been here a long time?" Eduardo asked.

"Yes. Several years. They're brothers and live here on the property."

"Okay," I said. "We'll leave the sketch with you and check back another time. Is that okay with you?"

"Sure," she said. Her smile was wide. Her blue eyes were

bright and guileless, like a child's. Maybe spending all her time with animals kept her innocent. "I hope you find him."

"One other question. Have you had any dealings with the people up the road?" I pointed in the direction of the compound.

A shadow crossed Reyna's face, the first hint of anything but calm on her unruffled surface.

"They're very odd," she said.

"Odd? How?" I asked.

"Maybe not so much 'odd' as different," she said, amending her spontaneous response. "They aren't like most people around here."

"Could you be a little more specific?" I asked.

Reyna giggled. "I guess I haven't been very clear, have I?"

"Not so much," I said with a smile to show I wasn't being judgmental.

"I'll try to put it into words," she said, sobering up again. "It's like this. We don't interfere with each other out here. There's a reason we live in the middle of nowhere on a big piece of land, right? We aren't interested in being in each other's back pockets."

She looked to see if I was with her, so I nodded for her to continue.

"When those folks first moved in, there was a lot of hustle and bustle, equipment and people coming and going. They installed that chain-link fence around the house; then it got very quiet. No one ever really goes in or comes out. But I thought I'd be neighborly, so I went over with a freshly baked cake. The man in charge barely even said thank you."

She looked at the three of us as if that was the worst offense anyone might commit against another. "I mean, who doesn't appreciate a freshly baked cake?"

She had a point.

"It's true most people keep to themselves, but their front gates are open. I might not invite you in for supper, but I'm not going to stop you from coming up to my front porch. And I'm certainly going to thank you for a cake. You see?"

Actually, I did.

"So they weren't welcoming," I said.

"Not at all. I could only come up with one thing to explain it."

"What's that?" I asked, contemplating what nefarious explanation Reyna had come up with for her neighbors' bad behavior.

"They have to be from California."

I'd keep that in mind.

"Okay, well, thank you for your help," I said, turning to Eduardo and Chava to see if they had anything to add.

"Beautiful place you have here," Chava said.

"Thank you. I'm sorry I couldn't be of more use to you."

"*Gracias*," Eduardo said, making me wonder why he used Spanish.

"*De nada*," she said. "*Buena suerte.*"

Her accent sounded pretty good.

We got back into the car and Chava headed back down the driveway. Our beautiful palomino escort had lost interest and was grazing at the far end of the pasture.

"So, what do we think?" I asked. "Are our odd folks up the road from California?"

"That could explain a few things," my father said. This time I was sure he was making a joke. I was starting to recognize the subtle signs.

"What are we going to do next?" Chava asked, apparently ignoring California as a viable explanation for strange behavior.

That was a good question.

Chapter Twenty-Eight

———•———

WHAT WE ENDED up doing didn't involve the investigation at all. Chava and I had only intended to stay at the resort for a long weekend, so we were running short on dog food. After I'd reassured my parents I was fine on my own for a few hours, we went our separate ways. Eduardo returned to his room to do a little work online. I wondered what all he did for his "employers." Maybe my father performed other odd jobs for the mob—web design and social media, for example. Chava went off to get a pedicure, and I borrowed the car to drive up to Leavenworth.

A Paw Above was a great little store where I was able to stock up on dog food, dog treats, and poop bags in brightly colored rolls. I also bought a car magnet that read I LIKE BIG MUTTS to stick on the Mazda. I wondered how long it would take Chava to notice and move it over to my Subaru.

I'd just finished loading up the car and was contemplating lunch in town when I heard someone calling my name. Looking around, I discovered Jake on the sidewalk.

"Hey," I said, clicking the lock on the Mazda. "What brings you up here?"

"Just dropping something off with my sister," he explained. "She lives not far away. What about you?"

I explained my errand and mentioned I was considering lunch. "Where would you recommend?"

"I was just going to go get a brat," he said. "Want to join me?"

Maybe I'd learn something about his trip up to the crime scene with Detective Campbell. "I'd love to," I said. Even if I didn't learn anything, it would be good to keep company with someone who knew what I had been through in the forest fire.

We walked down the street, which was bustling with tourists, and turned in at the München Haus, a small joint tucked into a corner of the main drag. They served brats, kraut, and beer. The outdoor seating area was furnished with wooden picnic tables, and pots and planters bloomed with a riot of bright flowers. A veritable Garden of Eden, hopefully minus the snake. Hearing that rattle last night was enough for me. Waiting on our food, we stumbled around for something to talk about. I wanted to ask if he'd learned anything about my missing dead man, but I thought I'd better be subtle about it.

"What got you working as a firefighter?" I asked. Using a straw to poke at the lemon in my iced tea gave my hands something to do.

"It's what my father did before he retired," he paused a moment before finishing his thought, "and what my brother used to do."

"Your brother does something else now?"

Jake dropped his eyes and gave a half shrug. "My brother died in Afghanistan."

"I'm sorry."

"Don't be. He died doing something he believed in."

"Did you believe in what he was doing?"

At first I thought I'd made Jake angry, but he just looked surprised at my question. I was a little surprised myself.

"No one has ever asked me that before," he said.

Most people had more tact.

Now it was my turn to wait. I focused on my tea, submerging the yellow half moon into the ice. Apparently I wasn't so good at light, fluffy chitchat.

"I don't have an answer for you," he said. "I respect what he did, but I hate that he's gone."

My fiddling finally flipped the lemon out of my glass. It landed next to Jake with a spray of diluted tea droplets. I could feel my face turn crimson. *Wonderful.* No good at party talk and now I'd flung citrus at the man.

Jake laughed and pushed the lemon off to one side.

"No one has ever thrown a lemon wedge at me either," he said.

"I'm not very good at casual conversation," I said.

"You're doing all right."

Our food appeared. I dug into my Jalapeno & Cheddar Sausage and German potato salad—I was on vacation, after all—and thought about his brother being a vet. Had his family received his Purple Heart after he died? Was *Fulano's* Purple Heart something someone he loved had earned? Or had he gotten it himself, only to die in a fire after he'd returned home?

"How did things go yesterday after we left?" I asked.

That was subtle, right?

"You want to know if I learned anything from the detective?" Jake asked.

"Occupational hazard."

"I thought you might be curious. I considered calling you afterward, but I didn't have your number. We went back up to that ravine, and you were right, the body was gone."

I hadn't really doubted that at all, but it was nice to have the confirmation.

"Did they search the area?"

"I assume so," he said. "My job was done after I'd directed them to the location."

"Aren't you even a little curious," I said after a beat, "about what happened?"

"Okay," Jake said, "I admit it. I am." He dropped his voice and looked around as if someone might be listening in. "Your parents weren't gone very long, so I keep wondering how that body got moved so fast."

Leaning forward, I told him I'd been wondering that too. "You're a local, familiar with these mountains. Any ideas?"

Jake shook his head. "Nothing I come up with makes any sense. There was no sign of an animal dragging him away. We didn't hear an off-road vehicle. Even a strong man would have trouble carrying a dead body over such rough terrain." He shrugged, and I could tell something else was on his mind. I waited.

"I'm glad I ran in to you," he said, focusing his attention on his food. Whatever he wanted to say, he felt awkward about it.

"Yeah?"

"Yeah. I wanted to say I was sorry." This time he looked up, his eyes meeting mine.

"About what?"

"That we didn't believe you … that *I* didn't believe you about that man being up there. I keep thinking if we'd taken you seriously, we might have found him earlier, and whatever happened to his body wouldn't have happened."

"I appreciate that," I said. "I have to admit, I was starting to doubt myself. But don't beat yourself up about it. I wouldn't have believed me either."

We spent the rest of lunch talking about less dramatic things. He told me about his wife and two kids, even showing me photos—the boy in a Little League uniform, the girl in a sparkly tutu. I asked how he'd feel about his children following in his footsteps.

"I'd worry, of course," he said. "It's dangerous out there. But I'd understand it if they did. Mostly, I just want them to be happy."

His wife was an elementary school teacher. I watched his face light up when he talked about her. I wondered if Chance had ever looked like that when he talked about me.

"Your wife must worry about you," I said, remembering what it had been like to be involved with a police officer. Chance wasn't a patrol officer, but that didn't mean he wouldn't put his life on the line. I remembered a few sleepless nights, waiting for him to get home. Worrying he wouldn't.

"She does, but she knew what she was getting into when she married me. Her brother is a firefighter; that's how we met."

"You're lucky," I said, "to have someone who supports you."

"It works both ways," he said.

We finished lunch, and Jake walked me back to my car. I gave him one of my cards. "Just in case you learn anything else," I said. He gave me one of his as well.

"If you find out what happened to the man," he said, "I'd like to know too."

Driving back to the resort, I thought about Chance. He'd probably gotten back from Orcas Island by now, so he might be hearing about what happened to me. I wondered what his reaction would be. Our history together circled around in my mind. Memory is a strange combination of those things we work to remember and the things we can never forget. I'd relived the final days between us over and over in my mind. My few belongings packed in my Subaru while Chance was at work, the note I left. The highway out of town. I'd fled for a number of reasons, and I'd always thought the primary one was guilt, because I'd been with Chance when I was supposed to have been with my mentor. As if that would have stopped Coop from killing himself. But that was a lie. The primary reason I'd left was fear. The pain of losing Coop made me want to protect myself. Living with a cop, loving a cop, felt too dangerous. I didn't want to lose him to an act of violence too.

It wasn't logical—leaving him to keep from losing him—but it meant I was in control. I was the one who'd left. Unlike Coop, who's death I hadn't seen coming. I had now become more aware of my own mortality, so my perspective had undergone a change.

After acknowledging that, I let other memories come. The way his presence made me feel. Like he was north and my heart was a compass that always found its way home.

I hummed along to the radio. When I got back to Bellingham, I was going to talk to Chance. I was going to explain why I did what I did and find out if there was any room for forgiveness. For a second chance at us.

Arriving back at the cabin, I opened the door to find Chava and Eduardo huddled around his laptop again.

Chava glanced up as I put the dog food away, an inquiring look on her face. "Are you all right?"

"I am," I said, "or at least, I will be."

She started to ask another question, but I didn't want to get into it with Chava. I needed to talk to Chance first.

"What have you two been up to while I've been gone?"

"Wait until you see what we found," Chava said, her attention pulled back to the laptop.

Nothing like a good investigation to take Chava's mind off other things.

Chapter Twenty-Nine

———◆———

EDUARDO AND CHAVA had been going back through the drone photos. They'd made a note about the two vehicle license plates they'd been able to read, along with the make and models of the cars. Eduardo had access to places I didn't want to know about. My best guess was the Department of Motor Vehicles, though the source of the most reliable information about automobiles in the country was NCIS. I didn't want to think about what it meant if my father had access to the Naval Criminal Investigation Service.

"Both vehicles are registered to a security service company," he said.

"You were right, Eduardo," I said. "There's no way these guys are just running a cattle ranch and a few apple orchards if they've brought in hired guns. So what are they doing?"

"There are a lot of possibilities," he said. "We know they have increased power and water to their outfit, with the solar panels, a wind turbine, and the extra well."

"And we know they're doing something underground, which is why they have vents," I said, completing his thought.

"What would they be doing underground?" Chava asked.

"Growing marijuana or manufacturing drugs seems the most likely explanation to me," I said. "The extra electricity could be for grow lights or processing. Though it's weird they've hired a professional security team if they are up to something illegal."

"Is it possible the security team doesn't know what's going on underground?" Chava asked.

"That wouldn't say much for their skill set," I said, which made Eduardo laugh.

"Why generate their own electricity?" Chava asked.

"Lots of reasons why a group would want to do that," I said. "Staying under the radar, for one. If they have probable cause, the police could ask for a warrant to check power consumption through the local utility. If the police deem the records suspicious, that could allow them to get a warrant to search the premises."

"So do we think *Fulano* worked at the compound and got caught up in whatever is going on there?" Chava asked. "Or just knew too much, so they decided to get rid of him?"

"Maybe he started out a participant, then decided he wanted out," I said, more to myself than my parents. They both nodded. At this point, anything was possible. "And they abducted his daughter to keep him quiet."

"Or, he was competition in some way. Maybe he worked for someone south of the border and he was sent to, what … negotiate? Challenge?" Eduardo's voice drifted off as he considered the possibilities. We'd moved further into his territory, not mine.

Silence descended as we contemplated what steps to take next.

"I don't suppose you have any way to find out who the security company is working for out there?" I asked Eduardo.

He shook his head. "No. Companies like that, they never reveal who their clients are, and I don't know anything about that particular organization. Even my contacts only go so far."

"It seems like we have to get back on the property and find out for ourselves," Chava said.

"That may be easier said than done," Eduardo said. "We know they have cameras. We saw one at the front gate. We can assume there are others. There are armed guards, and maybe dogs behind the fence. I saw evidence of them on the photos—dog bowls and a doghouse, but not an actual dog. Not something we want to get tangled up with if we can help it."

"Do you think we can figure out a route to dodge the cameras?" I asked. "You took a lot of pictures of the trees around the buildings. I assume that was in part to locate any cameras or security measures they have in place."

"Yes," Eduardo said, "but I think it would be better if we took out their power supply. That would both interrupt their systems and cause confusion."

Chava and I stared at him. Was he serious? It felt like I was starting down a slippery slope to committing a felony.

"What did you have in mind?" I asked, not sure I wanted to know the answer, or how willing I was to go along.

"Transformers are vulnerable," Eduardo said with a shrug, as if this was information everyone would know. "One well-placed shot from a high-powered rifle will suffice."

"I'm not sure I can participate in that," I said, trying to keep any sound of judgment out of my voice.

"If they're criminals, what's the problem?" Chava said, surprising me with her quick response. I'd have thought she'd at least think about it before electing to commit a major crime.

"But we don't know if they *are* criminals," I said. "What if they aren't doing anything illegal and we shoot out their power supply? And what if they have backup generators? Not to mention anyone else reliant on that transformer. I assume they're expensive and hard to fix."

"About a million dollars," Eduardo said, "and they take several months to replace."

Even Chava blanched at the casualness of his response.

"That's a little more than I want to be liable for," I said, not to mention that I was anxious to avoid having a felony on my conscience.

Eduardo smiled. "We wouldn't get caught."

Of that I had no doubt, but I still wasn't on board.

"There's got to be another way," I said.

"Well … you could shoot holes in the vacuum tank of the breaker," he said. "That would be less expensive to replace than a transformer."

"How much money are we talking about now?" I asked.

"A quarter of a million dollars," Eduardo said, "and a few days to repair."

Still a little out of my comfort zone. How did he know these things?

"I think we'd better find another way to get past their cameras," I said, though I wasn't sure why I was willing to do one thing but not the other. I was apparently okay with trespassing and committing the occasional breaking and entering—often at Chava's urging—but I balked at shorting out a power transformer or a breaker. It might have to do with the amount of money involved, but it also felt like a line in the sand I didn't want to cross. I guess I was unethical by degrees and I was only now discovering those parameters. What did it say that my parents were the ones encouraging me to break the law?

Eduardo thought a long moment. He could be considering the problem at hand or just as easily how his daughter's morals were getting in the way of his fun.

"I can continue to use the drone photos and see if I can identify the camera locations. Knowing what type of camera and where they are located, I can do a basic map showing any areas without coverage. They probably don't have every inch of the property covered. It is a lot of ground. They may have other security measures in place, sensors or alarms, but I can do my best with what we have. And see if I can determine about the dogs."

"That sounds like a plan," I said.

"It carries much greater risks," Eduardo warned. "We are

more likely to get caught or shot. We know these men are armed. If they are involved in the drug trade, killing us won't be an issue."

How much *did* I want to risk? Was this just about some dead guy I didn't know? The missing, potentially abducted girl? Or did I need to prove something to my father?

That was a disturbing thought. Was his opinion of me really so important?

Now it was my turn to fall quiet while I mulled over what I wanted and more importantly, why.

"Perhaps we should start with some of our other leads and leave the more … questionable tactics for a later time," Chava said.

Interesting time for my mother to be the voice of reason.

"Okay," Eduardo said, not waiting for my response. "That seems best."

Hesitating, I caught my father's attention on me, a question in his brown eyes.

"I thought you might be disappointed in me," I said. "That I didn't rush to take out a transformer."

Eduardo's smile was genuine, not the sly one I often saw on his face.

"You never disappoint me, *mija*. We all have our own ways of doing things. Until those ways don't work anymore."

I wondered what it would take for me to do things my father's way. And more importantly, was that what he hoped to find out?

Chapter Thirty

AFTER MY SOMEWHAT disturbing conversation with my parents about our next moves, we agreed on a plan of sorts. Eduardo would go back to his room and follow up with his assessment of the security in place at the compound. Tomorrow, we would follow up at the Langston Ranch with Reyna's father, Luis, and the other two workers. Plus, we'd return to the compound to see if the security guards had asked around about the sketch we'd shown them as they'd promised. I continued to believe we did not want to tip our hand about the missing woman. If she was being held, but was still alive, I didn't want anyone to know we were looking for her.

To clear my head, I went for a short walk with Franklin at my side. Not into the woods, just around the grounds of the resort.

At one point I stopped and watched some ducks in a pond when I caught movement out of the corner of my eye.

It was the teen runner I'd seen on the trail. The one I'd gone off track to try to find, starting this whole adventure. He was jogging along a path, moving at an impressive clip. I flagged him down.

"Are you okay?" he asked, jogging in place and breathing hard.

"I'm so glad to see you," I said.

"You are?"

"The day of the fire, you ran up that trail." I pointed off toward the direction of the trailhead we'd both used.

This stopped him in his tracks.

"That was you. On the cellphone," he said.

See, he *was* impressed I'd had cell service.

"It was, then I didn't see you come down, but …."

"You were the person looking for me, right?" he said. "The police called here and the resort figured out who I was."

"Sheriff, not police, but yes." I said. "I'm just glad you're okay."

He scowled. "You got me in a lot of trouble."

"I did?"

"My parents found out I'd gone off the trail because of you."

"If you had a good reason to, how much trouble could you get into?"

The teenager said nothing, but his body was tense, his fingers clenching and unclenching. I had a moment of clarity.

"Smoking? Weed? Did you take a flask?" What else could a teenage boy do by himself to get his parents so worked up? But why not simply lie to them?

"It was just a joint. Now I'm grounded for a month."

"You could have gotten killed up there," I said.

"You could have gotten killed too," he said over his shoulder as he went back to his run.

It would have saved me a lot of grief if I hadn't gone looking for him, I thought as he sped away. But then *Fulano* would have died without any witness. And no one would be looking for Gabriela. I guess it all turned out all right in the end. Or it would, if we found the missing woman … alive.

DEBBIE AND INDY met up with me while I was out. We were far

away from anyone else or the road, so we sat down on a bench to watch the two dogs run around off-leash. I got her fully caught up on events, including the mysterious disappearance of our dead guy.

"Someone was there when you found him?" she asked. "And hid in the woods until you left?"

"That's what we think."

"That's terrifying. Do they know who you are?"

"No way," I said, to reassure my friend. "It wasn't like we called each other's names out while we walked around out there."

"What if they saw your car and found out who you were that way?"

That gave me pause. And then there were all the people here at the resort who already knew who I was.

"I can't imagine that would be true," I said. "It would require multiple people. Someone up in the woods and someone down near the car, who just happened to be there when we arrived, who also realized there was some reason to track us down."

"You think you arrived when the killer was moving the body and he just slipped into the trees until you left?"

"Basically."

Picking up where I'd left off, I recounted the rest of the story, including our reconnaissance at the compound.

Debbie thought for a moment. The dogs had wandered over while we were talking. Franklin leaned against me but pushed his nose under Debbie's hand.

"Hello, sweet boy," she said, rubbing his bearded chin and ruffling his ears. A moment later, when she stopped, he shook his head, gray dreadlocks flinging out bits of fur in all directions.

"Sorry about all the hair," I said. "Your room must be covered in Franklin puffs."

"Not to worry," Debbie said. "I love having him around. It's not like I don't already have hair floating around from Indy."

I knew she was just being kind. A Goldendoodle, Indy didn't shed like Franklin.

We sat in silence another moment, both of our minds whirring with my complicated tale.

"What do the folks at the horse farm have to say about their neighbors?" she asked.

I chuckled, remembering Reyna's words. "They're odd, according to one," I said. "She's the young woman who lives at the ranch next door. But she's not much over eighteen, so 'odd' could mean a lot of things that aren't illegal."

Debbie laughed, but got serious again. "Please be careful," she said, as we got ready to walk back to our rooms. "Franklin would never forgive us if something happened to you."

"I promise," I said.

"Have you visited the closest Catholic church that does services in Spanish?" she asked as we put the leashes back on the dogs.

"I hadn't thought of that."

"Well, your guy is Catholic and Latino; you said he spoke Spanish. There probably aren't that many places he would go. Someone might recognize him."

Looked like I had to put "visit the Catholic Churches in Wenatchee and Leavenworth" onto our list of things to do.

But how much useful information could we get out of a priest?

Chapter Thirty-One

———•———

I FILLED CHAVA and Eduardo in about Debbie's idea over dinner, including the info I'd researched on the local Catholic community. There was one Catholic church in Leavenworth and two Catholic churches in the greater Wenatchee area. We decided to visit the ranch and the compound first, to see if anyone at either place would identify *Fulano*; then, if that didn't work, we'd head over to visit the churches.

"Your friend, Debbie, she is a wise woman," Eduardo said. "She is important to you, no?"

I trusted her with Franklin. It didn't get more important than that.

THE NEXT MORNING, we left Franklin with Debbie and drove back up the valley to *el recinto*. When our car reached the front gate, I waved at the camera again. A few minutes later, the same white pickup truck appeared with the same two gunslingers. They stopped a short distance from the front gate, but this time got out of their vehicle without pause.

"You're back," the driver said.

"We are," I said. "We're wondering if you had the opportunity to show the sketch around to the others who work here."

"We did. No one recognized him. Sorry." He began to hand the picture back, but I stopped him with a gesture.

"Hang on to that just in case," I said. "Thank you for your time."

Getting back in the car, Chava put the Mazda in gear and we headed over to the Langston Ranch.

The same big palomino stood sentry near the gate. Once again, he ran alongside the fence all the way down the long driveway.

We could see Reyna in one of the small pens, working with a light-brown horse, his shiny dark mane and tail flashing in the sunlight. The rest of the place was quiet. Getting out of the car, we made our way over to the girl, who saw us coming and slipped gracefully through the bars of the pen to meet us.

"*¿Bonito caballo. Es un* grullo, *verdad?*" Eduardo said as she walked up.

"*Sí*, you know your horses, Mister ..." she trailed off, waiting for my father to fill in the blank.

"Eduardo," he said. "*Me llamo* Eduardo."

"Eduardo," she said. "Right, I remember." Her eyes flicked over to Chava and me. I still wondered why he was using Spanish with Reyna.

"Grullo is the color of that horse," Eduardo explained to us. "It's an unusual color for a Quarter Horse."

"Very pretty," Chava said.

"We're wondering if we can speak to your father," Eduardo said. "And perhaps the other men who work here?"

"Sure. Let me just find out where everyone is." Reyna pulled a cellphone out of her pocket and speed-dialed a number. "Hey, Dad," she said into the phone. "Those people I told you about, the ones with the picture? They're back. They want to talk to you." She listened for a moment, before saying, "At the round pen," then clicked off the phone.

"He'll be out soon," she told us. "I should have asked, would you like to get out of the sun?"

"We could wait in the barn," Eduardo said, pointing to the large building not far away. "I'd love to see more of your horses."

"Not much going on in there right now," she said, leading us away. "It will be more comfortable on the front porch anyway; it's hot in the barn."

"What about him?" I asked, pointing to the horse still lose in the pen.

"He's fine," she said.

I paused to watch the horse, who stood, eyes closed, back leg cocked, sleeping in the sun. As she said, he looked fine.

The four of us walked up onto the porch. Chava and I sat on a bench swing hanging from the ceiling, while Eduardo perched on the rail.

"Can I get you something to drink?" Reyna asked, ever the helpful hostess.

We demurred, and waited, the quiet of the place settling in around us.

"¿Y Luis? ¿Dónde está?" Eduardo asked Reyna, wanting to know if the other trainer was here.

"He's with Dad. They'll both be here shortly."

As she spoke, we could see the figures of two men come from around the side of the barn and skirt a few horse trailers parked on the wide section of driveway. One was an older white man, his pale hair sticking out from under his hat. I assumed he was Reyna's father. The white straw hat threw his face in shadow, but we could see the leatheriness of his skin from where we sat. With the right segue, I could imagine Chava chastising him for not using proper moisturizer and sunscreen.

Next to him, a short, dark-haired man walked with the bowlegged gait of a cowboy. Reyna's father moved slowly, like an old man or someone in pain, his steps tentative, as if he wasn't sure how much each action would cost him. They made their way to the porch, the younger man matching his stride to his boss's.

"Afternoon," Reyna's father said as they drew closer. "Takes me a bit, but I'll get there," he added, grasping the handrail at the steps and climbing up to us. "Johnny Langston." He reached out to shake our hands. His grip was firm, stronger than I expected for someone who moved so gingerly. We introduced ourselves in turn.

"This here is Luis," Johnny said, clapping the younger man on the back, his accent making it Looey instead of the soft Lu-iss, as his daughter pronounced it. "Best trainer of horses in the entire state of Washington."

I'd continued watching Reyna's face as her father said these words. Her eyes darkened and I wondered if the words hurt her, as I'd expect them to. Did her father discount her training abilities because of her age, her gender, or her relationship to him? Perhaps Luis was just that much better and it had nothing to do with her.

"Reyna gives me a run for my money," Luis said. "You taught her well."

Smart man. He both praised his boss and put him in his place. Interesting dynamic at work among this trio.

"Your horses are very handsome," Eduardo said. "How long have you been here?"

"This *rancho* has been in my family for four generations," Johnny told us. He pronounced "rancho" like a gringo, and I tried not to cringe. Why did this man keep using poor Spanish? Was he really so tone-deaf? Was he showing he was trying to be inclusive? Or that he didn't care about getting it right?

"My great-grandfather rode with the Pony Express back in 1860," Johnny continued. "That ended in 1861 when the first telegraph came through and he found himself out of work. He worked his way north until he ended up homesteading this land. The Langstons have been here ever since."

"Horses run in your blood, it would seem," Eduardo said. Chava and I remained silent. Something told me Johnny would respond better to Eduardo than either one of us.

"That they do, pardner," Johnny said, and it occurred to me

he wore his "cowboy" persona like a costume donned for a Halloween ball, horse trainer or no horse trainer. "So, what can we do for you? I heard tell from my daughter here, you're looking for someone? A missing man?"

"We are. Did you have a chance to look at the sketch we brought in yesterday?"

"I did," Johnny said. "And I'm sorry to say, I didn't know the man. Wish I could be of more help."

"And you, Luis?" Eduardo said.

"I'm sorry, no."

Eduardo nodded, pursing his lips as if thinking about something uncomfortable. "Perhaps you recognized him though?" he said, looking at Johnny intently, then back at Luis. His voice carried an edge of steel.

"I said I didn't know him," Johnny said, flashing a little steel back. Reyna looked back and forth between our fathers with her brows drawn together, as if she too felt the tension.

"Yes. This I understand," Eduardo said. "You did not know the man, but perhaps you have seen him somewhere. Maybe my English is wrong—I make mistakes sometimes—but I think 'knowing' someone and 'recognizing' him are two different things, no?"

Johnny's eyes narrowed. From far off I could hear the neighing of a horse and another's answering call. From the corner of my eye I could see the blur of the big palomino dancing across the pasture, another reddish-brown horse meeting him. The two stood on hind legs, crashing into each other in what looked like a death grip, but they both landed back on four legs and circled each other again.

"Boys will be boys," Reyna said, her eyes on me. "They're just playing."

"What?" Johnny looked sharply at his daughter, then out at the horses. "Oh, yes, the geldings. They'll do that all day long."

"You have stallions too, yes?" Eduardo asked.

"We do," Johnny said, "but of course we keep them separated."

"Of course," my father said. "They will fight each other for the girls."

"To the death," Johnny said, his eyes now turned out to the field, where the two horses dashed across the pasture, feet flying, hooves pounding on the baking ground.

Chava looked at me, and I could feel the question in her glance.

What were we talking about now?

Chapter Thirty-Two

---◆---

THE REST OF the conversation with the Langstons and their employees went nowhere. Luis and Johnny both restated they'd never seen the man before. Not much later, Johnny retired to the house, his daughter explaining he struggled with chronic pain from his accident. Guillermo and Alejandro came in on three-wheelers from wherever they were working and also told us they'd never seen *Fulano*.

I contemplated asking about Gabriela, but it still felt too dangerous to say her name. If she were being held by someone who then learned we were asking about her, it could just get her killed.

The Langston Ranch appeared to be another dead end. If losing the corpse was strike one, I think we'd just had strike two.

As we were wrapping up our conversations, Eduardo's eyes scanned the property again. "This is very rugged country out here. Do you have trouble with predators?"

"I'm not sure what you mean," Reyna said.

"Oh, *coyotes,* for example," Eduardo said with the Spanish

pronunciation. "Perhaps even *lobos* out here. You know, wild animals bothering your horses?"

"We don't have wolves," Reyna said. "They've started showing up in the Cascades, but I've never even heard one. You're more likely to find them out in Coleville," she said, referencing a small town near the Canadian and Idaho borders. "Coyotes we have, but they rarely bother us."

"You probably keep a good rifle around, just in case," my father continued. "I'll bet you are even a better shot than your father." He said this last comment with just the right amount of appreciation, making it sound like a compliment rather than fishing for information about their gun ownership and abilities with firearms.

"Sure. We've got a rifle in the barn." She gestured toward the building on the hill. "I've never shot anything but rattlesnakes."

Reyna went back to work with her grullo in the round pen, and the two field hands returned to their labors. Only Luis remained to see us off. He walked us toward the car and stopped, looking back at the house as if he might catch someone in the window.

My father spoke to him in Spanish, asking if he had something he wanted to tell us.

"No," Luis replied in English. "Nothing. Just, I wish you luck in finding this man."

He turned, and we watched him disappear behind the barn. With nothing else to do, we headed toward Leavenworth to see if we could find what we were looking for at church.

"What do you make of that crew?" Chava asked as she settled in behind the wheel. Eduardo got into the backseat without complaint and I rode shotgun.

"Many undercurrents," Eduardo said, sliding on his dark glasses, which made him even tougher to read.

"Why do you say that?" I asked. I'd picked up something wasn't right at the ranch, but I wondered what Eduardo had seen.

"Mr. Langston, he doesn't like to show weakness, but he will when it suits him."

"You don't think he's as injured as he claims?" I asked.

"I think he's in a lot of pain," my father said. "He wasn't inventing that. But that's not the kind of man who leaves strangers on his porch, no matter how much he wants to lie down."

"Unless he doesn't want to talk to them," I said.

"Exactly," Eduardo responded.

"Do you think he's lying about knowing our *fulano*?" Chava asked.

"Someone's lying about something," I said at the same time Eduardo said, "Yes."

Chava laughed.

"What's funny?" I asked her.

"You and your father," Chava said. "You two think alike a lot. It's a little disconcerting."

I realized it was.

What I didn't mention to them was a detail I'd noticed when Johnny turned his back and went into the house. The band of his hat was decorated with the rattles from snakes. Could he have made the sound I'd heard? If so, why would Johnny have been out in the woods after dark?

THE CATHOLIC MASS held in Leavenworth took place in different locations. Churches in Leavenworth and Cashmere, then also at a convalescent center in Cashmere. There were times listed for Mass and Reconciliation, which Eduardo explained was another term for Confession, at the church locations, and then another address for the priest's office hours. The office hours for Thursday were at the Leavenworth location, so we went there first.

The priest—a nice older gentleman with a fringe of gray hair, decided paunch under his black shirt, and a wheeze in his voice—was helpful, but knew nothing useful. I even showed him Gabriela's photo; it seemed unlikely he'd abducted her, though these days one couldn't be too sure. She wasn't familiar to him either. He made sure we had the addresses of the two churches down in Wenatchee.

THIRTY-FIVE MINUTES LATER, we were pulling up outside the first church, the one on the east side of the river. This church didn't have office hours listed on their website. The buildings sat on a rise and looked out over the valley, the Columbia River splitting it down the center a few miles away, and the browned hills rising farther to the west and south. The main Church building was concrete and round, like a giant hatbox with a cross perched on top. We walked up to the smoked-glass front doors, which curved under arches, breaking up the façade.

The doors were locked.

"I didn't know you could arrive at a church like this and find the place empty," I said. "What if we were in the middle of a spiritual crisis?"

"It appears we would be out of luck," Eduardo said.

The huge parking lot was empty, though a sprinkler ran on some rose bushes closer to the street. We walked around the side of the building, following a sign that read OFFICE. It was so quiet, we could hear the traffic on the highway below.

The office was also locked. We weren't going to learn anything here today.

The second church was located not far from the hospital, so we crossed back over the river. This church was wooden, less grand, but with a warmer, more welcoming feel than the last one.

"It might be best if you wait in the car," Eduardo told Chava. "I think we are less … intimidating if it's just the two of us."

"I'm not intimidating."

Eduardo laughed. "You are to me."

"Fine."

Chava's smile showed a hint of satisfaction. I think she liked the idea she intimidated my father. As I got out of the car, I noticed Eduardo looked a touch satisfied too. I guess everyone got what they wanted.

At least the door was unlocked. The interior was hushed and the air was cool compared to the heat outside. Eduardo and I stood a moment, letting our eyes adjust, before we walked farther into the sanctuary. We opened the double doors leading to the main room, with its rows of pews and an altar. The ceiling soared above us, full of heavy beams and dropped lighting. Eduardo dipped his fingers into a font near the front door. I watched him out of the corner of my eye as he crossed himself with holy water.

I'm not sure why I was surprised. Even hit men for the mob could be complex.

And look for moments of grace.

We walked down the aisle, the pews stretching out on either side of us, empty at this time of day. With the lights off, the room was dim. On our right, a few small structures that looked like phone booths were lined up under stained-glass windows. I assumed those were confessionals.

"Think anyone's hanging around in there hoping for a penitent?" I asked, pointing at the stalls.

"People don't confess as much as they used to," Eduardo said. "It's more likely we'll find someone …." Before he could finish the thought, we both heard the sound of a door opening and closing, followed by muffled footsteps on the carpet. Someone was coming our way.

A short, blond man carrying a clipboard came into view. He wore a black dress shirt with the sleeves rolled up, suit pants, and a clerical collar. He stopped abruptly, apparently surprised to find anyone here. As he looked back and forth between my father and me, a troubled expression crossed his face.

"Can I help you?" he asked, continuing forward after a moment of assessment. I wondered briefly if he'd felt threatened in some way. He appeared uncomfortable with our presence.

"My name is Eddie Shoes," I said, holding my hand out.

"Hello, Eddie," he said, shaking my hand before he turned and looked expectantly at my father.

"This is my father, Eduardo," I said after a beat.

"Welcome," the priest said. "I'm Father Terry Doyle."

"We're wondering if perhaps you know this man," my father said, holding out the drawing we had of *Fulano*.

"Why are you looking for him?" The priest's eyes remained locked on my father's. He had not yet looked down at the image Eduardo held out.

"We have reason to believe he may have been hurt in a recent forest fire," Eduardo said, "as my daughter was."

The priest looked at me now, with that same appraising intensity. I pulled off my baseball hat and lowered my head so the shorter man could see my bandages.

"That looks bad. Are you all right?"

"Much better, thank you," I said. "But I'm concerned this man may not have come out as well as I did."

"But you don't know his name?"

"I came across him in the forest, already injured. I tried to help him," I said, letting my voice sound as husky as I could. I considered coughing too, but thought that might be overkill. I had the sense this priest didn't miss a trick.

"Let me see," he said, stepping closer and taking the paper from Eduardo's hand. He walked over to where the light was better and spent a few moments scrutinizing it. Bright, colored squares of light filtered through the image of a saint in the glass, turned his fair hair red and blue.

"I'm sorry, I don't. Did you have reason to believe he's a member of this church?"

"We know you perform services in Spanish," Eduardo said. "Perhaps there is another priest? The one who speaks Spanish?"

"*Ése sería yo*," said the priest with, at least to my ear, a very good accent. The man laughed at the surprise on Eduardo's face.

"Yeah, I get that look a lot. I grew up in Los Angeles, in a primarily Mexican neighborhood. Then, after my ordination, I spent five years at a church in Puebla, Mexico."

"And you're sure you would recognize him, if he attended here?" Eduardo asked.

"We are a large building, but a small congregation," the priest said. "Have you tried the church in East Wenatchee?"

"No one was there for us to ask," Eduardo said. "We will try there again another time. Thank you, Father."

"There is another possibility," the priest said before we could turn to go. "A place migrant workers go for Mass. It's not a formal church, so you wouldn't find it through the yellow pages or Google."

"Where is it?" I asked.

The priest hesitated.

"We mean this man no harm," Eduardo said. "If that is your concern."

"You have to understand," the priest said. "Wenatchee has its problems, just like any other city. The economic decline has hit us hard and racial tensions are high right now."

"Latinos have been targeted?" Eduardo asked.

The priest looked uncomfortable. I wondered if it was difficult for a white man to be having this conversation with two brown people, no matter how good his Spanish might be. "I don't have any reason to believe you'd be a danger to him," the priest said, "but I think there's more going on here. Why is your friend sitting back there in the dark, pretending she doesn't know you, yet listening so intently?"

We all turned and looked at Chava, slouched down in the last pew. Knowing her bat-like hearing, I was sure she hadn't missed a thing.

She waved at us, proving my point.

"That's my mother, Chava," I said, with an exasperated sigh. "She was *supposed* to wait outside."

"In my experience, mothers don't always do what we expect them to," the priest said, to which Eduardo chuckled.

"Chava, why don't you come over and say hello," I said. My mother walked down to meet the priest, hand outstretched.

"Hello, Father. Can I call you Father, even though I'm a Jew?"

"You can. Some of my favorite people are Jews."

Chava laughed as she took the priest's hand. I could see his body language change. He relaxed a bit. My mother had that effect on people.

"Why are the three of you really looking for this man?" he asked.

"We think he died ... in the fire," I said, deciding to put our cards on the table. "But proving that has become a little complicated, as we don't know his identity and no one has found his remains."

At least not a second time, but I wasn't going to tell that to a priest.

"We want to confirm he is missing," Eduardo said. "And make sure his family knows what happened to him. We are not convinced he is anyone's priority."

I wasn't sure I agreed with that assessment, but I let it go. It might make the priest more helpful.

"I'm sorry to hear this," the priest said. "Why aren't the police investigating?"

"They are," I said before Eduardo could disparage the sheriff's department. "But I'm a private investigator. We are doing a parallel investigation, to assist the authorities." I pulled one of my cards out of my wallet and handed it over to the priest.

"In that case, I'll help you if I can." He went on to describe the other location. It was a community center located in Peshastin, a tiny town on Highway 2, back toward Leavenworth.

He drew us a crude map on the back of one of our flyers.

"Will you let me know?" he asked. "If you find him?" He added a telephone number to the directions on the flyer.

"We will," I promised. "One more thing," I added, making a decision to trust him and holding out the other photo. "Do you know this woman? Her name is Gabriela. We believe she is his daughter."

"Was she caught in the fire too?" he asked.

"No," I said. "We just don't know her last name or how to reach her."

He looked at the photo but shook his head. "I'm sorry. I don't know her."

I thanked him for his time.

"I will be praying for him," the priest said as we turned to go. Then he added, "Has it been a while?" We all turned back, but it was clear he spoke to Eduardo.

"*¿Qué?*"

"Since you've been in a church? Has it been a while?"

I wondered why he zeroed in on Eduardo and not on me, though maybe he thought I was a Jew, since my mother was.

"I am at peace with God," Eduardo said. I admired how neatly he'd sidestepped the question while simultaneously wondering if it was true.

"*Entiendo.*" The priest nodded. "*Vaya con Dios.*"

"*Y contigo,*" Eduardo said as we stepped out of the dark church and into the light.

Chapter Thirty-Three

————•————

EDUARDO WAS QUIET as we made our way back to the car, where he once more got into the backseat. We drove in silence as we crossed the mighty Columbia, its waters blue and calm today. Our road crisscrossed the Wenatchee River in its path to join the Columbia on the way to the sea. Orchards and farms stretched out on either side of us with homes perched on top of the steep hillsides. As we went farther into the mountains, the hills turned from brown to green.

Arriving in Peshastin, we discussed our plan of action as we exited the highway and turned up into a hilly neighborhood of small but tidy homes. We found the location the priest described to us, a single-wide trailer in the middle of a dirt lot. Several vehicles were parked out front—mostly pickup trucks with balled tires and rusted paint jobs, and fifteen-year-old American coupes encrusted with dirt and rust. Chava parked near the entrance to the lot, closest to the road, with the nose pointed out. "In case we need to make a fast getaway," she said.

I was starting to think Chava watched too much TV. I had noticed she'd been saving old *Rockford Files* episodes on our DVR.

Walking up to the front door, we could hear the sound of a man speaking in Spanish, his voice resonant, though I didn't catch many words. Eduardo took a seat on the front steps, and Chava and I joined him.

Twenty minutes later, we heard the noises of people standing up and gathering their belongings to leave the building.

"They're coming out," I said, holding out a stack of flyers. "Time to go to work."

On the drive, we had decided that the best way to proceed was to show our sketch of the man around and pay attention to the responses we got. It was likely no one would admit to knowing him, but hopefully we were all astute enough to recognize the signs when someone had information they didn't want to share. If nothing worked today, we'd start over again with Gabriela's photograph next time. At some point we might need to mention her name, even though it could put her in danger.

"We can finish by speaking to the priest," I said. "He may not have a lot of information for us, but I don't think he'll out and out lie."

Eduardo laughed at this, but he didn't elaborate, and I didn't ask.

The congregation began to exit the makeshift church, heading to their various cars. The three of us split up, attempting to catch everyone before they left for the night. The group was a mix of men and women of varying ages. There were a few teenagers in the throng, but not many older than sixty. These were hardworking individuals who toiled in the orchards and ranches and fields.

"*Con permiso*," I said, stopping a man who'd gotten past Eduardo and Chava, both busy with other people.

"*¿Sí?*" he said, looking at me with suspicion.

"*¿Conoces a este hombre?*" I held out the sketch, but the man ducked his head.

"*No. Lo siento.*" The man tried to move away.

"Please, I'm trying to help him. *Quiero se ayudar*," I said. I knew I didn't have the words quite right, but apparently he understood.

The man stopped and grudgingly took the flyer. He looked at the picture, then at the other people in the lot.

"*Por favor. Necesito tu ayuda*," I said. "*Creo que el hombre esta en peligro.*" Telling this guy I believed *Fulano* was in danger and I needed his help was the most Spanish I'd attempted with anyone other than my father. I felt like a fraud, with my terrible accent. But I must have sounded sincere because he dropped his voice and leaned in toward me.

"*Es el padre de Gabriela*," he said.

"*¿Conoces el nombre última?*" A last name might go a long way. I didn't think I had the right words there, but I hoped he'd understand my meaning.

"*¿Apellido? No se.*"

"*¿Donde vive Gabriela?*" Was I about to get a line on our missing woman?

The man shook his head, "*No se.*"

"*¿Adonde trabaja Gabriela?*"

"*No se.*"

"*¿Estás seguro?* I asked. *You're sure?* If he did know where she worked, it would be our first break.

The man shook his head again and ducked away. I believed he didn't know any more, so I let him go. Besides, what else was I going to do? Tackle the guy? I didn't want to spook him, and we could always come back here to try again. Maybe the priest would know more.

Within a few minutes, we'd questioned as many of the people who'd attended the church as we could, and Eduardo and I arrived back at the car together. The priest had come out in front of the building to say goodbye to his flock and stood watching us.

"Did you learn anything?" Eduardo asked.

"I found one man who recognized *Fulano*. He knows he's

Gabriela's father," I said. "But he didn't admit he knew his name or where she works or lives."

"No time to talk," Chava said, rushing up to us. "We have to follow them." She pointed to two guys getting into one of the trucks in the lot. "Now."

Hearing the urgency in Chava's voice, we hopped into the car as the men pulled out onto the road.

"Why are we following them?" I asked as Chava pulled out behind them. "Did they know *Fulano*?"

"They know something," Chava said. "When I showed them the flyer, they both panicked. They couldn't get away from me fast enough. They very conveniently went from speaking English to '*no se, no se.*'"

"We have to be getting closer," I told her. "I found a guy who recognized *Fulano* and knew of Gabriela. They must have attended church here. Or he came here looking for her before he died."

Plus, it was the only lead we had, and sometimes you had to have faith.

Chapter Thirty-Four

—————————

THE DEPARTING VEHICLES left in a stream, half turning southeast toward Cashmere, the rest turning northwest toward Leavenworth. The car we followed headed toward Leavenworth. As we continued up the road, people dropped off on side streets, and soon it was just one other car between our quarry and us.

A few minutes later, the men swung onto a smaller dirt road. Chava continued past the turnoff and slowed to a stop on the side of the road. We rolled our windows down and listened to the loud, muffler-challenged vehicle getting farther away. Chava made a U-turn and crept up to the turnoff, which vanished into some trees. We could see the vehicle disappearing around a bend in the road, the left taillight out, giving it a distinctive, one-eyed look.

Chava followed them, using the cloud of dust and noise as a guide. We continued our slow, steady climb for a couple of miles. I told Chava to stop again when we heard the loud growl of the men's truck shut off. Turning our own engine off, the three of us sat, listening to the quiet.

Eduardo pulled his phone out.

"What are you doing?" I asked.

"Getting our latitude and longitude," he said. "If we can figure out where we are, we can figure out who owns this property, which will tell us who these men work for. I'm guessing they work on a ranch or farm, and this is the back way into their encampment or housing area."

"That's pretty smart," I said. "You'd make a good private investigator."

Eduardo laughed. "Perhaps our jobs haven't been so different after all."

I wasn't sure how I felt about that. We did both track people down, just for very different reasons.

"So what now?" Chava asked. "Do we go in and ask more questions?"

"I think we should get more information first," Eduardo said.

"But they're here now, and they know something," Chava said. "We should strike while the iron's hot."

My father laughed and said, "They wouldn't speak to you outside the church. They are even less likely to tell us anything now that we followed them all the way here."

"What do you think, Eddie?" Chava asked, turning to me.

Both my parents looked expectant, waiting for me to be the tiebreaker.

Did this mean I had to take sides? That was pretty darn uncomfortable. What was I supposed to do?

This was a practical decision, I told myself, not a personal one. So why did I feel like I was going to hurt somebody's feelings? I'd worked hard over the years to set my life up where I wasn't in this position.

Life was a lot easier without personal entanglements, or apparently, parents.

"What have you found with your coordinates?" I asked Eduardo, who still had his smartphone out.

"It looks like we're on the property of *el recinto*," he said. "One more reason to get a closer look at that place."

That made our next move clear.

"These guys clearly have ties to this community," I said. "They attend a church and probably live here. They aren't going to disappear on us in a day. They don't know we followed them. Let's see what else we can learn about the compound. If these guys work there, all the more reason to discover what we can about that place before we approach them."

"You're the expert," Chava said. I couldn't gauge her mood from her tone. The tall hillsides put the car, and her face, into shadow. I wished I could see her expression.

"You did good identifying they had more information," I said.

"That's true," Chava said. "You're lucky I'm here."

"I am," I said. "I'm lucky both of you are here."

I just hoped I wouldn't end up wishing this was a solo investigation.

Chapter Thirty-Five

---•---

THE RESORT WAS quiet when we returned. It was only seven at night, but being mid-week, it wasn't too busy. We decided on dinner at the fancier restaurant.

"My treat," my father said as we settled into the leather chairs.

"Thank you, Eduardo," my mother said, scanning the wine list as if she wasn't going to have a martini on the rocks with a couple of olives. I thanked my father too as I looked over the menu.

An enormous stone fireplace took up one wall nearby, the heat of the dancing fire welcome as the night air turned cool. The smell and crackle reminded me of my ordeal, but my heart rate didn't even bump. It just felt good and looked safely contained.

We ordered steaks and drinks. The conversation was casual, with no comments about the puzzling dead man or anyone we'd interviewed. It was the first time in my life I'd had a nice meal with both my parents. What would it have been like to grow up with both of them? How different would things be? Could Eduardo have been happy as a butcher? Coming home to the wife and kid? Or would he still have found work that skirted conventional society and the law?

Of course, it was unlikely Chava and Eduardo would have stayed together no matter what paths their lives had taken. Or perhaps, Chava would have gone and worked for the mob. They might have moved to Vegas together.

There was a picture for me to contemplate: a child of two criminal masterminds.

"You're quiet," Chava said as I took a sip of wine to dispel the thought.

"Just enjoying our meal," I said, smiling at the two of them. Whatever choices we had all made over the years, we were together now, for better or worse.

We topped off our steaks by sharing a couple of desserts. I definitely was going to have to work to get back in shape after we returned to Bellingham.

As we finished up the chocolate lava cake and a creation that involved candied rhubarb and vanilla beans, I asked Eduardo if he'd scouted out a safe route onto the compound property that would allow us to avoid getting picked up by surveillance cameras and motion detectors.

"I have a route," he said. "Let's leave here about two in the morning."

"I suggest we all take naps," Chava said. "It sounds like a late night."

"I am thinking that perhaps Eddie and I should go alone," Eduardo said, locking eyes with Chava.

"Alone? You mean without me?"

"That is what alone means, yes," Eduardo said, his tone light and teasing.

I waited, watching Chava's face shift through a variety of tiny expressions before it settled into what I can only describe as stubborn.

"And just why would you want to do that?"

"This venture, as I mentioned before, is much more dangerous than just asking questions in daylight."

"So you can put our daughter at risk, but not me?"

And here I'd been so hoping I'd get left out of this little confrontation.

"Eddie understands the risks."

Chava looked at me like I might be behind the idea of leaving her at home. "Oh is that so?" she said, eyes turning to slits. "Do you understand the risks, Eddie?"

At this point I figured my biggest risk was damaging the tenuous bond I'd formed with each of my parents. Whoever killed *Fulano* was the least of my worries at this moment.

"I think what Eduardo is saying is that we will be trespassing on a heavily secured piece of property where something illegal is probably going on and a murderer and kidnapper might be housed. I think he's just worried about us getting caught."

I'd meant it to sound reasonable, but as soon as I stopped talking, I knew I'd said the wrong thing.

"And I'm going to be the cause of that?"

"No, I didn't mean that, I just meant—"

"If we do not come back or we get caught and arrested, someone has to sound the alarm or bail us out," Eduardo said, his tone still light, as if we were discussing a trip to the store, not a trip to a felony. Though at least we wouldn't be shooting out a transformer or shorting out their electrical service.

Chava sat back in her chair.

"Well. I certainly don't want to be a burden to anyone," she said, setting her spoon down on the plate so gently it didn't even make a clink.

She pushed her chair back and tossed her napkin onto the table.

"I'll just go back to our cabin where I can't cause any problems."

"Chava ... Mom ... wait."

"I'll go collect Franklin," Chava said, speaking over her shoulder as she exited the room.

I started to get up, but Eduardo put his hand on my arm.

"I'm sorry, *mija*. I misjudged how much your mother would take this personally. Give her a moment to cool off and let me talk to her."

Torn, I debated what to do. Chava and I had done pretty well since she moved into my place back in December, and I didn't want that threatened. But my relationship with my father was new and felt more fragile than the one I had with Chava.

"Go on over to my room," Eduardo said, handing me a key. "Take a nap. I will talk to Chava. I think I am the one she is upset with, not you. No matter how it feels right now."

Any place out of the middle of the triangle felt like safer ground, so I agreed.

"I will come wake you when it's time to go," he said.

I just hoped that when he did, peace would be restored.

Chapter Thirty-Six

———•———

I THOUGHT I'D have a hard time falling asleep, but no sooner had I lain down on Eduardo's bed when someone shook me awake. Expecting my father, I clicked on the bedside lamp and was surprised to find Chava looking down at me.

"Is it time to go?" I asked, wondering if she'd killed my father and stuffed his body in the Jeep along with the expensive drone.

"I wanted to talk to you for a minute before we did."

I noticed the use of "we" in the sentence. If there had been a battle between my parents, Chava had won.

That wasn't surprising, of course. The mob had nothing on Chava.

"What's up?" I asked casually. Maybe I could still get out of being in the middle of whatever this was.

"About earlier …" Chava said, looking away. It was rare to see Chava uncertain, so I kept still. "I just wanted to say I'm sorry."

"That's a first," I said, teasing her.

"I'm serious, Edwina," she said, slipping back into my childhood name.

"Okay. What is it you're sorry about?" I asked.

"I shouldn't have jumped on you, or your father for that matter. He's right, after all. We shouldn't all go. Someone has to stay on the outside in case something goes wrong."

"That's probably true," I said. Though it was clear she wasn't finished.

"I guess I'm a little envious of your relationship with Eduardo."

"Why?"

"Because you two get each other. Even though you don't know him and he doesn't know you, there's some … bond I can't be a part of."

I reached out and took my mother's hands in mine. Mirror images, hers just a size smaller. The same long, thin fingers, hers adept at shuffling cards, mine at pointing cameras at cheating spouses. "Don't you think he could say the same about us?"

Chava smiled at me, smoothing my bed hair, carefully avoiding the burnt part.

"Eduardo and I decided I'd go along," she said, "but stay in the car. If something happens, I can't help from the resort. We think our phones work on the property—we used them when we launched the drone and they worked fine at the Langston place—so we can stay in contact over text. If something goes wrong, I can react quicker from nearby."

"That," I said getting out of bed, "is a great compromise. Let me just swing by our cabin to change." I had some darker clothes and a heavier jacket that would work better for a late-night raid at the compound. "Where's Eduardo?"

"He's meeting someone before we go. I think he called in a few more favors and got some articles he wants to bring with us."

That should be interesting.

Standing up, I pulled Chava into an embrace, taking us both by surprise. We weren't physically demonstrative people.

"You'll always be my best friend, Mom," I said into her sticky beehive of hair.

* * *

THE NIGHT-VISION GOGGLES lit the world up in shades of green. Looking across the open land, I could see hot spots where the cattle lay. Nothing person-shaped appeared in my field of vision. I knew Chava was chaffing back at the car, but it was for the best. As much as it would suck to get arrested for breaking and entering, it beat dying in some underground room. Detective Campbell might be pissed off about what we were doing, but she could get a warrant based on our disappearance. And Chava had to be there to call it in.

We stopped near where we'd launched the drone and I sent a quick text, letting Chava know we were all right. We'd decided I'd text her every twenty minutes. If I went longer than forty minutes without a text, she'd call Detective Campbell.

Falling in behind my father, I let him lead the way. Scanning the land around us as we crossed toward the chain-link fence, I kept expecting armed guards. But apparently Eduardo's homework had paid off.

The dog appeared, Eduardo making tschssing noises through his teeth. Reaching down to the chain-link fence, he held his hand to its nose. The dog wagged and bounced around like it had found a long-lost friend.

"Not really a guard dog, is it?"

"No," Eduardo said, a genuine smile on his face. "I think perhaps for the livestock. It …" the dog rolled over, showing his belly, "*he* is an Australian Cattle dog. Excellent herding animals."

"Why do you think they don't have actual guard dogs?"

"They may think they have enough security in place. This is hardly the south side of Chicago." Eduardo continued to converse with the dog in his strange noises. Then he made some gestures and the dog dropped down on the ground, quivering with excitement.

"What would you have done if he hadn't been so friendly?" I asked.

"I have some pills wrapped in something delicious."

"You would have poisoned a dog?" Despite knowing my father's career choices, I was stunned.

"*Mija*, I don't poison dogs. Just a little sedative. We'd have waited a few minutes and then we could have walked past even the toughest of dogs. But with this boy, we will be fine." Eduardo had already done pretty well keeping him from barking. I'd have to trust he knew what he was doing. I guess my father really was an animal whisperer.

Eduardo dropped his backpack and pulled out a tool that cut through the chain links like they were made of butter. I needed to get a set of those. It must be another item he'd gotten from his "friend," along with the night-vision goggles and the bulletproof vests we were wearing.

Once he had made a hole big enough for us to crawl through, he put them away and held the hole open so I could follow. The dog watched Eduardo with rapt attention. Eduardo tossed him something and made a shooing gesture. The dog trotted off.

Once he was out of sight, Eduardo followed a zigzag pattern the rest of the way to the buildings. He explained he'd memorized the path we'd need to take to stay clear of the cameras. He was pacing off specific distances before heading a new direction. We reached the vent we'd seen on the photo. So far we hadn't set off any alarms or showed up on any video feed, or we'd have already been stopped.

"The cattle are our best friends," Eduardo had said as we were planning this foolhardy raid. "There are no motion detectors or booby traps outside the fence because the animals would always be setting them off."

After asking me to stand guard, Eduardo removed his backpack again and pulled out an electric screwdriver. He changed the tip out to match the hardware and unscrewed the bolts on the vent cover. The vent was just large enough for us to fit through so we could see what was going on underground.

Removing the cover, we discovered light bleeding through

from underneath. The cover had overlapping slats that allowed air to pass through, but blocked light from showing.

Eduardo had already removed his night-vision goggles and set them aside. I did the same. He carefully leaned into the vent, which was shaped like an upside-down L. He managed to keep his feet on the ground, but his entire head and chest disappeared into the vent, the ninety-degree turn about waist high.

After a few minutes, he retracted out of the tight space and motioned for me to poke my head in, letting me know he'd keep his eyes and ears out for any sentries who might be patrolling the grounds. Pushing myself into the vent, I had a moment of disorientation. The space underneath our feet was much larger than I expected. The cavernous room was brightly lit, the floor a dizzying distance below. The floors and walls were a brilliant white. The air was warm and humid and smelled of sulfur.

Before seeing the room, I'd have bet on marijuana or some other kind of drug being manufactured on the premises. That would make sense, given the amount of electricity being generated, the armed guards, and the secrecy. But unless marijuana growers had discovered a new way of producing buds, what I was looking at didn't line up with anything I was familiar with.

Tanks. Huge water tanks glowed neon green in the bright fluorescent light.

Pulling myself back out of the vent, I turned to my father. "What the hell is all that?"

"I have no idea."

Chapter Thirty-Seven

EDUARDO REPLACED THE cover on the vent. Picking up our night-vision goggles, we started back to where we'd left Chava. We'd both snapped photos of the tanks in hopes of figuring out what we were looking at. After crawling back through the fence, Eduardo stitched it together with a roll of baling wire. But before we could get to the car, we heard raised voices off to our left. We stopped, straining our ears to hear what the fight was about.

"I'm going to ask you one more time. What are you doing on this property?" The male voice was clearly agitated. He sounded young to my ears, and angry, not scared.

"I told you. I just got lost in the woods. I'll go back the way I came and get out of your hair."

That voice, unfortunately, was very familiar. Chava had apparently chosen not to stay in the car. I checked my phone. My last text had gone out. Why had she gotten out of the Mazda?

Next to me, Eduardo sighed.

"What do we do now?" I whispered in his ear.

"It looks like we may need to rescue your mother."

"Do you think she's in danger?"

We both heard her voice again. "Where are you taking me? Let go of my arm!"

Eduardo didn't answer my question, just moved off toward the sound. We came upon Chava in a small clearing, tangling with a man I didn't recognize. Clearly there were more than two security guards on the premises. Despite the security guard being twenty years younger and built like a WWE wrestler, she wasn't making it easy for him. I thought he might get his eyes gouged out if he wasn't careful. I might have been tempted to let Chava free herself from the situation just for pure entertainment value, except that another security guard showed up with a gun.

"Freeze," the second guard said, pointing his weapon at the other two. I heard another sigh from Eduardo standing next to me, though he didn't sound distressed. At least not yet. More irritated than concerned.

Before I could make a decision about what to do, Eduardo sprang into action. He stepped forward out of the trees and into the small clearing, a rather large gun of his own pointed at the armed security guard. Glimmering gold in the faint moonlight, Eduardo's weapon looked downright wicked. What was that thing?

"I wouldn't do that if I were you," Eduardo said. "Drop the gun."

It looked to me like everyone could get shot in this little scenario, but I didn't have a better option. There had to be some way for me to give us an advantage. After all, no one knew I was there.

The guard with the gun out shifted his aim from Chava to Eduardo. I recognized him from our earlier visits as the driver of the truck. "Why should I?" he said, his voice carrying only the slightest hesitation.

Eduardo didn't move a muscle and the trio fell silent. Everyone was tense; the heavy breathing sounded like ocean waves in the still of the night.

"Because I've got a gun pointed at you too," I said from my cover in the trees. "You might shoot him, but you won't shoot me."

I just hoped he didn't demand I walk out into the light of the moon where my lack of a weapon would be obvious to everyone involved in this little kerfuffle.

The big guy holding Chava couldn't easily get to the weapon strapped on his hip without dropping his hold on her. Plus, he'd be too slow against Eduardo and his big gun, and me in the shadows.

"It's not worth getting shot over," the man holding Chava said to his partner.

The security guard with the gun held his weapon up in surrender.

"Lose the magazine," Eduardo said, and the guard complied. He popped the magazine out and started to lower it to the ground, along with the gun. "And the one in the chamber."

The man set the magazine down, then racked the slide back into the open position and ejected the cartridge.

"Now, you," Eduardo said, turning his gun toward the guard holding Chava. "Let go of her."

The man let go.

"Now, hold your hands up while she takes your gun."

I thought for sure the guy would fight about that one, but he complied. Chava did as Eduardo asked. I forced myself to keep breathing. We were almost out of the woods, literally and figuratively.

"Now you three can be on your merry way," said the driver of the truck.

"First, please pick up the other weapon," Eduardo said to Chava. "We don't want them putting it back together and following us out of here."

Chava started to bend down, when another voice came out of the trees behind her.

"I wouldn't do that if I were you."

Apparently, someone else had joined our little group.

"Why not?" Chava asked, with just a hint of quaver in her voice. It wasn't very often I heard fear from my mother.

"Because my gun is bigger than his and I can shoot you both before you get a chance to reload the guns on the ground."

Crap. Now what?

Chapter Thirty-Eight

————•————

MY FIRST THOUGHT was that I should blend back farther into the trees and hightail it out of there. I could try to spring my parents if they were taken hostage by these guys or contact Detective Campbell to come out and bring the cavalry. I really should have asked Eduardo for a weapon, though I wasn't sure adding one more gun to the mix would solve the problem.

"We seem to be at an impasse," Eduardo said, his firearm never wavering.

"I suppose you could understand it that way," the newest voice said. "Though considering that I can see you, but you can't see me, I'd say I have the advantage."

"Perhaps we should come to some kind of mutually beneficial end to this little … problem," Eduardo said, his voice never revealing an ounce of concern. You'd never know an armed conflict was unfolding around him. I really did need to have him teach me how to stay so calm.

"What do you have in mind?" the voice asked.

"We would like to leave, and I believe you would like us gone, so why don't we all put the guns down and go our separate ways," my father said.

The pause lasted long enough that I thought the lone gunman had fallen asleep out there, but he finally responded.

"Why are you here?" he asked.

That was a tricky bit of business, wasn't it? How much of our hand did Eduardo want to show? What if Gabriela was being held captive on the grounds?

"We are still looking for the missing man," Eduardo said.

The driver had no doubt recognized Eduardo, so there was no reason to lie about that. But still no reason to bring up that our missing man was actually dead.

"What missing man?"

That was an interesting response, since he sounded honestly curious.

Eduardo appeared to think so too, because I caught the tiniest waver in his gun hand. So, something could surprise him ….

"Do you mean to tell me this gentleman here didn't show you the police sketch we brought around two days ago?" my father asked, gesturing toward the security guard with a casual flick of his gun.

"Police sketch?"

The driver shifted his weight back and forth, and I was sure that if I could see his face, I'd note that his skin had gone a little pink.

"I didn't think it was important enough to tell you about," the leader of the duo said.

"If it concerns this property, the decision about how important something is belongs to me, but we can discuss that later. Who is this missing man?"

"I'm going to lower my gun," Eduardo said. "I suggest you do the same. We can continue our conversation like civilized men."

Without waiting for a response, Eduardo dropped his

hand to his thigh. And though his gun didn't disappear into its holster, everyone's body language relaxed a bit. I held my breath. Who remembered me out here hiding in the trees?

"Can you step out," Eduardo said to the disembodied voice in the forest, "where I can see you? So we can resolve this thing?"

"Don't do it," the driver from the truck said. "They also have someone in the trees with a gun."

One person remembered I was here.

"How about the two of us who are hidden step into the open together?" the voice said.

"Okay," I said. "I'm putting my gun away."

"I will too," came the other voice. "We'll step out on the count of three. One. Two. Three."

As I arrived not far from Chava, a short, squat man with his hands in the air stepped out of the dark. Everyone countered so we ended up in a rough circle, equidistant from one another. We looked like a group of school kids getting ready to play a game of Duck, Duck, Goose.

"So why are you creeping around my property at night?" the new guy said. "And who is this missing man?"

Did that mean he didn't know anything about *Fulano*? Or was he the one who killed him, and he wanted to ascertain what we knew before he killed us too?

Chapter Thirty-Nine

———•———

THE NIGHT TOOK on a surreal feeling. I explained about the fire and *Fulano*.

While talking, I monitored everyone in our little group. Chava was slowly edging her way backward into the trees, though I wasn't sure what she planned on doing even if she did escape. The two security guards were watching my father, having apparently discounted Chava and me as potential threats.

"Tragic," the short man said with regards to the man who died, "but I still don't understand what you're doing wandering around my property in the middle of the night."

"We have reason to believe he worked here, on your ranch," I said. "Or at least knew someone here. We want to find out who he was, so we can tell his family what happened."

That was sort of true.

"No one who works for me went missing in the fire," he said. "And why not just come and ask me?"

"We did," my father said. "You are already aware that your security guards didn't pass that information on since you know nothing about our earlier visits. We could tell in our conversations with them they were hiding something and not being helpful. This made us very suspicious."

"You spoke to them more than once?"

"Yes. Well, we spoke to *him*," I said, pointing out the driver. "Twice."

More shifting around from the security guard. Looked like someone might be getting into a little trouble with his boss after this was all over.

"I'll deal with you later," he said, directing the comment to the driver. It's comments like that which make me glad I work for myself.

"You said you have a picture of this man?"

"A sketch I did with the authorities when I reported him missing," I said.

"Let me see it."

I pulled out a copy of the sketch and handed it over, and the man clicked on a small flashlight. The light was bright and my eyes burned, a red hotspot showing as an afterimage when I shut my eyes. Turning away, I focused on the driver to save some of my night vision. Chava had gotten even closer to the trees.

"Could you please ask your friend to stop trying to sneak away?" the short man said, apparently tracking my mother's progress as well.

Chava stepped back into the circle without a word.

The man took his time looking over the drawing.

"I don't know this man," he said. "I'm sorry."

"But your security guards know something about his disappearance that they are not sharing with us," Eduardo said, putting a few more of our cards on the table. "Or at least that someone is missing. They definitely know more about the situation."

"Is this true?" the man asked his employees.

The two men stood awkwardly for a moment, exchanging what glances they could with each other in the dark, unsure what to say. From the body language, I was guessing the security guard who hadn't been in the truck didn't know what was going on.

"It's possible the man has a daughter named Gabriela," I said, curious if that would get a reaction. "We are hoping to speak with her."

The new guy gave a startled look toward the security guards. "You knew about this?"

"No," the driver said. "Her name never came up."

"But you thought there might be a connection? Between this man and Gabriela."

Neither man responded.

"I think this has just become a longer conversation," the short guy said to us. "You all had better come back to the house."

Were we about to learn more? Or were we now going to walk into the killer's den? After all, we still didn't know what this guy had going on here at the compound. If he was doing something illegal, why invite us in? Unless it was to get us exactly where he wanted us.

Chapter Forty

"**D**O WE THINK that's such a good idea?" Chava asked.

"I'm not sure we have much choice," I said.

My father nodded. "Eddie's right."

"How do we know we'll ever get out alive?" Chava asked. "Everyone in this little group pulled a gun on us."

The boss apparently came to some kind of decision.

"Look," he said, "we are not criminals. I can prove it." He pulled his coat open, then lifted it above his waist and turned around. "I'm not actually armed. That was a bluff. I don't carry a gun. I'm a scientist."

"A scientist?" I said, confused by this turn of events.

"What happens here is proprietary information, which is why I have a security team. Usually you'd have to sign a nondisclosure agreement before I let you into these buildings, but I'm going to trust my instincts you aren't here to steal my concepts. We're not doing anything illegal out here. I'm heading up a research and development team into alternative energy."

The tanks.

"What kind of alternative energy?" Eduardo asked, curiosity

in his voice, at the same time Chava said, "Why all the secrecy?"

The scientist raised an eyebrow.

"Forget it," I said. "You're right, we don't care about that. We aren't interested in your science, just in identifying this man and locating his daughter."

"*Sí*, my daughter is right," Eduardo said. "You keep your R and D to yourself. We will come back to your place and you can tell us about this Gabriela; that is all we are interested in."

"Okay then," Mr. Scientist said. "Keep all your weapons tucked away. Follow me."

A silent battle raged as everyone determined the order of the march. Eduardo clearly wanted to fall in behind the security guards, but they were having none of it. The scientist got farther ahead as everyone else stood around refusing to get in front of anyone else.

"Oh, for the love of God," Chava finally said, speeding to catch up with our host. The security guards were torn, not wanting her to get too far out in front, but not trusting Eduardo. Deciding the guards weren't going to shoot me in the back, I fell in behind Chava.

When we arrived at what appeared to be the main house and went through a gate in the fence, I found the guards behind me, with Eduardo bringing up the rear.

I wasn't surprised he'd taken the tactical advantage. Compared to my father, these two men were amateurs.

"Lock the gate," the scientist said to the last security guard in line. My heart bumped at the thought that we were now locked in, but there wasn't much I could do about it now.

"Welcome to my home," the scientist said, as he crossed the front porch and opened the front door, gesturing for us to enter. "At least for as long as this project goes. I am Dr. Varine, and you are …?"

"Chava," my mother said, wiping her feet on the mat and walking in as if she'd been invited over for tea.

"Eddie," I said as I followed her inside.

The two security guards started to come in behind me, but Dr. Varine put up his hand. "I don't think I'll be needing you for this. We're just going to talk. You can go back to your quarters."

The guards looked uneasy, but followed orders and disappeared around the side of the house. I saw Eduardo watch them before entering behind us.

"Eduardo," my father said, pausing to shake the scientist's hand. "It's a pleasure to make your acquaintance."

The scientist laughed. "It's been a rather strange night, hasn't it? I've never pretended to have a gun before."

He sounded pleased with himself and I had to bite my tongue not to add that I'd gotten away with the same thing.

As he was speaking, the dog trotted up to the house.

"There you are," Dr. Varine said. "I wondered what happened to you." The dog crossed the porch and came into the building. "He's not much of a guard dog, but I like having him around."

Eduardo gave the dog a scratch behind the ears before we all trooped farther inside. At least Dr. Varine didn't know we'd already met the dog the first time we'd come through his fence. I wondered how long it would take him to find his fence had been cut open. Currently, he didn't know how far onto his property we'd come, or that we'd seen down into the space with the tanks. If he did, he might not be so helpful.

"Can I get you anything?" our host asked as he led us toward the back of the house. We arrived in the kitchen. "Cup of tea? Beer? Or something a little stronger? I think I could use a drink myself."

"Tea would be lovely," Chava said.

"Nothing for me," I said.

"A cold *cerveza, por favor*," Eduardo said.

"Where are you from, *mi amigo*?" Dr. Varine asked.

"Many places," my father said.

Dr. Varine laughed again. "I should know not to ask a man too many questions when he shows up sneaking around my place with a gun. Speaking of guns, that's quite a pistol you have. Is that thing gold-plated?"

"A Magnum Research Desert Eagle," my father said.

"What's the caliber?"

"Fifty."

"Can I see it?"

"No."

The scientist filled an electric kettle with water. "Looks like I need a better security team," he said. "Perhaps I should hire you?"

Eduardo smiled, with a brief nod of his head at the "joke," but I thought the scientist might be serious. He dropped the idea and turned away to pull a box of tea out of a cupboard. "There's beer in the fridge," he said to Eduardo. "Help yourself."

My father opened the vintage refrigerator, and I could see a six-pack of Dark Persuasion from Icicle Brewing Company in Leavenworth. The box had one bottle missing. Next to that was a carton of milk, a dozen eggs, and some takeout boxes. Eduardo pulled out a beer and twisted off the top.

"You don't want to join me, *mija*?" he asked.

"Sure," I said as the dog settled under the table at our feet. This couldn't get any weirder; why not have a beer? The more relaxed we all were, the less likely this little soiree would be to turn into a gun battle.

Eduardo handed the bottle he had over to me and pulled out a second one. Meanwhile, Dr. Varine had gotten out a teacup and handed a teabag to Chava.

"Sit, please," he said, gesturing to the retro kitchen table, gray Formica with silver around the edge and four red padded chairs. Though I guess it didn't count as retro if it was the original furnishings; then it was just old. "Would you like something else?" the man turned toward a Tupperware container on the counter. "I have some very good cake."

The three of us declined and we sat and waited in silence while the water heated for Chava, though my father and I clinked our bottles together and I could see a sparkle in his eye.

It dawned on me that Eduardo was enjoying this little

detour in our evening. My father apparently loved adventure, whatever the adventure might be.

At least no one had gotten shot. So far. But just as I started to feel safe, I heard footsteps coming down the hallway.

How long would it take for Eduardo to get to his gun?

Chapter Forty-One

———◆———

EDUARDO HEARD THE noise as well, because he was up and out of his seat. He began to move toward the hallway, hand on his hip, no doubt where he'd stashed that big gun.

"Whoa, whoa, hold on there," Dr. Varine said, his hands up in supplication, but putting his body between Eduardo and the person in the hall.

"I hear someone else in the house, and yet from you I believe we are alone." Apparently, Eduardo's syntax got a little strange under stress.

"I never said anything about who else was in this building," Dr. Varine said, his voice taking on a quality I hadn't heard before. The undertone was a little more sinister, not what you'd expect from the lighthearted scientist who'd ushered us in for tea.

"Why should we believe we are safe sitting in here with you?" Eduardo asked.

Chava looked ready to back Eduardo up, fingering her cup as if it might stop a bullet. Or maybe she just planned to hurl it at anyone who threatened us. I remained seated. What else could I do? I wasn't armed, and there was no easy way out of the room. If someone down the hall was gunning for us, there weren't a lot of options. Sometimes the best thing to do in a situation like this is stay calm and not make things worse.

Whoever lurked in the hallway had stopped walking toward us, presumably because of hearing strange voices in the kitchen. They could also be preparing for some kind of ambush.

"No one is interested in hurting any of you. Just … wait here a minute." Dr. Varine made no move to go; he was waiting to see if we were going to do as he asked.

Eduardo didn't sit back down right away, but commenced a staring contest with Dr. Varine. Something must have been reassuring about the man, however, because after a tense moment, Eduardo took his seat. He picked up his beer and gave a slight signal to Dr. Varine to go chat with the person in the hall. It was clear Dr. Varine considered Eduardo the leader of our little group, even if I had been the one doing most of the talking. Or maybe he just saw Eduardo as the greatest danger. If they'd been rams, they would no doubt be banging their heads together.

Chava started to speak as the scientist left the room, but Eduardo hissed at her, a noise not unlike the one he'd used to shush the dog. She leaned back against the counter and held tight to her cup, though at this point I think she was considering throwing it at Eduardo.

The whispered conversation in the hall gave us no information about the other person. I couldn't guess age or gender from the muted tones. A few minutes later, Dr. Varine reentered the room.

"We won't be disturbed again," he reassured us.

What else was there to do except trust that the man was who he said he was, a scientist growing some kind of bioenergy source, using geothermal heat, if the smell and humidity were any indication.

The kitchen was quiet. We all settled in to our drinks and our ragged breathing returned to normal. It dawned on me that Dr. Varine had been surprised by the incident as well, as I watched him take a bottle of bourbon down from a cupboard with a shaky hand. He poured himself a bourbon and water and joined us at the table.

"Now, let's get back to this missing man of yours," Dr. Varine said as he spread the sketch out on the table, smoothing the paper under his hands. He took a sip of bourbon, and I noticed a brief expression of concern cross his face. He was having a rough night. First he'd come across three random people sneaking around his supposedly well-guarded property. Then he'd pretended to wield a gun. Finally, he'd been unexpectedly interrupted by one of his own people. Most unsettling, one of the interlopers to his compound had a beehive hairdo and smelled of Aqua Net.

"Where to start," Dr. Varine said.

"How about Gabriela," I said. "Tell us what you know about her."

Dr. Varine nodded. "Let me just say upfront, I'm not going to tell you who I work with or any details of the research we're doing." He looked around the table, confirming again we weren't spies sent in by a competitor in the high-stakes game of alternative fuel. "I want to make sure we're clear on that."

The three of us nodded. Eduardo gestured for the man to continue.

"An investor in my research owns this property. It's perfect for our work, but uses little of the total acreage."

I could see where this was headed.

"The investor decided to use the rest of the property for cattle and agriculture. That was its original purpose, and there was no reason for that to change. That's why there's a herd of cattle here and fruit trees. I've heard the rumors we use the agriculture to cover illegal activity, but it was a financial decision, not a misdirection. We're being discreet, not disingenuous."

Though it didn't hurt that the cattle served both purposes.

I guess in his world, it was better for people to think he was growing pot than solving the world's energy crisis.

"Didn't you worry that all that speculation about what you're up to would actually make people more curious about what you're doing here?" Chava asked.

Dr. Varine shrugged. "Not really. We're a long way from the city. None of our competitors are neighbors, so it's not like they're going to discover us. The people who live out here are the kind who keep to themselves. That works in our favor. Our neighbors aren't interested in what we do."

"With rumors of illegal activity, you weren't worried about the police nosing around?"

"We have nothing to worry about," he said. "Keeping a low profile isn't against the law."

True. Plus, maybe Detective Campbell already knew what this crew was about. Maybe that's why no one had visited *el recinto* yet; they weren't such a mystery after all. She wouldn't have had any reason to fill me in on it. I *was* just a private investigator, not a member of law enforcement. And there certainly wasn't any reason for the fire department to know.

"So, who is this Gabriela?"

"Yes. Well. There is a group of farmworkers who live on the property to take care of the animals and the trees. We have very few interactions with them, but I needed a housekeeper."

"Gabriela was your housekeeper?" I asked when Dr. Varine fell silent a beat too long.

"She was, until a couple weeks ago. She didn't show up one day."

"How long had she worked for you?" I asked.

"About a year," he answered.

"Weren't you worried about her?"

"Yes, I was concerned. After a few days passed without any word, I made inquiries. I was told she went back to Mexico."

"And it was easier not to look too closely," Eduardo said. His tone didn't make it a value judgment, but the words clearly did.

"What would you have had me do?" he asked, his voice taking on a plaintive note. "She was an adult and I had no reason to believe she'd come to any harm. It was *her* friends who said she was fine."

"But you didn't report her absence to the authorities," Eduardo said.

"Report what? That the woman who cleaned my house didn't show up one day?"

"You were worried you would get into trouble?" Eduardo's voice stayed level, with no indication of his internal state. It appeared to work with Dr. Varine, who didn't seem insulted by the direction of the conversation.

"She had a green card."

"But you don't remember her last name?"

Now the pause in the conversation verged on uncomfortable.

"I was paying her cash," Dr. Varine said finally.

"But you had doubts about her disappearance," Eduardo said.

Dr. Varine sighed heavily, slouching back in his chair. "I'll be honest with you. I did."

"Why is that?" I asked.

"Something felt off. Gabriela is a fantastic cook. I hired her for additional hours. She'd come and cook a week's worth of food, which I kept in the freezer and heated up. Working for me as a housekeeper and a cook, supplementing what she earned as a farmworker, she was earning more money than she ever had before. She told me she wanted to start her own restaurant in the Wenatchee area. I don't understand why she'd go back to Mexico when that dream was getting closer."

It was looking more and more like Gabriela had been abducted. Or at least left the area under suspicious circumstances.

"We need to talk to the people who know her—the other migrant workers," I said to my parents. "And find out if we can get a last name."

"You're sure you don't recognize this man?" Eduardo asked, tapping the sketch on the table.

"I was telling the truth. I've never seen him before."

"Do you recognize this?" I held out the rosary, which I'd taken to carrying in my pocket. Dr. Varine took it and looked at it closely.

"It's similar to the one Gabriela carried. I saw her with it once and asked her to show it to me."

We fell quiet again.

"What about the other people who live here?" I asked. "Can you show them the sketch, at least? I'm not sure your security guards showed it to anyone else."

"Sure," Dr. Varine said, "but I can guarantee the others interact even less with the workers than I do. If the security guards and I don't recognize this man, it's doubtful they would. But give me your cell number. I promise I'll call you if I learn anything. And I'd like it if you'd do the same."

"We should definitely go visit the camp," Chava said when it became clear the scientist had nothing else useful to add. Not a surprise, as that had been her plan all along. At least she didn't say I told you so.

"I'm not sure that's the best way to go," Eduardo said. "They have no reason to trust us, even if I do speak their language. If they are concealing the whereabouts of this girl, they might not want to tell us. We are assuming she was abducted. It could be she's hiding."

"Or *they* did something to her," I said.

"What's our alternative?" Chava asked.

"We need to know a little more about them," my father said. "Find a way to talk to them that doesn't look like we're just trying to find Gabriela."

"Short of joining them to pick fruit, how would you recommend we do that?" Chava asked.

"They must have other places they go, besides the church," I said.

"Any ideas?" Eduardo asked the scientist, who had been following our back and forth with interest. "You saw Gabriela every week."

"We didn't overlap much," he said. "But she did mention a restaurant she liked, Carmelita's Cantina. She said she wanted to model her restaurant after them, but with better ambiance."

"Have you ever been there?" Eduardo asked.

"No," he said. "But I might start. With Gabriela gone, I'm slowly starving to death."

Chapter Forty-Two

D R. VARINE HAD one of his security guys drive us back to our car. Someone had to unlock the gates to let us out. Either Dr. Varine wanted to demonstrate to us that he had a bigger force than we'd already seen or he figured we'd had our fill of the other guards. We hadn't exactly gotten off on the right foot with his core crew, and this guy was someone we'd never met before.

We got into the Mazda, and Chava started toward the resort.

"Why did you get out of the car?" I asked her, keeping my tone neutral so she wouldn't get defensive.

"I heard a motorcycle. I thought I might be able to see who it was or where they had stopped."

"A motorcycle? Did they drive into *el recinto*?" I asked. "Or pass by?" As far as I knew, there wasn't anyone living farther down the road; I thought it ended at *el recinto*. Was I wrong about that?

"I wasn't sure. That's why I got out, to try to see."

"You're sure it was a motorcycle?" I asked.

"It wasn't a car."

"How about a quad or a three-wheeler?"

Chava thought a moment. "It might have been, why?"

"Because the Langston Ranch has a few of those," I said.

"Why would anyone from the Langston Ranch be driving around on a three-wheeler in the middle of the night?" Chava asked.

Good question.

We'd arrived back at the resort. It wasn't yet light, and everything was quiet as we pulled into the spot in front of our cabin. Franklin was sleeping over at Debbie's and I missed his face waiting for me in the window.

"I believe Dr. Varine is telling the truth," Eduardo said. "With what we saw in the tanks, some kind of biofuel grown with the aid of the naturally occurring hot springs makes sense. But someone told him Gabriela went back to Mexico. We should find out who recommended her to him in the first place."

Someone who knew Gabriela and also knew Dr. Varine, or someone working with him.

"It could be someone who works for the Langstons," I said, mostly thinking out loud.

"Now what?" Chava asked.

"Sleep?" I said.

"I agree," Eduardo said, getting out of the car. Chava got out as well and began to walk toward our cabin. When she was out of earshot, I turned to Eduardo, who had waited, apparently knowing I had a question for him.

"What would you have done if they'd taken Chava hostage?" I asked, curious about my father's loyalty to a woman he hadn't seen in over thirty years, even if she was the mother of his child.

Eduardo shrugged. "I would have left you outside," he said, with his sly smile, "so you would never need to know."

WHEN I AWOKE several hours later, Chava had already left. A note propped up on the counter said she'd gone over to get

Franklin. She'd meet me for lunch at one o'clock. I checked the time. I had half an hour, so I lay back and stretched.

The bruises on my body were fading, though the one on my hip had turned the color of an angry plum with a corona of yellow.

At lunch, we decided to visit the Mexican restaurant, though we also needed to return to the informal church to ask about *Fulano* and Gabriela; maybe the priest knew their last name and where they were from. We decided we could cover more ground splitting up. Chava didn't argue this time because she had a job of her own. She'd head over to the makeshift church, find out what the priest knew, and ask any parishioners about Gabriela. Eduardo and I would blend in at the restaurant.

THE AFTERNOON WENT by too fast as I hung out with Franklin, Indy, and Debbie Buse. "Be a good boy for Debbie," I said to Franklin as we finished our romp in the grass.

"These two are going to crash," Debbie said, looking down at both dogs, panting up at us, tongues lolling out of their mouths.

I loved that Franklin had a best friend. I gave Debbie a hug as I left. Almost dying in a fire was making me very thankful for my friends, two-legged and four-legged.

We thought mass at the church was at six, so Chava had already left when I met up with Eduardo. I climbed in next to him in the Jeep.

"Should we just go in and start asking people about *Fulano* and Gabriela?" I asked.

"I trust your judgment."

"Let's park outside for a bit first."

Arriving in front of Carmelita's Cantina, we found a divey-looking restaurant with all manner of old cars parked out front. Eduardo cruised through the parking lot, which was rutted, hard-packed dirt, and continued around back for more of the same. We didn't see any vehicles that looked familiar, so Eduardo drove around the building and back out onto the street. He parked on the other side, where we could see anyone who pulled in.

The men from the church were easy to identify. From where we were parked, we could see them come up the street, then pull into the lot and continue around to the back, the broken taillight like a brand. Though we couldn't make out their faces, we could see three straw cowboy hats in a row. It looked like the two from the church had brought along a friend.

"We know they're going in. Let's get ahead of them," I said. Eduardo nodded and got out of the Jeep.

The Cantina was even more of a dive than the exterior promised. Tables were scattered across a floor covered in peanut shells, which crunched under our feet as we headed toward the bar. Booths lined the walls, many of their red-vinyl padded benches hemorrhaging stuffing. The rest were lumpy and misshapen from years of use.

The joint was about half full. Though men made up the majority of the patrons, a few women were there as well, including waitresses wearing peasant blouses and full, brightly colored skirts.

Eduardo crossed to the far end of the room and leaned against the bar, signaling to the bartender.

"*Negro Modelo*, he said. "*Y para tí …?*" Eduardo looked at me for my order.

"*Lo mismo*," I said, hoping my accent did him proud.

The bartender slapped a basket of peanuts down on the bar and wandered back to the beer cooler to grab our drinks. Looking around, I saw Eduardo had been right about one thing. Chava would have stood out here like a sore thumb. Between her clothes and her ash-blonde beehive, she would have been a beacon of whiteness and velour.

Lively music blasted, startling me, and I noticed a bright orange-and-yellow jukebox in the corner. A young, skinny guy bent over it, dropping in quarters and pushing buttons. The rapid-fire lyrics were too quick for me to translate in full, but the male voice appeared to be singing about a broken heart if I understood *mi corazón roto*.

Our vantage point at the end of the bar allowed us to monitor the front door, so we saw when the men entered the building. They sat at a table near the front and a waitress soon brought them menus, chips, and salsa. I guess the peanuts were just served to folks at the bar.

Eduardo dropped a ten-dollar bill when the bartender returned with our beers and waved off any change, walking over to the booth closest to the table the men had chosen, with me trailing along behind, carrying the peanuts.

The chips and salsa were excellent, and my mouth watered as I looked over the menu. Eating would make us blend in even more, right? It would look weird if we just sat here drinking our beer and eating chips and salsa and peanuts. I'd never had that combination before, but it was pretty darn good. We both placed orders when the waitress came back. Leaning back, Eduardo smiled at me, raising his beer.

"What should we drink to?" he asked.

"*La familia*," I said, without thinking about it, but it felt right when I did.

"To *la familia*," Eduardo said, clinking his bottle against mine. Then fell silent as we strained our ears to listen to the table next to ours. The music made eavesdropping difficult, and we were only catching a few words.

"We could just walk over and talk to them," I started to say, when the man whose face I hadn't seen yet shifted in his seat. Eduardo and I recognized him at the same time. It was Alejandro, the ranch hand from the Langston Ranch who we'd spoken to the previous day, along with Reyna, Johnny, Luis, and his brother Guillermo.

"Now what?" I said. "We think the two men from the church recognized *Fulano* and Alejandro knows them both. Was he lying about knowing the man in the sketch?"

"This is a question I believe we need answered," Eduardo said. "Perhaps we should go talk to them."

"I wish we had a better idea about who to trust here. If Dr. Varine was telling the truth, the people who know Gabriela don't want to report her missing, which might include Alejandro."

Eduardo nodded. "They are from a community that is trying not to draw attention to itself right now. They may think they are protecting her."

"So what do we do?" I asked.

"Those men from *el recinto* know Gabriela. Alejandro knows them. Maybe it's time to take a closer look at the Langston Ranch."

"That's what I'm thinking," I said. "Does this mean I get to use the fancy night-vision goggles again?"

"*Sí*," Eduardo said, amusement making his eyes sparkle. "You are enjoying the technology?"

"I am. I don't usually get to play with the expensive toys."

"I'm glad I could be of service," he said, bowing his head in an exaggerated gesture. "It's nice to work together, no?"

It was, but I hoped that didn't mean Eduardo was grooming me to take his spot with the mob when he retired.

"Should we reconnoiter first?" I asked, not letting my mind go to any ulterior motives Eduardo might have.

"I don't think they have security like *el doctor* has at *el recinto*."

"I don't either. Plus, I'm starting to worry about how long Gabriela has been missing. I thought it might only be days, but Dr. Varine said weeks. I'm afraid we're already looking for another murder victim."

The waitress arrived with our dinners and we kept an eye on the men at the other table. They paid little attention to their surroundings and we didn't worry that they would recognize us in our booth. The food was as good as we'd expected. I just hoped tonight wouldn't go sideways on us, making this my last meal.

Chapter Forty-Three

AFTER DINNER, WE got back to the resort and caught up with Chava, who'd struck out at the makeshift church. No one was there, and the sign on the door stated there was no mass on Friday nights.

Knowing we'd have another late night, I rested in the cabin, while Chava went over to get dinner.

I had just closed my eyes, when the phone rang and I looked down to see Chance's ID on the screen. My heart skipped a beat.

"What's up?" I said in the most nonchalant voice I could muster.

"Is this a bad time?" His voice was hesitant, not something I was used to where Chance was concerned.

"No, it's good."

"How's the vacation going?"

How should I answer that? I was guessing Chance had heard by now about at least some of the events. No doubt his partner Kate Jarek had told him about the phone call from Detective Campbell. Was he trying to find out if I was breaking any laws? Or concerned about my welfare?

"I'm probably not going to get photographed for any of the resort's brochures," I said, scrambling for time. "Especially with the bandage on my head." Humor usually works for me as a way to deflect.

"Yeah. I heard something about your experiences ..." his voice trailed off. I still couldn't get a gauge on what he was after.

"You heard about the fire."

"I did .... Look, I'm just calling to find out if you're all right."

"You are?"

Chance laughed. "Is that so hard to believe?"

Well ... yeah. He picked back up when I didn't respond.

"I hear from Kate a crazy story about you getting caught in a forest fire and trying to save a guy's life. It didn't occur to you I might be concerned about your welfare?"

Well ....

"I wasn't sure," I said. "Plus, I knew you were out of cellphone range."

"Eddie. You can be so dense sometimes."

Great.

"What's that supposed to mean?"

"It means ... I haven't forgotten what things used to be like between us."

Gulp.

"You haven't?"

"Of course not. I'm not the one who walked away."

True. Plus, he had shown up in Bellingham a few years later. I never thought our relationship might have played into that decision, but could he have moved, in part, to reconnect with me?

"It wasn't you I was leaving."

"Yes, Eddie, it was. Whatever else you might have been running from, I was the person you left behind."

He didn't sound angry, just resigned.

"I've missed you," I said.

There was a pause.

"So, are you all right?" he asked. "I heard you suffered from some burns and smoke inhalation and a long list of other unpleasant things."

Letting out a breath I didn't realize I'd been holding, I launched into details about my experiences.

When I wound down, I realized how good it felt to tell someone what I'd been through. I wanted to talk about more serious things, but I hated not being able to read body language. Phone conversations always make me feel like I don't know what is really going on.

"Are you back to work then?" I wasn't quite ready to end the call.

"It's all hands on deck for the march this weekend. Did you hear about it from Iz?"

I told him I had and that I was worried about her safety.

"Everything will be fine. Bellingham's finest will be out to keep the peace."

Great. Now I'd worry about Chance too.

"We talked about getting together when I get back," I said, finally getting up my nerve to broach the subject before our conversation ended. "Is that still a plan?"

"Sure," he said. There was a pause and I wished I could see the expression on his face. "What did you have in mind?"

How should I know? I was making this up as I went along. "A first date?"

Chance laughed. "We lived together. Don't you think it's a little late for a first date?"

"I think we've been apart long enough that we get a do-over," I said, holding my breath.

"Do you remember our first date?" he asked.

"Are you counting the baseball game?" Chance and my mentor Coop used to go to baseball games together. After I started working for Coop, I usually went with them. One night, I arrived to find Chance alone. Coop had given him some lame excuse for why he had to leave. We'd watched the Mariners lose to the Yankees and ended the night making out in my car.

"I did buy you a hot dog," he said. "So I'd call that a date."

"How about I take you to a game?" I said. "I'll buy the dogs this time."

"That might be fun," he said. "I'll check the home schedule."

I thought the call was over, but caught his final words just before he hung up.

"I've missed you too."

Chapter Forty-Four

A FTER MY CALL with Chance, I was too keyed up to rest anymore, so I went to see what Chava was up to. I found her finishing dinner. I sat down just as she signed off on the bill.

"Something's on your mind," she said after one look at my face.

"Want to sit out on the porch?" I asked rather than answer her question.

"Lead the way."

We walked out to the same spot where I'd been sitting when I called Iz. The night was quiet. The sounds from the restaurant around the corner were muted. We each sat down in one of the wooden rockers. It was fully dark out, and the hooting of an owl emphasized how far we were from city life.

"Could you live somewhere like this?" I asked her.

"Meaning at a resort?"

"Meaning on this side of the mountains. A more rural lifestyle."

"I don't know," Chava said. "I've never thought about it.

Moving to Bellingham felt like a big enough adjustment. Why? Are you thinking about living somewhere new?"

I rocked a little more before answering her.

"No. I'm not thinking about that, but I guess I'm thinking about forks in the road. Wondering if I've made wrong choices my whole life."

This time Chava rocked a few beats before responding. Her words, when they came, surprised me. " 'Two roads diverged in a yellow wood, and sorry I could not travel both, and be one traveler, long I stood, and looked down one as far as I could.' "

"Are you quoting poetry at me?"

Chava laughed, her genuine laugh, the one that tinkled like bells. The one I didn't hear very often. "I am."

"What's your point? That I should always take the road less traveled?"

"No. That's not what the poem's about."

"It isn't?"

"It's not the road less traveled, it's the road not taken. Those are two very different things."

"I'm not following you," I said, feeling adrift. Since when did Chava analyze the poems of Robert Frost?

"That poem is about the fact that the person at the crossroads realizes the two paths are interchangeable. Whatever road he takes is how his life will unfold. There's no mysterious destiny. At some point in the future he'll tell everyone 'I took the road less traveled' as a symbol of his bravery or individualism, but that's all an illusion."

"Is this supposed to make me feel better?"

"Are you feeling bad?"

That was an interesting question. Was I feeling bad?

"You always say I overthink things. Do you really believe that?"

"The fact we're having this conversation kind of proves my point," she said, albeit gently.

"I'm not sure what to believe about Chance. I'm apparently lousy at intimate relationships."

"Oh, sweetie. None of us are good at those. We're all just faking our way down the road and taking whatever fork seems like the right one at the time. Except ... it's more of a bend than a fork. The other road doesn't really exist."

I sighed. And rocked. And realized she was probably right. Before I could say anything else, Eduardo arrived.

"I thought I might find the two of you here," he said. "Can I sit with you?"

"We'd love that," Chava said.

"What are you two discussing?"

"That we have miles to go before we sleep," I said.

"On the road less traveled," Chava said.

"I thought it was 'not taken,' " Eduardo said. Then he just looked confused as Chava and I laughed.

"You are absolutely right," Chava said, reaching out and patting his hand. "So what's our plan for tonight?" she added, smoothly changing the subject. I sat back and listened to the sound of my father's voice, Chava carrying the conversation for me. I let thoughts of my past and future slip away and focused solely on the present. It seemed like the right thing to do at the time.

WE PARKED BACK at the same spot we'd used when we snuck onto Dr. Varine's property. Eduardo and I struck out once more through the trees with the aid of our fancy night-vision goggles, but this time we stopped much sooner. Arriving at the edge of the trees that skirted the Langston's pastureland, Eduardo removed his, so I did the same.

"We won't need these," he said, pointing out into the field. Though the moon wasn't full, there was enough light for us to see across the expanse.

"Don't you think someone will see us?"

"It's certainly possible. But at least here we aren't cutting through a chain-link fence, dodging security guards, or hiding from surveillance cameras."

Eduardo made trespassing sound so easy. I didn't remind him that the people who lived on the ranch were armed and probably very good shots. He didn't need me to tell him.

We stood for a while, listening to the sounds in the dark. Horses nickered and whinnied. A loud banging sound made me jump, but Eduardo reassured me it was just a horse kicking the side of its stall in the barn.

We noticed one of the trucks was missing from where they'd been parked before. Maybe no one was home? Or at least, not everyone. We decided to start with the barn closest to the driveway and snuck across the open area, coming up against the side farthest from the house. Pausing, we listened for the sound of someone announcing our presence, but the night remained quiet. The smell of hay mingled with the scent of horse manure and animal sweat, a combination I found surprisingly pleasant.

Slinking around the end of the barn, we came up on the giant rolling doors, which were closed. We continued past them and edged around the side of the barn that faced the Langston's home.

No one appeared to be awake. The sky was lit only by a pale quarter moon. No lights were on inside the house, but a very bright, ice cold, bluish light mounted on the barn, shined across the expanse between us and the other building. If anyone happened to look outside while we crossed the open land, they couldn't miss us.

Eduardo continued forward, pressed against the side of the barn, to the single door we'd seen during our previous visits. He tried the doorknob, only to find it locked. Kneeling down, he pulled something out of his pocket and there was a clicking sound before the door popped open. He was quicker with lock picks than I was.

He ducked through the open door, with me hot on his heels.

"It's strange that they lock their barn," Eduardo said after we got inside.

I didn't reply. He knew the habits of horse people better than I did.

Once in the barn, the animal smells got much stronger and I could hear nervous movement.

"Wait a moment," Eduardo said into my ear. My eyes began to adjust to the dim light inside the building and I could see him moving down among the horses. He murmured and they quieted down. A few minutes later, he arrived back at my side.

"What were you doing?" I asked.

"The horses don't know us, so they were nervous. I just introduced myself and let them know I wasn't going to hurt them." My father really was a horse whisperer. "Now, they will remain quiet while we take a look around."

Eduardo clicked on the red light clipped onto his CCFD hat. It was just bright enough to light up the area directly in front of him, but wouldn't impact our night vision. I turned mine on as well. The horses reached their heads over the tops of their paddock doors, eyes glowing, bottomless, but my father's magic seemed to work. They didn't appear bothered by our presence.

"Does this mean you vouched for me too?" I asked, nodding in the direction of the animals.

"*Sí, como no,*" my father said, reassuring me he had me covered. I still couldn't tell when he was joking.

We each took one half of the barn to investigate. I'd already gone through bins and bags and buckets without anything catching my interest when I noticed a door into a sectioned-off portion of the barn.

Opening the door, I flashed my light around enough to know there weren't any windows in the small room, so I searched for a light switch, finding it close to the door. Eduardo came up next to me on those silent feet of his. The two of us stepped in, closed the door, and I turned on the light.

There were neat shelves of containers and boxes on one wall of the room and rows of saddles on the other. On another wall, I observed what looked like a stack of colorful blankets and various leather straps with bits of metal hanging on hooks.

"Tack room," my father said.

"What are all these?" I asked, pointing at the shelves of various items, many of them bottles and plastic tubs.

"Bute, banamine, Mare Magic—these are all medicines and supplements for horses."

"Anything that doesn't belong?" I asked.

"Nothing obvious," Eduardo said. "But that doesn't mean there isn't something here." He began to look through the items on the shelves, opening various containers. Occasionally he would pause, giving a sniff—or even at one time, a taste— of the various powders and creams and liquids. But nothing raised a red flag.

Then I came upon a padlocked box underneath the pile of blankets. It was in a corner and too heavy to lift easily.

"Can you open this?" I asked. Eduardo took his fancy cutters out of his backpack. They were short enough to fit inside, but thick. I recognized them as the same ones he'd used to cut through the chain-link fence at the compound. They worked remarkably well and he had no trouble cutting off the lock. Opening up the box, we found glass vials, labeled HYDROMORPHONE.

"This is very interesting," Eduardo said, holding one of the bottles in his hand.

"What's hydromorphone?" I asked.

"An opioid."

"Is this something a horse owner would have?"

"*Sí*, it would be used on a horse in pain, recovering from an accident perhaps."

"Can a person use an equine opiate?"

"The drug doesn't know whether it is used on a horse or a person."

"Wouldn't it be dangerous? To use something designed for such a big animal?"

"Drug users would be unlikely to care."

"Do you think the Langstons are dealing in opioids?"

"This feels more like a personal stash," Eduardo said. "Mr. Langston is a man in pain. Perhaps he is medicating himself."

"Do you think it's enough to kill over?" I asked.

Eduardo said nothing, just tucked one of the vials into his backpack.

"Why not simply take a picture of the label?" I asked.

"It might be useful to have the contents analyzed," he said with a shrug.

Nice to have those kinds of resources. Maybe I *should* start working for the mob.

We'd gone through the rest of the tack room and found nothing else suspicious, so we put everything back where we found it and got ready to go.

When I picked up the cut-off lock and tucked it into my backpack, Eduardo looked at me quizzically. "They will wonder why the lock is off, but there's an offhand chance they'll think someone else did it. If they see it cut off, they will know for sure someone broke in."

"*Muy inteligente.*"

We switched off the light and turned the red lights on our caps back on, slipping out into the main section of the building.

"Time to head up to the other barn?" I asked as we crept out.

"There's one stop we need to make first."

"Where's that?"

"The horse trailers. Perhaps they are hiding something there."

From where we came out of the barn, it wasn't far to the open area on a spur from the driveway where the Langstons parked their trailers. I'd noticed them when we came the other day, but had not paid a lot of attention. There were three of varying sizes. The first looked to hold only one or two animals, the second about four, and the last had room for at least six. Eduardo and I each took one of the smaller vehicles, planning to meet up at the back of the big one. I looked through the smallest trailer, but found nothing. Eduardo walked up, shaking his head; he hadn't found anything suspicious either.

The back doors on the big trailer, which opened into the holding area for the horses, had latches but no locks. Eduardo twisted the handles and opened one door, stepping up with me on his heels. Once inside the back, we could see it was a huge space, and very clean. There were some shavings on the ground in neat piles and moveable dividers to separate the animals, but other than that, the floors where the horses would stand were clear. No place to hide anything.

After going over the inside of the trailer, we climbed back out and walked up to the door on the side.

"This one has an extra lock," I said, tugging on the padlock.

"That in itself is interesting," Eduardo said, taking his cutters back out. "It's possible they lock it because they keep expensive saddles or other things, but it seems excessive, given there is also a lock built into the door." Eduardo made fast work of the padlock, which went into my backpack. It was getting less and less likely the Langstons or their employees wouldn't notice someone had been poking around. Eduardo pulled a set of lock picks out and handed them over to me with a grin. "Would you like to do the honors?"

I was very proud to have the door open in record time.

We stepped up into the trailer and looked around. There was a bunk built in and a small kitchen area. The trailer was designed for both horses and riders to be gone longer than a day.

"There's one last place," Eduardo said as we closed the trailer door behind us. "I believe there is a pull-out drawer for hay storage," he said. "Based on the section here." He gestured toward a space about three feet by three feet square that ran under where the bunk was inside. Kneeling down, I could see another built-in lock, which I successfully picked, though it did take me a little longer than the door. I told myself I wasn't used to having an audience for my questionable behavior.

It rolled open very quietly, the sweet smell of hay coming up out of the space. Eduardo reached in. "This is interesting," he said.

"What's that?"

"This hay. It's as if it was put in sideways. The flakes are horizontal. They should be vertical."

I had no idea what he was talking about, but he was the expert.

Reaching in, he lifted up an armful of hay. I could see it came out in a dense section even though it wasn't tied together—that must be a flake. Leaning over from the other side, I looked down and found a layer of the glass vials we'd seen in the tack room, laid out on top of the remaining hay.

Eduardo let out a low whistle. "So that's how they are transporting the drugs," he said.

"Every time they transport a horse, they can drive around with these," I said.

"No reason for anyone to get suspicious. Even a drug dog would miss them, as they would be unlikely to be taught this smell."

Drug dogs have to be taught individual smells. This was an area of police investigation I knew little about, but I'd started to do some research. Now that I had Franklin, who exhibited signs someone might have trained him as a cadaver dog, I wanted to learn more about how dogs could be used.

"Glass is also the most impermeable substance, so the scent would be well-contained," he said.

I thought about why my father might know what a drug dog could or couldn't identify.

"Okay," I said, dismissing thoughts about my father's areas of expertise, "so we can guess what they are up to around here.

Maybe now is the time to get this information to Detective Campbell and let her deal with it."

As we stood there contemplating what to do next, we heard a scream.

Chapter Forty-Five

————◆————

"THAT SOUNDED LIKE it came from the other barn up on the hill," I said, tucking back down behind the trailer and peering out into the dark.

Eduardo and I waited, but we heard nothing more except the rustle of a light breeze and an occasional snort, whinny, and nicker from the animals.

"We should go check," I said just as the barn door slid open. A moment later the outline of someone on a horse shot out. We could see the rider had something slung over the saddle in front. Something the size and shape of a person.

Eduardo sped out from behind the trailer, but the horse was quicker and headed away from us off the ranch. The pounding of hooves blocked out any sound of us running behind.

"Do you think that's our missing Gabriela?" I asked, stopping to catch my breath. "Or is she the one doing the riding?"

Eduardo said nothing, just turned and ran back the way we came.

"What are you doing?" I asked, rushing to keep up with Eduardo, who raced toward the barn we'd already searched.

"You get on the phone to Chava and the police. I am going to follow that rider."

"Follow? How?"

By this time, we'd reached the barn and Eduardo flipped on the lights. Stealth was no longer our concern.

"On a horse, of course," he said.

I don't think he noticed he sounded like Dr. Seuss.

Pulling out my phone, I called Chava, who sat parked back on the dirt road where we'd left her. I filled her in on the situation while watching Eduardo. He went into the tack room and came back out with a bridle. Then he walked past each horse in the barn, speaking softly as he went. Apparently one of them spoke back, because he went into a stall and came out with a tall, brown horse with a black mane and tail.

"What about a saddle?" I asked as Eduardo began to lead the animal out of the barn.

"Not enough time," he said. "Whoever that was doesn't know we're behind them, so they aren't concerned about us following, but they still have a head start."

With that, Eduardo launched himself onto the horse's back and the two shapes merged into one as he sped off up the driveway after our nighttime rider.

I guess if I wanted to keep up with Eduardo, I'd have to learn how to ride a horse. Bareback. In the dark.

"What's happening? What's going on?" Chava's voice over my cellphone pulled me back. I explained what we'd seen and what Eduardo had done and told her to call Detective Campbell to tell her the mystery rider, with Eduardo following, appeared to be heading up the forest road across the street from the ranch.

"But don't tell her we started at the ranch. I don't want her to know we were wandering around on private property. I'm going to be in enough trouble as it is. Tell her we saw this from the road, and make sure you come and park the car somewhere that will support our story."

"I'll be there as soon as I can," Chava said.

Ending the call, I remembered something I'd seen the last time we visited. I just hoped it would help.

Chapter Forty-Six

———◆———

THE THREE-WHEELERS WERE parked in one corner of the
barn. Hopping on the closest one, I found the key in the
ignition. I rocked it back and forth and confirmed it was full of
fuel. Looking around to see if there was any kind of weapon to
take with me, I discovered the rifle propped up in the corner.
Probably the one Reyna mentioned they used for rattlesnakes.
I checked to make sure it was loaded.

With the rifle strapped across my back, I climbed up onto
the machine, started it up, and rolled out of the barn, down the
hill, and up the fire road, hoping I would be able to see which
direction the two horses had gone.

The headlight on the three-wheeler lit up the ground enough
that I could see hoof prints in the dirt. Racing up the fire road,
I remembered the big ditch just in time to keep from pitching
myself into it. Carefully navigating through, I slowed down,
looking for where the horses might have gone off the road. I
passed the area where we'd gone off toward the fire and the
meadow where I'd found *Fulano*. About a mile farther up the
fire road, I could see recent hoof prints heading into the woods.

I turned off onto what looked like an animal trail, hoping it wouldn't get too narrow for the back tires of my three-wheeler. Stopping, I used my jacket tied to a tree as a marker. If my luck held, Chava and the authorities would see it and recognize it as the place to turn. Even if I'd had the time to call and leave directions, my cell service had dropped out.

Continuing slowly on the uneven terrain, I thought briefly of trying to maintain a stealthier approach on whatever waited for me, but there was nothing I could do about the loudness of an off-road vehicle.

A few minutes later, the trail had become too tight for a three-wheeler to pass. I shut off the engine and listened. There were voices ahead of me, shouting. The wind had also picked up, blowing into my face. Perhaps no one had heard me drive up.

Creeping down the trail, I soon recognized Eduardo calling for someone else to give up. The sky was growing brighter, as I came out in another small open area. At one end, both horses were standing together eating. In the middle, two men faced each other about thirty feet apart.

Eduardo stood closest to me, his back turned. Johnny Langston stood behind a large rock, with the object he'd carried slung over the horse balanced in front of him like a living shield. At least, I hoped whoever it was still lived. If it was Gabriela, I had yet to see her move. Or was it the corpse of *Fulano*? Had Johnny been hiding him in the barn?

"The police are on their way," Eduardo said. "You aren't going to get away with what you've done."

"I'll just kill you and hide you too," Johnny said, though I heard the note of desperation in his voice.

"Like you did the man in the meadow?" Eduardo said. "It was you, wasn't it? Who was hiding in the woods on your horse? Waiting for us to go so you could get rid of his body?"

"You just had to come back up here …. Why couldn't you all just leave it alone?"

"You'll be arrested and tried for three murders," Eduardo

continued. "Is that what you want for your daughter? To see her father executed?"

"Washington never executes anyone," Johnny said. "Besides, with you gone, there's no proof for any of this."

"You are assuming I won't shoot you first," Eduardo said, and I knew he had that big Desert Eagle pointed at Johnny.

"Except," Johnny said, holding his gun against the figure in front of him, "you aren't sure if she's still alive, and you might just miss me and hit her. Do you want that on your conscience?"

He said "she," so I assumed it was Gabriela balanced on the rock. As long as she might be alive, Eduardo wouldn't risk Johnny shooting her. Though Johnny must have brought her here to kill her, it didn't mean she was already dead.

Moving slowly through the trees, I worked my way around to get a clean shot at Johnny. Maybe we could still talk him out of whatever he planned to do. Then Gabriela, or whoever was wrapped in the canvas, moved. She was still alive, and it was up to me to keep her that way.

Chapter Forty-Seven

——◆——

JOHNNY FALTERED WHEN a moan escaped from the person on the rock. Either he'd thought she was already dead or that she wasn't going to regain consciousness so quickly, because the sound seemed to surprise him as well.

"I don't think you're really a killer," Eduardo said. "I have known many in my time, and you are not one. I believe the first one was an accident. You didn't mean to hurt the man."

"You know me so well?" Johnny said. "You don't know anything, my friend."

"The man we found, he wasn't burned. I think you tried to save him, by moving him out of range of the fire."

Johnny fell silent. Had Eduardo gotten that right?

"I had no idea the tent would burn so fast," Johnny said. "It just went up like a … a … inferno."

"You went back and tried to help…" Eduardo prompted Johnny to keep talking. I guessed this served multiple purposes. It might keep Johnny from killing Gabriela, plus it gave me time to get into a better position.

"At first I wasn't going to," Johnny said. "I was just going to leave him there. But I couldn't let him die that way. I circled around on my horse and went in after him. That palomino of mine will go anywhere I ask him to. I got ahold of the man, but he was already dead. I left him there, in the ravine. To come back for later."

"Then you went back to move him again, in case the Forest Service came across him during their investigation. But you found us instead."

"I heard you all coming down the ravine and hid until you left, then dragged him onto my horse and moved him where no one will ever find him."

"You have been holding Gabriela a long time without killing her. I don't think you want to."

"You're pushing my hand," Johnny said, his voice a little stronger. He stuck his gun a little harder against the figure in front of him. "Now you just back out of here and let this go, or I'll shoot her, and it will be your fault."

"Why would I leave?" Eduardo said. "You are going to kill her anyway. And me too, if you can. I assume you brought her out here to bury, now that you know we are getting too close to you."

Johnny crouched down behind the form. If he really was disabled from his accident, he had to be in a lot of pain by now. He'd carried the body, ridden on the horse, and was trying to hold onto a gun. Even if he was doping himself with hydromorphone, maybe we could just wait it out and he'd drop the weapon.

"I should just shoot you," Johnny said.

"Do you want to know what I think happened?" Eduardo said, his own gun never wavering, its barrel pointed toward Johnny as if he hadn't just threatened him.

"Not really," Johnny said.

"I think Gabriela discovered your drug sales. Perhaps she worked for you too and saw something she shouldn't. You panicked and grabbed her, but you couldn't kill her, so you just kept her locked up. How am I doing so far?"

Langston said nothing, so I guess Eduardo was doing pretty good.

"You told your workers she'd gone back to Mexico, and they believed you."

"You're just guessing."

"Then her father came looking for her."

"How was I supposed to know he'd come all the way from Mexico?" Johnny said, his voice pitiful, as if a man worrying about his own daughter was an inconvenience.

"You discovered she had given something to him, before you grabbed her up. And you knew you had to get that item back."

"She'd written him a letter. Telling him everything," Johnny said. "I had to get that letter."

"So you followed him—"

"I never followed him. I knew where he was. I told him Gabriela liked to go hiking in the woods and she must have fallen; that's the way I explained how she'd gone missing. I told him she was confused about the drug sales. That she'd disappeared on her own, nothing to do with me. He was camping out there to search for her. That's what I thought he was doing when I arrived at his campsite. He was in this country illegally, so I knew he wasn't going to rush to the police, to report any of this. But I had to get the letter back. With no letter, it would just be his word against mine."

"It was an accident, wasn't it, when you hit him in the side of the head."

Johnny was quiet so long I thought he wasn't going to answer. He might not want to admit the truth.

"He surprised me," Johnny said. "I thought he was gone when I searched his camp."

"The police will understand," Eduardo said. "They will have mercy."

"I had no idea it would burn so fast. I wasn't thinking clearly. I found the letters, the ones Gabriela had sent her father, but they were written in Spanish, so I didn't know which ones would incriminate me. I only knew she'd told him what I was doing. So I put them all in a pan he had in the tent and set fire to them. But the flames went higher than I expected, and the breeze came through and pushed some of the burning paper out of the pan. I tried to put it out."

That must have been the rustling I'd heard in the tent, Johnny trying to put the fire out but hampered by his lack of mobility. Though he could be lying. Perhaps he'd set the fire deliberately to cover his crimes but didn't want anyone to know.

"We can explain all this to the police."

"No, *you* don't understand," Johnny said. "That man died while I was committing other crimes. That makes it felony murder, whether I intended it or not. And I am not going to jail because some stupid border bunny stuck her nose where it didn't belong."

That's when I smelled smoke.

"Looks like it's too late for all of us now," Johnny laughed.

"What did you do?" Eduardo asked, stepping closer.

"I'm not going to leave any evidence this time."

He'd started another fire. A cloud of smoke rolled over him. Then I heard a muffled shot. Had Johnny just killed Gabriela? Right in front of me? Or fired at Eduardo?

"Eddie, no!" my father yelled as I broke out of the trees and streaked toward the rock.

There was no way Johnny was sticking around now, but I wasn't going to telegraph where I was hidden in the smoke, so I said nothing. Tripping over the still form, which had rolled onto the ground, I grabbed on and hauled, dragging the body out of the fire. Johnny was nowhere to be seen.

Eduardo appeared next to me. "We've got to get the flames out," I said. He began stamping on the ground as I unwrapped the motionless form. After unwrapping the canvas and finding the woman from the photo, I searched her for a pulse and found that she was breathing. Whatever Johnny had fired at, it wasn't Gabriela. There was no way he would have missed. Had Eduardo really tried to shoot the man?

Leaving her long enough to help Eduardo, we managed to extinguish the flames.

"Where would Johnny go?" I asked, looking around for the horses. They both stood at the far end of the clearing. Johnny couldn't have gotten far. Eduardo and I fanned out, looking for him.

Eduardo found him first. "It's over, Mr. Langston," I heard him say. "Put the gun down." Johnny sat with his back resting against another rock, blood pouring from a wound in his leg. Eduardo must have shot him. We were the only ones out here.

Johnny didn't see me, but he fixed his eyes on Eduardo, who stood not far away. Johnny started to raise his gun toward Eduardo.

Everything became very clear, as if my eyesight improved a thousandfold in that instant. My extremities got cold and my hand shook.

But I knew what I had to do.

"Hey, Johnny," I called out, everything now in slow motion. The arm with the gun lurched in my direction. I fired. Johnny slumped to the ground.

The horses bolted as the earsplitting gunshot sent an entire flock of ravens streaking into the air above the trees, the woods exploding in a flurry of black wings.

Eduardo and I both rushed forward. We turned Johnny over, looking for where my bullet had pierced him.

The bullet had gone through his right shoulder, just under the collarbone, and I worked quickly to staunch the blood pouring from the wound.

"How is she?" I asked, as I pulled off my sweatshirt and pressed it against the wound. Eduardo went back over to Gabriela's side.

"She is alive and coming around," Eduardo called out. "How's he?"

"Goddamn that hurts," Johnny muttered, his breath coming in short gasps as he struggled to take in air. I suspected he had a collapsed lung.

"He might survive if we get him help," I said. "One of us should try to call Chava again and get the medics in here by helicopter." Eduardo put his belt around Johnny's leg, to slow the bleeding from that wound.

"I'll ride out until I can get cell service," Eduardo said. He pointed to the horses, who had only gone as far as the end of the meadow and were foraging again.

"Hurry," I said, knowing my arms would start to fatigue. If I didn't keep the pressure on Johnny's wound, he would bleed out quickly. As Eduardo left, I could see the ravens had returned and watched us from the trees.

Chapter Forty-Eight

———•———

EDUARDO DIRECTED THE helicopter to our location. He'd already secured the horses. The blast of air under the rotors hit me like a cyclone, and I crushed Johnny's body under mine to protect him from the dirt and leaves and everything else the windstorm rained down on us. One medical team leaped from the chopper to work on Johnny in the field. They had to pull me off him; my hands had cramped against his chest in my efforts to keep more blood inside him than what stained the earth red beneath us.

Another team worked on Gabriela. I could see an IV hooked to her arm, which looked as thin and frail as a child's. Eduardo and I managed to talk to her for a moment after she was stabilized and both teams worked on Johnny.

Gabriela told us her name was Gabriela Del Toro. We described *Fulano* to her and she burst into tears. Incoherent with grief, she couldn't tell us anything else now. We'd have to hope she recovered and we could learn more at the hospital. I pressed the rosary into her hand before she was loaded into the helicopter. Perhaps it would bring her some comfort.

Eduardo and I looked at each other after the helicopter lifted off.

"The bullet is still in Johnny's leg," I said. "We should get rid of your gun."

"I didn't shoot him," Eduardo said. "I thought you did."

Another shooter? Who was left?

"Who else has the most to lose?" I said, musing out loud.

My father and I spoke at the same time.

"Luis," my father said, just as I said, "Reyna."

"It has to be," I said. "She and her father were working together."

"It could also be Luis. He is the heir apparent. He travels with Johnny; he could be part of the drug deals."

My father was right—either one could be our shooter.

First things first. Eduardo went off to hide his weapon, our night-vision goggles, the vial of hydromorphone, and all the other paraphernalia that would be difficult to explain when Detective Campbell arrived.

Not long after Eduardo returned, Chava showed up, huffing and puffing from her half walk half sprint up the Forest Service road.

"I found your marker and the three-wheeler," Chava said, plopping down next to me to catch her breath. "But I left them for Detective Campbell."

"Good," I said. Eduardo came over, and the three of us put our story together. It went something like this.

Our own investigation had made us suspicious of the Langstons. Without more proof, we'd decided to simply watch the farm. We didn't go onto the Langston property until Johnny rode out in the middle of the night with his mysterious bundle, visible to us because we were parked nearby. At that point, Eduardo had gone onto the Langston property and commandeered a horse. I'd grabbed the three-wheeler and the rifle and followed after.

As far as what happened in the field, it was clearly self-defense. Not only was Johnny holding Gabriela hostage, but he'd admitted to killing her father and had been pointing a gun at Eduardo. When I'd come forward trying to talk sense into him, he'd swung the gun toward me.

Fearing for my life, I'd shot him. Which was true, even if I'd made him do it. It would keep me from a manslaughter charge if the man died. The medics hadn't said whether he would make it before they loaded him on the helicopter, though he'd been alive when they left.

"What do we do about the other two?" I said, looking at Eduardo. "Either Luis or Reyna must have shot Johnny in the leg. Who else could it be?"

Chava wanted to go down and singlehandedly stop whoever it was from destroying evidence, even if it did jeopardize the shaky legal ground we stood on or put us in harm's way.

"They should pay for what they've done," Chava said. "Whichever one it is."

"We saved Gabriela; now our duty is to Eddie," my father said. "Our job is not apprehending a criminal. I'm not going to do something that will get Eddie arrested or make her lose her license."

"Don't you tell me how to protect my daughter," Chava said, eyes flashing, fists clenched.

"*Our* daughter," Eduardo said.

"Stop," I said, before this got any worse. "You're both right. But we are not running down to the ranch. That shooter is armed and dangerous and desperate. But the ranch is going to get searched. It's where Gabriela was held. Let Detective Campbell do her job."

Eduardo and Chava dropped their defensive postures, then looked at each other with something like affection. Chava spoke first.

"Our girl is pretty smart."

"She takes after her mother," Eduardo said.

* * *

DETECTIVE CAMPBELL ARRIVED and took our statements. Eduardo handed over Johnny's Smith & Wesson SW 1911, which he'd secured before he hid our stuff in the woods. Then the detective sent us down to Wenatchee with a couple of deputies.

"The horses—" my father started to say.

"Will be taken care of," Detective Campbell said. "We do know how to do our jobs, no matter how much you three don't want to admit that."

Walking out, we found my coat had already been put into an evidence bag and another CSI was checking the three-wheeler. My fingerprints on the ORV made me even more confident we'd done the right thing by admitting I was the one who shot Johnny in the field.

Getting down to the road, we discovered fire trucks and other emergency vehicles.

"What happened here?" I asked one of our deputy escorts.

"Someone set fire to the barn on the hill."

Chapter Forty-Nine

—◆—

AFTER BEING INTERROGATED for several hours, Chava, Eduardo, and I were all let go. It didn't appear that any charges were going to be made against me, but Eduardo promised an excellent lawyer if there were. By the time I was released—the last of our little crew to be set free—Chava and Eduardo had gotten her Mazda back and were waiting for me in the parking lot.

Chava rushed to my side and pulled me into an embrace. "I'm so glad you're all right."

And not under arrest.

"Let's make one more visit to the Langston Ranch," I said after Chava let go. "The pieces have started to fall into place."

"Won't the sheriff have made their arrests?" Chava asked. "Will there be anyone there?"

"The house will have been searched for anyone else in danger or need of medical help, but whether it's been searched for evidence depends on whether they've gotten a warrant. Everyone living or working on the property will be under suspicion, but it doesn't mean arrests have been made. The sheriff needs to build a case about the drug dealing, the murder of Gabriela's father, and the abduction of Gabriela. Things don't move as fast as *Law & Order* would have you believe. The barn is a crime scene, but the house may not be."

"Let's go see what has risen from the ashes," Eduardo said, and Chava put the car in gear.

THE RANCH LAY quiet in the late afternoon sun. The barn on the rise was blackened. Part of the roof had collapsed, and yellow crime tape covered the entrance. Luckily it hadn't housed any horses at the time of the fire. The horses were only kept in the barn closer to the house. The one Eduardo and I had searched. I wondered if that was by design, so no one had any reason to go into the location where Gabriela had been held. The area around it was untouched, and the rest of the place looked exactly the same. Even the big palomino rushed to greet us, running along the fence as we pulled up in front of the house. A deputy sat parked in the driveway, but he didn't prevent us from walking up to the front door.

Reyna came out on the porch. She didn't seem too happy to see us, her expression wary. "What do you want?" she asked.

"To ask you a few questions," I said.

"I'm not interested in talking to you."

"I don't doubt that," I said. "How about you just listen? I'll tell you a story, and you tell me if I've got it wrong."

Reyna said nothing, which I took as the closest thing I'd get to a yes.

"You're romantically involved with one of the security guards next door."

That took her by surprise, though she said nothing.

"Gabriela did housekeeping for you, and when Dr. Varine was looking for help, his security guard asked you for a recommendation."

With Gabriela alive, there was no use in disputing that. Reyna looked out at the pasture in front of her, but she didn't stop listening. Maybe the burden had become too much. Her eyes focused on a car turning into her property. I recognized Detective Campbell's SUV, and we all waited in silence until she parked next to her deputy and walked over to where we stood.

"Why am I not surprised to find you here?" Detective Campbell said to me. "I should have added this address to the list of places you can't go."

"I was just getting a few last facts straight from Reyna here."

Detective Campbell looked back and forth between the young woman and me. I expected her to kick me off the property, but she waited, so I turned back to Reyna.

"After Gabriela disappeared, the security guard you're sleeping with asked you if you knew what had happened. You're the one who told him she'd gone back to Mexico. You probably went down to where she lives and cleared out some of her stuff. To make it look like she did."

Detective Campbell didn't seem surprised. Something told me she already knew this part of the story.

"You are the one who grabbed Gabriela," I continued. "After she discovered your father was dealing drugs from the ranch. You'd do anything to protect this place."

"You can't prove that," she said.

"I don't have to," I said. "Detective Campbell will."

We all turned to look at the sheriff's detective.

I waited to hear what the charges would be. I knew Detective Campbell would eventually prove Reyna had committed the murder. It was Reyna who hit Gabriela's father over the head, leaving him to die in the mountains, though I anticipated the murder charges would come later, after the detective had gathered all the evidence against the woman. Johnny had gone looking for the letters and set the fire, but it was his daughter who had caused the man's death. He'd said he thought the man was out searching for his daughter when he arrived at the campsite. I believed that was true. He didn't know the man was lying unconscious in the field until after the fire had started. While he had been prepared to get rid of Gabriela on his daughter's behalf, things had changed.

"Reyna Langston, you are under arrest for the abduction of Gabriela Del Toro."

"Wait, what?" Reyna looked shocked.

"Anything you say can and will be used against you in a court of law."

"But my father admitted to the abduction."

Detective Campbell continued giving Reyna her Miranda warning.

My parents and I waited until Reyna had been put into the back of the deputy's car for transport down to Wenatchee. Luis had walked up and stood watching as well. Detective Campbell turned to the four of us.

"I hope this means you're going back to Bellingham," she said, looking at me.

"Johnny sold his daughter out?" I asked.

"He did," Detective Campbell said.

I hazarded another guess. "He discovered it was his daughter who shot him. The bullet in his leg matched a rifle you found on the ranch."

Detective Campbell said nothing, so I continued. "I'm betting you'll be adding charges about the death of Gabriela's father, right?"

Detective Campbell looked at Luis and back to me, her face giving nothing away.

Johnny hadn't known *Fulano* had been hit in the back of the head, and he would have if he'd done it. Eduardo had said the man had been hit in the side of the head and Johnny didn't notice. Adding that to his belief that the man hadn't been there when he searched for the letters and his hesitation about telling his side of events, I believed he was just trying to protect his daughter. Until he learned how far she would go to save herself. The truth would come out, of that I had no doubt.

"What's going to happen out here?" I said, with a gesture toward the horses in the pasture.

Luis said, "The farm is in rough shape. Johnny borrowed heavily against the land and it's going into foreclosure. I am going to try to buy it from the bank."

I looked at Detective Campbell. Had Luis been involved in the drug trade? Her face still gave nothing away.

"I have an alibi for when Johnny was shot," Luis said, reading my disbelief. "And I wasn't here when the fire was set."

He wasn't under arrest; he might be telling the truth. Someone had to care for the horses. If Luis wasn't guilty of a crime, who else would it be?

"I hope you can," I said to Luis. To the detective, I said, "Yes. We'll be heading home in the morning. You know how to reach me if you need to."

Back in the car, Chava turned to me.

"How did you know about Reyna and the security guard?" she asked.

"I wasn't completely sure, but it made sense. The guards were hiding something, but I didn't think they were involved in Gabriela's disappearance. Someone recommended Gabriela to Dr. Varine, and I figured it had to be someone who lived out here. Gabriela didn't clean at the resort, because Chava had asked about her there, and no one recognized her. That left the people here at the ranch. I doubted Johnny Langston would have paid attention to a housekeeper, let alone known her name. Lastly, there was the cake."

"The cake?" Chava asked. "What cake?"

"When Reyna talked about the "strange" people who moved in next door, she said the Dr. Varine didn't even thank her for the cake. Gabriela had been gone for weeks, and Dr. Varine didn't cook. Yet there was a homemade cake in Tupperware on the counter. I figured Reyna lied about her interactions with them. I think she's taken plenty of cakes next door. Dr. Varine just doesn't know where they came from. The security guard wasn't going to admit he was seeing her—it might jeopardize his job. I think they've had some rendezvous on the property.

That was the three-wheeler you heard, Chava. Reyna was visiting her boyfriend. When Reyna talked to us, she thought she'd throw suspicion on Dr. Varine. She probably has no idea what he's really doing over there. She hoped to sidetrack us until she could scare us away by other means."

I didn't tell my parents about the sound of the rattlesnake or the laser sight, which I was sure Reyna had used to scare me into leaving.

"Plus," I said, "she was the one who set fire to the barn. Johnny didn't do it, and Luis wasn't home. She wanted to destroy any evidence from where Gabriela was held. Which means she knew about it to begin with."

"Had you figured all that out?" Chava asked Eduardo.

"I didn't trust her," he admitted, "but I didn't catch the bit about the cake."

I'd missed her lying to us in our earlier conversations. I guess I wasn't as good at reading deception as I thought. But I'd impressed Eduardo with that final detail. That was worth something.

"What now?" Chava asked. "Is it time to go home to Bellingham?"

"First I think we should see if Gabriela can have visitors," I said. "I'd like to piece together the rest of the story, and we have one more item to give her."

GABRIELA WAS IN a private room. Her injuries were not life-threatening. She suffered from dehydration and starvation. She'd been fed during her ordeal, but not very well. It would take a while for her to recover from all the drugs pumped into her by her captors. The knock she'd taken on her head had caused a mild concussion, but nothing serious. She should make a full recovery and agreed to see us.

"Thank you for letting us visit," I said as I pulled up a chair to sit next to her in her hospital bed.

"No, I'm glad you are here. I wanted to say thank you. If you hadn't been there, I would have ended up like—" her words were cut off by a sob.

"I'm so sorry about your father," Chava said. She stood behind me, hands on my shoulders, while Eduardo leaned against the wall.

"Thank you for this." Gabriela held up the rosary. "How did you get it?"

I explained about my job as a private investigator and told her the story of finding her father—how his last words had been about her.

"He just wanted you to be safe," I said. "He loved you very much."

Gabriela's tears shook her body, and Chava went over and placed her arm around the woman's shoulders until she regained her composure.

"There is something else we found with your father," I said, gesturing to Eduardo. He pulled the Purple Heart out of his pocket and handed it over. "Did this belong to him?"

"Yes. He earned it. He was a soldier in Iraq and Afghanistan."

"Why didn't your father report you missing to the police?" I asked. "We thought he didn't because he was here illegally."

"He was here illegally. My father lived in this country many years. He worked hard, but didn't have a green card. He went into the military to help get citizenship. He thought he had done everything he needed to do, but he missed some paperwork. He had trouble holding down a job after serving in combat. He made mistakes. He got caught forging a check. He served his time in jail, but was deported. He's been living in Tijuana, working with an organization to try to get citizenship or at least his veteran's benefits."

"But you are here legally?"

"Yes. Only my father was sent back."

"That doesn't seem fair," Chava said. "He served honorably in the military and he did his time for a minor, nonviolent crime."

Gabriela looked at her, a sad smile on her face. "Nothing about any of this has been fair."

That brought the conversation back to the events that led us here, a natural segue for me to question her.

"You discovered drugs were being sold through the Langston Ranch?"

Gabriela nodded. "I've explained all that to the police."

"Did you know if Reyna was involved?"

Gabriela shook her head. "I have no idea. I never thought any of this would happen. I was trying to do what Justino," she paused a moment, choking back a tear, "what my father, Justino, would have done. The honorable thing. And for that he died."

My parents and I did what we could to reassure her, but our words would never be enough. Her situation was tragic. She and her father had both tried to do the right thing. His mistakes didn't warrant the cost he paid.

We left her with the rosary clutched in one hand and the Purple Heart clutched in the other.

TURNING INTO THE resort, I felt a sense of satisfaction. I'd done my duty to Justino. I'd found his daughter and identified him. Reyna and her father would duke it out in court, each blaming the other, but I had faith the detectives would figure out who was guilty of which crime and the legal system would run its course. They would both pay for what they had done.

We decided to spend one last night at the resort and head for home in the morning. I had dinner with my parents and Debbie. We spoke only a little about the events that had put us in danger, though we filled Debbie in on the basics. Mostly we just enjoyed each other's company.

After dinner, Chava and I were walking back to our cabin with Franklin, when Eduardo stopped us.

"I'd like a moment with our daughter," he said. Chava nodded and went ahead alone.

"*Mija*," he said, "after everything we have been through, there is something I want to give you. Something that has brought me great comfort over the years. But I will need to explain—it does not symbolize what you will think."

He held out his hand. Dangling from his fingers was an icon on a chain, similar to a rosary but without a crucifix. I studied the medallion. A skeleton, dressed in robes, with a scythe in her hand.

"What does she symbolize?"

Surely my father wasn't giving me something to represent death at a time like this.

"Santa Muerte," he said. "She is a folk saint and very old."

"Who does she protect?"

My father folded my fingers around the dainty figure. "She protects criminals … as well as people who live with danger, like police officers. This, I believe, should also make her the patron saint of private investigators."

The metal was warm in my hand.

"*Gracias, papi*," I said. Eduardo smiled at the endearment as he pulled me into a hug.

EDUARDO WALKED ME to the door, where we found Chava standing in the doorway, waiting. She waved goodnight to him as she ushered me inside.

Tucked into bed that night, with Franklin at my feet, I felt Santa Muerte against my skin. I wore her around my neck, a reminder of everyone I held dear. Debbie, Iz, my parents, and Chance. Always it had been Chance. And I would see him soon, so I could tell that to him. I hoped he felt the same.

For now, my heart pointed north, as if it knew the way home.

Photo by Mark Perlstein

ELENA HARTWELL STARTED out her storytelling career in the theater. She worked for several years as a playwright, director, designer, technician, and educator before becoming a novelist.

She lives in North Bend, Washington, with her husband, their trio of cats, and the greatest dog in the world. When she's not writing, teaching writing, or talking about writing, she can be found at a farm down the road where she and her husband keep their horses.

For more information about Elena, please visit: www.elenahartwell.com.

You can also follow her on Facebook, Twitter, Instagram, Pinterest, and Tumblr.

An Eddie Shoes Mystery, #1-2

One Dead, Two to Go

Available in 5x8 trade paperback, multiple eBook formats, and audiobook

PI Eddie Shoes photographs her client's husband in a seedy hotel with his girlfriend. It should be an easy case, but the girlfriend is killed and the client goes missing. Is Kendra in danger or is she the killer? Not usually one to carry a gun, Eddie is soon dusting off her Colt 45. To complicate matters, her rowdy mother shows up on her doorstep, and her ex is the new homicide detective in town.

Two Heads Are Deader Than One

Available in 5x8 trade paperback, multiple eBook formats, and audiobook

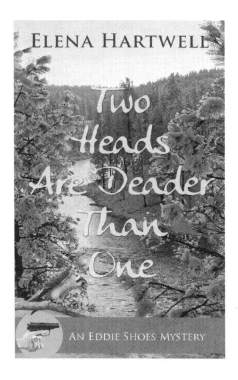

Dakota, PI Eddie Shoes' best friend from high school in Spokane, has surfaced in a Bellingham jail. Eddie covers her bail, but as soon as her friend is free, she disappears. Why did Dakota jump bail? And what are Eddie's business cards doing on the bodies of two murder victims? To find answers and clear her own name, Eddie must dig into the past.

From Camel Press and Elena Hartwell

T HANK YOU FOR reading *Three Strikes, You're Dead*. We are so grateful for you, our readers. If you enjoyed this book, here are some steps you can take that could help contribute to its success and let you stay in touch with the Eddie Shoes series:

- Please think about posting a short review on Amazon, BN.com, and GoodReads.
- Check out Elena's website and join her mailing list at www.ElenaHartwell.com.
- Spread the word on social media, especially Facebook, Twitter, and Pinterest.
- "Like" Elena's author Facebook page: www.facebook.com/Elena.Hartwell and the Camel Press page: www.facebook.com/CamelPressBooks.
- Follow Elena (@Elena_Hartwell) and Camel Press (@camelpressbooks) on Twitter.
- Ask for your local library to carry this book and others in the series or request them on their online portal.

Good books and authors from small presses are often overlooked. Your comments and reviews can make an enormous difference.

Read on for the opening to Book 1,

One Dead, Two to Go

Chapter 1

———•———

CALL ME EDDIE Shoes. Not a very feminine moniker, but it suits me. My father's name was Eduardo Zapata. My mother, Chava, in a fit of nostalgia, named me Edwina Zapata Schultz, even though by the time I was born she hadn't seen my father in seven months. Edwina was a mouthful to saddle any child with, and at the ripe old age of six, I announced to Chava I would only answer to Eddie. I didn't have any nostalgia for a guy I'd never met, so Zapata just seemed like a name no one ever spelled right the first time. I also didn't care much for Schultz, and Chava wasn't particularly maternal in any conventional sense, so not a lot of nostalgia there either. At eighteen I legally changed my name to Eddie Shoes.

That said a lot about my sense of humor.

Chava and I had come to an understanding. I kept her in my life as long as our contact was minimal and primarily over email. It was just enough to allay her guilt and not enough to make me crazy, so it worked out for both of us. She'd always been down on my choice of career, but what did she expect from a girl who called herself Eddie Shoes? If I hadn't become a private investigator, I probably would have been a bookie, so

I figured she should have been a little more positive about the whole thing.

My career was the reason I sat hunkered in the car, in the dark, halfway down the block from a tacky hotel, clutching a digital camera and zoom lens, waiting to catch my latest client's husband with a woman not his wife. I'd already gotten a few choice shots of the guy entering the room, but he'd gone in alone and no one else had arrived, so I assumed the other woman was already waiting for him. I'd been tailing the guy for a few days, so I had a pretty good guess who the chippie would turn out to be. I didn't think he'd hired his "office manager" for her filing skills, and sleeping with the married boss was a cliché because it happened all the time. I could already prove the man a liar. He told his wife he played poker with the boys on Wednesday nights, and I didn't think he was shacked up in this dive with three of his closest buddies, unless he was kinkier than I imagined.

But then, people never ceased to amaze me.

December in Bellingham, Washington, often brought cold, clear weather and that night was no exception. Starting the engine to warm up sounded tempting, but I didn't want anyone to notice me sitting there. Nice it wasn't raining, but if the thermometer crept much over twenty, I hadn't noticed. To make matters worse, my almost six-foot frame had been scrunched down in the driver's seat for more than two hours. Even with a blanket wrapped around my shoulders, I was half frozen, and I desperately hoped my mark didn't have more stamina than I'd pegged him for. All I wanted was to go home and go to bed.

And at some point I would need to pee.